Zazen

Zazen

Vanessa Veselka

Red Lemonade
a Cursor publishing community
Brooklyn, New York

Library of Congress Control Number 2011921296
ISBN 978-1-935869-05-4

Cover & Interior design by Fogelson-Lubliner
Printed in the United States of America

Red Lemonade
a Cursor publishing community
Brooklyn, New York

www.redlemona.de

Distributed by Publishers Group West

10 9 8 7 6 5 4 3 2 1
Zazen

War A is going well and no longer a threat, small and mature. Like a Bonsai. War B is in full flower. Its thin green shoots reaching across the ocean floor like fiber optic cable. The TVs are on all the time all the time now. The lights dim and everyone moves in amber. They flicker like votives. That's what we will all be one day, insects in sap, strange jewels.

This novel is really for Violet Veselka

I went to work and a guy I wait on said he was leaving. He said everyone he knew was pulling out.

"Canada is just not far enough. Mostly Mexico. A bunch to Thailand. Some to Bali."

He always orders a Tofu Scramble and makes me write a fucking essay to the cook. No soy sauce in the oil mix, no garlic, extra tomato, no green pepper. Add feta. Potatoes crispy and when are we going to get spelt. He holds me personally responsible for his continued patronage. I hope he dies. I'd like to read about it.

My brother Credence says people who leave are deluding themselves about what's out there. I just think they're cowards. Mr. Tofu Scramble says I should go anyway, that it's too late. I want to but I can't. Maybe when the bombs stop, or at least let up. Nobody thinks it'll stay like this. I call it a war but Credence says it isn't one. Not yet. I say they just haven't picked a day to market it. Soft opens being all the rage. My last few weeks down at grad school it was so bad I thought everything was going to shake itself apart. I tried to focus on my dissertation, follow the diaspora of clamshells but every night it got worse. It's not any better here—here, there, now, tomorrow, next Wednesday—geologically speaking it's all the same millisecond. The gentle rustle of armies crawling the planet like ants. Anybody with any sense knows what's coming.

I was in yoga yesterday and this girl started crying. Raina, who teaches on Mondays, went over, put her hands on the girl like a faith healer, her fingers barely grazing her shoulders. She closed her eyes and let the girl cry while she breathed. Everyone was watching like they were going to see sparks or something. I was anyway. I would have liked that. The girl calmed down. Her breath was hard and her eyes swollen. Raina talked about being okay with how you find yourself on the mat and I thought there's no one here who's okay with that. If you took the roof off we would all look like little gray worms, like someone lifted the rock; too close, hot, bent and wet. Well, maybe not hot because of the mud but that's still what I thought when the girl was crying. I was glad it wasn't me.

Credence says if half the privileged white marketing reps in my yoga class voted for something other than reductions in their property tax, something might actually happen. I'd like to see something happen. Something big that wasn't scary, just beautiful. Some kind of wonderful surprise. Like how fireworks used to feel. Now I'm no better than a dog.

Still, there's something true in that yoga manifestation thing because I feel different when I believe different things. Only I don't know how to go back to feeling how I did because I can't re-believe. When the first box-mall-church went up in the blackberry field I wanted some kind of rampant mass stigmata with blackberry juice for blood. It didn't happen. It's not going to. They win; they just roll, pave and drive over everything that's beautiful: babies, love and small birds. On summer nights with the windows open I hear joints cracking like crickets.

I wake up sometimes and feel the nearness of something but then it's gone and I've started to wonder if it was ever there. Lately, I've become afraid that the feeling I used to feel, like something good was waiting, is what people mean when they say "young" and that it is nothing more than a chemical associated with a metabolic process and not anything real at all.

I waited on Mr. Tofu Scramble. He had a date at lunch and they both ordered blackberry smoothies. Vegan. I thought about slipping his date a note telling her that he was a big old cheese eater when she wasn't around. But who am I to stand in the way of love?

I went into the kitchen and pulled a five-gallon bucket out of the fridge. They stack the tofu in soft blocks at the bottom of a bucket of water. With dirty hands I scooped out the tofu and threw a handful into the blender, little white clay hearts. Then I filled it to the brim with blackberries. I pressed the "chop" on the blender because it's louder and takes longer and in a second the blackberries stained those little white hearts and turned them dark as a bruise. I left the blender on. It took over the restaurant. Everyone tried harder and harder to ignore the noise but the more they did, the longer I let it run. There should be some price to pay for all of this ugliness, especially the pretty kind; especially the kind you don't always see.

Mr. Tofu Scramble looked around and I thought, yeah, that's right, it's you, you Big Old Cheese Eater When She's Not Around. His cheeks reddened and his jaw shifted side to side. He started to look so much like a little kid staring down at dirty candy that I turned the blender off. It's not all his fault. It's not his fault he's in love and wants quiet blackberries. It's just not his fault.

Even Credence fell in love and got married although I think he secretly wants a medal for falling in love with a black woman. Our parents were so proud. Now, if I could only abandon my heterosexual tendencies as uninvestigated cultural preconditioning and move in with some sweet college-educated lipstick-dyke bike mechanic, they could all finally die happy.

I've lived with Credence and Annette for almost three months now. At first I thought that because Annette was black I wasn't ever supposed to get mad at her. It was like living with an exchange student who spoke English really well.

"Jean-Pierre, what do they call baseball in France?"

"Annette, do you like macaroni and cheese?"

"Daisuke, how is the rebuilding going?"

Credence has a missionary belief in community organizing. He says "grassroots" like Bible thumpers say Jesus.

Hallelujah.

Credence and I stopped a Wal-Mart from opening once. It was earlier in the year and it lasted about a minute. Four months of door-to-door organizing, leafleting, town meetings, petitions, land-use hearings, senators, phone calls, cold, free doughnuts and sermons to the choir in the rain with balloons whipping around our faces in the wind while we chant and people drive by in heated sedans and look confused. Take pictures and send it out to everyone who couldn't come to the rally. And it worked. For about a minute. It's hard to do the same thing twice. It's hard to feel the same way you did, especially when you really want to. We just set them back a couple of months on their timetable. Chipped teeth, flags, crosses and white sugar.

I moved in with Credence and Annette the week of Wal-Mart's Grand Opening. That was back in May when we found out Annette was pregnant. They said I could stay until the twins are born. They gave me the attic. It has dormer windows and a leaky skylight. When I go to sleep I stare up through the glass and pretend that none of us are here.

Out of a desire to understand, I began collecting maps and putting them on the walls. Gift shop maps with sea monsters on them and beveled, unfamiliar coastlines, cold war maps with the Soviet Menace spreading like leprosy. Pink East Germany. Red China. Maps of Pangaea and Gondwanaland from back before the seams pulled apart when we were still all one big continent—Deep Time, where countries turn to silt, silt turns to stone and we can now tell time by comparing the rates of nations collapsing—Biostratigraphy? Patriastratigraphy? Following the law of superposition, one thing always follows another: map of the Trail of Tears, bike map, subway map, and one I drew when I was twelve and wrote "Della's world" in scented marker at the top. Historical, geological, topographical, ideological and imaginary. Sitting in Credence's attic I tried to figure out if culture was just geology. Maybe Rwanda was caused by mountain building. And the Russo-Japanese War by glacial till. Maybe you need pirated rivers in the headlands before you can have a Paris Commune.

I found a picture online of a man setting himself on fire. It didn't say where he was or what he was protesting. Next to his leg was a gas can. He must have just dropped the match because I could still see his clothes. His arms were raised and flailing. I thought of Buddhists who can sit, quiet as wellwater, and burn like candles, like in that famous photo where the Zen monk is sitting cross-legged on fire in the middle of an intersection while cars drive past and people watch. Everything near him is blurry, the cars, the people, because they're moving. But he's not. He is absolutely sharp because he is absolutely still. Every detail of his robe, his eyelids and the oil from the smoke is absolutely clear. I first saw that picture in high school. I remember telling Credence about it.

"On fire?"

"On fire," I said.

"You'd have to move."

"They don't move."

"Della,"—like I was doing it on purpose—"Della, their bodies would make them move. They'd have to."

His voice thinned and climbed.

"It's biological," he squealed. "They wouldn't have any control over it."

In 1969 in Prague it took Jan Palach three days to die because he wasn't trained to just sit there. It was more like what Credence said. He had to move. It was biological.

After I found the photo of the blazing man with the flailing arms, I began to look for eyewitness accounts of people setting themselves on fire. Hell, I figured, if you can't trust some hand-me-down, unverifiable, anonymous hearsay, what can you trust? There were more of them than I thought. There was one yesterday. He set himself on fire to protest a recommendation from a sub-committee to legislate a three percent quota in alternate grain production.

There were Americans, dancing around like sparklers on the fourth of July. There were Basque nationalists, German priests and Taiwanese publishers. One entry in Wikipedia said, "Kathy Change self-immolated to protest 'the present government and economic system and the cynicism and passivity of the people.'" And underneath, the afterthought, "MIT student Elizabeth Shin may have committed suicide in this manner."

One self-immolator was described as disgruntled. Following other names were comments like "supposedly for the same reason."

I started putting them up on the walls too. I bought a bag of fortune cookies and raided the fortunes. On the back of each I wrote, underneath their lucky numbers in red, the name of the burned.

Jan Palach
Your warmth encourages honesty at home:
718253741.10

Thich Quang Duc
Magic will be created when an unconventional friend comes to visit:
816223141.24

Elizabeth Shin
Your future is as boundless as the lofty heaven:
811283645.15

Norman Morrison

You will be reunited with old friends:

615213840.12

Kathy Change

Your nature is intense, magnetic and passionate:

712293644.27

Alice Hertz

Truth is a torch that gleams through the fog without dispelling it:

511243642.24

I taped the fortunes to pins like flags and stuck them in the maps. Each city that inspires immolation gets a tiny white flag to flutter. Tiny little surrender. Tiny little surrenders. Supposedly, the heart of the Vietnamese monk from '63 never burned but shriveled to a tiny liver. It is held hostage (kept safe as a national treasure) by the Reserve Bank of Vietnam. Tiny liver hearts. I pinned them to the walls. Katydids flutter all around.

Credence came in one day, looked at the wall and suggested I sign up for yoga classes. He offered to pay. I knew that Credence offering to pay for yoga classes was a sign of the box-mall apocalypse. Hey everyone, how about some yoga classes for Della and blackberry smoothies all around. Today, I'm feeling it. I'm feeling the Rapture! Credence waves magnanimously. A seal breaks and fire pours out.

Credence agreed it might be good for me to work in a more positive environment. I don't know why he thinks watching Wal-Mart crush impoverished communities isn't a positive experience. Listening to the snap of infrastructure? Cheering when something essential resists failure more slowly—strain… strain…(screaming fans)…strain…SNAP! The architecture of a new revolution now a palace of Popsicle sticks blasted to matted straw, each stick a darling to its mother who can now buy a full set of patio furniture for less than the cost of a box of tampons.

Once I burned an ant with a magnifying glass. It moved when it caught fire because it wasn't trained to sit there. The straw it crawled on, its very own Popsicle stick palace, blackened and burned. You have to sit there or it doesn't count. But it moved. That's how I knew it was alive; that's how I knew what I did was wrong. Little ant? Little ant? And me crying all night long with ash on my hands. Popsicle sticks. Matted straw. Grassroots. Hallelujah.

It was decided that it would be good for me to restrict my job search.

"Maybe just to restaurants," Annette said.

"Or even just vegetarian restaurants," said Credence. "Nothing too fast-paced. Maybe something run by a collective. You know, with art on the walls or some kind of theme."

I got the job at Rise Up Singing through Credence. He dated a cook there a few years back, a girl named Jimmy. It has a "we all work in hell but that's okay cause we don't have to take out our piercings" kind of theme.

Jimmy and Credence met at the Pride March. I was just home from my first year in grad school and told Credence I'd help him with this rally. We went to the march to pass out leaflets for a demonstration he was organizing to try to pressure Payless Shoes on labor standards (700 million Chinese watch transfixed as Credence and Della hand out lavender leaflets and strain to bridge the gap between identity politics and general global class-based oppression. Strain…strain…). Jimmy was on the back of the flatbed with a bunch of other half-naked women cheering on gay Christmas and passing out dental dams and candy.

I started whooping when the parade went by and forgot to hand out fliers. Not Credence. He made sure everyone who passed us had a lavender quarter sheet on sweatshops and fully understood the connection between gender and class. Someone was throwing glitter in the air and it rained on me and I started crying. I always cry at Pride. I can't help it. It's like everything's going to be all right and it's all going to end well. I just can't take it.

A big girl, as tall as me, and I'm tall, maybe 5' 9" or 5' 10", jumped off the back of a truck and ran over to us. Her hair was short on the sides like she'd shaved her head in the past few months. The ends were blonde and the rest, brown. I thought she was Latina but she's not. She was bare-chested, wearing jeans and suspenders. In her hand she had a plastic firefighter's hat.

"I'll take one," she said.

Credence gave her a stack and started to talk about the campaign but she ran back to the parade to catch up with her float. She swung up onto the back of the truck, put her fireman's hat on and smiled back at us before being swallowed by confetti.

Credence, whose hope never falters, didn't find her obvious gayness to be a stumbling block. She did come to the rally and they hung out. He convinced her that she was committing some form of gender oppression by shutting him down just because he was a dude. That lasted about a minute. I'm pretty sure, from what I know of her, that today she looks on her two months of recalcitrant bisexuality like some sort of Mandan piercing rite; a final trial before being declared gay for life. They stayed friends though and she's been a cook at Rise Up Singing since it opened.

So, I start waiting tables at Rise Up Singing. The walls on the outside are the color of egg yolk and there's a mural of neighborhood black people enjoying gentrification on the side of the building. I bet that was one big Popsicle stick snap. SNAP! Toaster prize: one mural honoring multiculturalism on egg yolk. Y'all eat soy, right? Annette, do you like macaroni and cheese?

The owner's name is Franklin. He started Rise Up Singing when every business on the street had bars on the windows.

"I like to think of myself as a coworker with lots of experience rather than a boss," Franklin said.

I like to think of myself as a boss more than a slave but mostly I prefer to not think about it at all because when I think about it, I can't stop.

"Okay," I said.

Coworker Franklin lowered his voice and leaned in a little.

"We are mostly vegan but we want to be friendly and welcoming to our meat-eating friends so please bear that in mind," he said.

I saw Annette's face looming black and carnivorous. Try to be friendly, don't make eye contact, back away slowly. Make macaroni and cheese. Side dishes are non-confrontational and potentially evocative of a southern heritage.

On my first day at Rise Up Singing I waited on both Mr. Tofu Scramble and his nemesis, Ed, Logic's Only Son. They each come every day and sit at the counter with an empty stool between them.

Mr. Tofu Scramble: So, Della, is this your first day? By the way, do you know if Franklin has ordered spelt yet?

Ed, Logic's Only Son: So what's wrong with butter and cheese? It's not like you have to slaughter a cow to get cheese.

Mr. Tofu Scramble: You know, spelt is better for you than wheat.

Ed, Logic's Only Son: And what about yeast? You drink beer, right? So is beer vegan? Is it okay to kill yeast?

My second day at Rise Up Singing I trained on the opening shift. I showed up early and Ed, Logic's Only Son was waiting for me in front of the restaurant. He had on a bomber jacket and a paperback of *The Martian Chronicles* was tucked under one arm. I could see the comb marks in his gray greased hair. Behind him on the mural wall an enormous black head with an elaborate Pan-African headdress floated in egg yolk.

He tapped a pack of Pall Malls against the butt of his palm and glared at me.

"You're late," he said.

"I'm on time. The person training me is late."

"Who's training you?"

"Mirror," I said.

"These fucking names," he said and shook his head.

Ed pulled the cellophane off the Pall Mall pack, crinkled it into a ball and threw it on the ground where it blossomed into a clear plastic flower.

Mirror was several blocks away biking up the center of the street, her pink ponytails fluttering behind as she pedaled. When she saw us she waved a friendly unhurried wave. I waved back.

"Fucking Christ!" Ed said and turned away.

Mirror coasted down to where we were and got off her bike.

"Sorry I'm late, Ed."

"This place used to open at seven."

"So go back in time."

Mirror unlocked the door and we followed her in. She flipped the lights and started showing me around. The walls inside Rise Up Singing were red, pink and purple. It was like being inside a placenta.

I got the bleach buckets out. Ed stood by the register locked in a staring contest with the unmanned grill. The cook came in, looked at Ed, and walked out back to have a cigarette.

Mirror took out her pigtails and started brushing her hair with an Afro pick. Little pink fuzz balls gathered on the comb teeth and she balled them together and threw them in the trash.

"Della, do you eat meat?"

"Sometimes."

"Well, don't eat it here. All the cooks are vegetarian. They either burn it because they get grossed out or leave it totally raw on purpose, it's disgusting."

Mirror threw another pink fuzz ball in the trash.

"Franklin said you were a geologist or something. Did you like, study at volcanoes?"

"No, invertebrate paleontology."

"Cool," she said, "I saw a special on deep-sea vents once. There were all of these white octopuses living down there that turned out to be totally gay," she rinsed the Afro pick off in the bar sink, "Probably not a great species survival plan, though."

Ed tapped his coffee cup with a spoon like he was an inmate but Mirror didn't look up. She has a pretty laissez-faire attitude toward customers in general. When I went to turn on the OPEN sign she told me not to because, "If you do that, they'll just come in." Flawless logic.

At the end of our shift Mirror dumped the tip jar out on the counter.

"I hope Franklin told you we pool tips," she said and began to separate the change. "He tries to pass it off as communism but it's really so he doesn't have to pay the cooks."

I adjusted the credit slips and Mirror counted the money into piles then went into the till and grabbed three ten-dollar bills. I thought she was going to make change but she just added one ten to each pile, "Slave tax," she said and paid us out. Jimmy came in through the back door. Her arms were full of lettuce.

"Hey you! I heard they hired you," she hugged me. "I'm so psyched."

I hadn't seen her for several years. Her hair was longer in the front and bleached out to a light orange. The back of her head was still clipped and brown. She dropped the lettuce on a nearby counter and came over. I could tell Credence had given her the update by the way she looked at me.

Jimmy had me help her break down produce boxes and we went out to a fenced area adjacent to the restaurant that smelled of rotten yogurt and urine. I ripped staples out of the boxes and Jimmy folded them flat and threw them in a pile. We talked about school and Annette and the Bellyfish and my parents.

"I always liked Grace," she said, "I'd love to see them again sometime."

She asked about the Wal-Mart campaign. I told her it was social bloodsport, which sounded like I was trying to be funny but I wasn't. Credence treats social justice campaigns like sand painting. Everything he does is a fucking seminar on impermanence.

"So do you have any plans?" she asked.

Hang out in the sub-cultural ICU with the free vegan donuts until my definition of the sparkling horror show matches everyone else's?

"See how it goes."

"Can you hold up the lid?" she asked.

I lifted the green metal top of the recycling container. Jimmy threw the flattened boxes inside, then I let the lid fall with a deafening clang.

"Well," she said, "Either way I'm glad you're here."

The way she smiled. I had this flash like it might be all right, like there might be a place for me and that I had maybe overlooked something, or lost some kind of perspective and that now it was going to get fixed. Her smile reminded me of my mom in this particular 1970s Polaroid where she's a young woman bending over to play with a cat. Her hair is light brown and the backyard grass is dry like straw, cropped and short. All that day I felt like that, like the sound of future bombs might dissipate, become no more than white noise like the freeway or the sea, or that I might stop hearing them altogether. Sleep like who I was before I knew any better.

I biked past the yoga studio on my way home. It was getting pretty dark but the streetlights weren't on because they had just switched to the new schedule. I know it's because of the war.

Credence says it hasn't started yet but he's wrong. They're rationing power and the TVs are on all the time.

I pulled my bike up onto the curb by the yoga studio and leaned it against the trashcan. I watched the yoga class through the glass. The lights dimmed and everyone moved in amber. They flickered like votives when the teacher crossed back and forth in front of the window and I thought, that's what we will all be one day, insects in sap, strange jewels.

The following week Coworker Franklin scheduled me to open the restaurant alone. The first day I got there early and it was still dark. I turned on the light in the pie case and it lit the whole room. I wiped the specials from the night before off the board. Outside the world was blue.

I went to get more bread from the back and was reaching into the pantry when I felt something near my foot. I jumped back and turned on the overhead light. On the ground in front of the pantry was a small brown rat. It was dying.

The rat held itself still and waited. Its fur glistened and it had tucked its paws in close so that its belly bulged out from the sides. I wondered if it, if she, was pregnant like Annette. I got down on my knees and slowly leaned over so I could see her face. She didn't move and didn't look at me. Her breath quickened and she looked straight ahead. I felt her fear like a wave of nausea.

Jimmy came in behind me.

"Franklin puts out poison. I think he thinks it's more humane than traps."

She leaned over.

"Has someone shown you what to do?"

"No."

She went into the walk-in and got a slice of cheese then had me scoop up the rat up with a dustpan and follow her outside.

We walked along a garden path toward the back fence. The sun was just hitting the green wet vines and red tomato skins. I passed a cluster of sunflowers. Behind them stretching along the fence was a row of dirt mounds with tiny homemade crosses sticking out of them.

"This is where we put them," Jimmy said.

I looked down a row of dew-covered twig crosses drying the morning light.

"If the health department comes just pull the crosses out and say it's squash."

"Squash? Really?"

She laughed a little, "Yeah, or something seasonal."

Jimmy took the dustpan from my hands and laid the pregnant rat in the furrow between two graves. She pulled the paper off the cheese, tore it into little strips and left it beside her.

"We'll bury her later. She'll be dead by the end of the shift."

The rat settled into the furrow of earth and tucked her paws underneath again. She put her nose down and shook. Jimmy pushed the cheese closer but the rat didn't move. Again, I felt her fear come like nausea.

Pregnant Rat

Your thirst for knowledge will impress your enemies:

563882981.23

Rumors of a heart unburnt and preserved in mud, buried inside a cage of ribs (kept safe as a National Treasure). Basta! Rat Golgotha, Presente! All around me were small snapping sounds that only a mother rat would hear and maybe only if the air were very still.

Up in my attic room the president came on the radio. Another special broadcast. Computers and digital cable hum in unison throughout the nation:

War A is going well and no longer a threat, small and mature. Like a bonsai. War B is in full flower. Its thin green shoots reaching across the ocean floor like fiber optic cable. Our only defense is attack. We will hunt them in destroyer disguised as a whaling ship.

Streaming the news is a signal of relapse.

I muted the computer.

Mr. Tofu Scramble says anyone who's leaving the country should go now. He's leaving in three weeks. It's Bali for sure, he says, the sale of his house is pending and as soon as it all goes through, he's gone.

I imagine people who leave turn to pools of light when they're over water. Circles of phosphorescent green appear and light up the Black Ocean then dissolve into silt and the silt turns to stone. We can now tell time by comparing the rates of people leaving—one thing always follows another—a timeline of events leading up and to and away from the central event, which in this case is the event of leaving.

I signed up for yoga classes the week I found the rat. I got a six-month membership. Credence said the consistency would be good. The woman behind the counter was wearing a tank top that had "Namaste!" written across the front of it like the Coca

Cola logo. Her hair was red and wrapped in an orange scarf. Her nails were pink glitter and she had a pendant of Guadalupe hanging from her neck.

"Can I help you?" she asked.

Yes. I want to look like you. I want to be so thoroughly anchored into some sort of pop culture aesthetic that nothing can knock me over or wash me away or make me hate everyone. I want to sleep again.

"I'd like to take some yoga classes," I said.

"Great! Let me show you around. My name is Devadatta."

She came around the counter and led me into a hallway that smelled of vanilla candles and dry leaves. She was like a beautiful collage, jagged and bright, and I thought I could be that, I could, but I can't and didn't know that then for sure but I thought it was probably the case. Still, I had some hope so I followed her down the hall.

"We have a really wonderful studio," she said and opened a door.

The room was large and empty with floors made of salvaged hard wood. People walked by the window outside, disembodied. Their heads sank and rose like glass floats upon the ocean or seafoam or apples.

"Do you prefer Vinyasa or Hatha?" Devadatta asked.

I prefer sleep and loud blackberries.

"I don't remember what I used to do," I said.

"I'd recommend Raina's class," she said, "She has a lot of yin energy, very gentle, you'll love her," and I remember thinking, like I do now, that I would love to love something, especially if I could do it without feeling like I was watching it die right in front of me, "Okay," I said.

Raina's class that day was full of women with quiet voices. I took a mat from the closet and set up next to two of them about my age. They were talking about the naturopathic school they were going to and how it was expensive but still worth it and how their parents didn't think so but who cared 'cause they ate frozen dinners and jogged even though it was bad for their joints. Raina came in and we started.

I slept through the night and didn't go to the Asian market for fortunes the next day either. Instead, I stayed home and helped Annette work on a mosaic she's laying down on the floor of the upstairs bathroom. She wants to finish it before the Bellyfish comes.

I brought in the boxes of broken tile I'd been collecting and a map of the design I drew on graph paper and blew up to scale. Annette was on the floor with her legs stretched out in either direction, jars of colored chips in between. She's gotten so big she can't sit comfortably any other way.

We were all shocked when Annette got pregnant. She's famous for saying there are too many of us already, comes from being a public health nurse. I think the whole thing was an accident and they decided not to terminate. Then found it was twins. I was working with Credence on the Wal-Mart campaign at the time. The joy almost killed our parents. Not only were Credence and I to be the Bobbsey Twins of Labor Unrest (300 million Americans watch as Credence and Della try to shore up failing infrastructure while simultaneously reinvigorating common discourse on the subject of THE PUBLIC as a reflection of collective will, as in REPUBLIC and not as in BIG GOVERNMENT), but to also be gifted with actual black grandchildren? It was a miracle in dark times.

Annette dumped the jar of red chips on the floor. We talked about the yoga class. She asked me what the new yoga studio looked like because it had only been open a few months. It used to be a shop that sold custom cut foam and had a huge bas relief foam flag in the window.

"The building's totally remodeled," I said, "You'd never recognize it."

I took a piece of paper and started to sketch it but then in my mind, the foam flag disintegrated. Golden sun and full spectrum track lighting flooded the old shop. The man at the counter grew girlish and began practicing forward folds, clothed in hemp and other organic fibers.

Map of Foam Store/Yoga Studio

1) *Foam flag area*: territory of patriotic working class, which emerged vanguardless from the masses i.e., without our permission.

2) *Yoga studio*: territory of micro-populists, who promise to make sure that everyone has forty acres and a mule upon which to build tiny rice paper houses which we shall call Jeffersons, like the democracy and not like a/the black family.

2a) *Subdivision of 2—Nowhere*: territory of the indigenous black.

Note: Patrons form the middle third, the scene of the battle, civilians and traitors. Torn between two visions of the future—
1) joint-cracking crickets following lucky numbers in red and
2) a glittering Popsicle stick palace, the architecture of a new revolution, tipping this way and that in the gentle breeze—they look at their shoes. Nice cement. Yeah, thanks. I poured it myself. Have you ever insulated with straw? No, I'm a cob man.

But that's not the map I drew for Annette. Her map had a box with Xs where they tore down a wall and hatch marks for windows. The real map was just forming on the edges of my thoughts. Flashing before me were new index fossils, like Taco Bell and Payless Shoes. And beyond that a shifting cartography, not like a series of snapshots, but like a hidden camera that never stops, never plays back and goes all the time, a living map.

Up in my room another presidential address came on the radio. It was just before dawn and contained no information.

We were to be prepared, but not nervous, yet alert. They tested the emergency broadcast signal and I threw up. Is that prepared or alert?

I finished the map, stuck it in my bike messenger bag and brought it to work. I spread it out on the counter in front of Mr. Tofu Scramble and Ed, Logic's Only Son.

Mr. Tofu Scramble: Did you draw that, Della? That's pretty cool, I particularly like the, uh...uh.

Ed, Logic's Only Son: What the hell is that? A spaceman?

Me: It's a map of colonialism as a cottage industry.

Ed, Logic's Only Son: What's that thing on its head?

The cumulative weight of a dense cultural mesh that prevents us from understanding whether the foundational problem is really race, class or gender? A hat?

Me: A hat.

Mr. Tofu Scramble: Well, it does kind of look like a hat. Now that I follow the, uh...uh.

Ed, Logic's Only Son: It would float off his head.

Mirror came in the door and walked over to us. She pulled off her knit cap and her pink hair, full of static electricity, crackled around her face.

"Hey Della," she said, "Franklin here?"

Tiny strands, like pink thread, pink and as thin as a spider's silk, stuck to her cheeks.

"He was here earlier," I said.

"Did he say anything about the work meeting?"

"Not to me."

Mitch, the morning cook, stuck her head through the food window, "He wants to talk about the future," she yelled.

Mirror handed me a flier for a sex party she was planning.

"I don't care what he wants to talk about. He scheduled the meeting for the day after my party and I'm totally not coming. No way."

Mitch came out of the kitchen and took some fliers. I looked at the one in my hand. It was a picture of an orgy drawn to look like a subway map with an arrow pointing to a tangle in the center that said *You Are Here*.

"We'll have lube, condoms and dental dams there. If you're allergic to latex you should bring your own gloves."

Mirror reached in her bag and pulled out a few more fliers. Mitch took some.

"You can take these and invite a couple of people but let them know that we're asking all fluid-bonded couples to use condoms and dams too," she said, "It's just more respectful that way."

I saw a broken horizon. Huge, jagged slabs in the distance under which people met and danced as though it was an actual dancehall and not a crack in the pavement.

Mirror grabbed a cookie from a basket by the register and unwrapped it. "When is Franklin going to fucking figure out that a chocolate chip cookie with milk chocolate is not vegan?"

Mirror picked out the chocolate chips and put them on a napkin, "Oh, by the way, I found another rat. Thankfully, it was already dead."

"You sure?" asked Mitch.

"Yeah. It had its head chewed off."

I went out to see where they had buried it.

The rain made the upturned earth look black. I found a hole near the back fence but there wasn't a rat in it. The other mounds had weeds growing out of them. Some of the crosses had fallen over in the rain but several were still standing. It had a miniature Buzz Lightyear lashed to it. I stepped around a rotten crate and went to the grave of the pregnant rat. I wondered if she was really in there and if I should have made more little white flags. I don't know how many baby rats she would have had, or how many are in a litter or even if they're called litters.

I left for the Asian market.

The windows of the Asian market were steamed and I smelled shrimp frying. Strings of packaged candy hung like beaded curtains and bowls of jade sat on dark lacquer shelves. I picked up a calendar that was lying on a wicker chair. It was full of Chinese girls wearing satin. When I flipped through it, it sounded like a fan whirring in another room.

On the grocery side a cook was stirring a pot and yelling in Chinese. Then he yelped and threw something. There was a huge clatter of thin metal, like a tray of spoons falling. A woman came out and they started arguing. The cook was holding a towel around his hand and kicking the oven door. I could see him through the hanging meat. He was just beneath two birds strangled and dangling with feet twined and tied to a crossbeam. The fluorescent light made the cook's skin look gray and yellow against his white shirt.

I looked through a basket full of Buddhas on the shelf next to me. Some were brass and others were gunmetal gray, no bigger than bullets. One was the size of a golf ball. I picked it up and thought about buying it and throwing it through the glass door of the box-mall-church. But that door wouldn't break no matter how hard I threw it. I couldn't do it anyway. I'd be afraid I'd hit someone or scare some kid so I put it back. I'm sick of how they always win.

On the floor was a basket full of fans. They had bamboo spines and collapsed like butterfly knives. Fans with flowers, pagodas, birds and the names of cities: Bangkok, Osaka, Tokyo on orange skies with burgundy suns and I thought, I need to get something, something for someone but I didn't know whom. I tried to imagine giving a fan to Annette. Maybe one that said Phnom Penh in red over a field of yellow. I could leave it on her nightstand and she'd put it somewhere special. But I couldn't take what it would mean to her. That would just be too much. I picked out a white fan with a single black branch on it. Good for all occasions.

The boxes of fortune cookies were at the end of the aisle. A recent shipment had come in. I usually get a bag, which has about thirty useable fortunes but I decided to buy a whole box, which has twenty bags. It was more than I'd ever bought until then and I felt a slight reeling in the deepest part of my abdomen. I took the fan and the box up to the register and paid. It started to rain really hard and they let me hang out inside to see if it would let up.

I was leaning against the gumball machines by the front window and trying to stay out of the way. Outside, under the awning was a red metal newspaper stand that had been tagged and dented. Through the glass and wire grid holding the paper I saw a picture of a woman crouching, aflame. A man and a young girl were running down a street. Behind them was a wall of smoke. On the side, down in the corner of the photo, was the person crouching. All around her fire, like a corona, spread into the black ink. She was as dark as an eclipse and held herself still and burned. Chinese characters ran in lines down the page around her. That reeling came again, only deeper, like something was shaking loose in a place that nobody had ever been before. The doors of the box-mall-church flashing like mica. The cook with the burnt hand, flailing. The glitter of progress; the sheen of nostalgia. Out by the older malls are huge Asian markets with the HDL screens by the register. They play videos of Filipinos running through Scottish castles in jodhpurs and trailing lace. He has a riding crop and she, an empire waist.

Unagi. Bonjour! Dónde está el arroz? But it's not some vibrant, new, glittering incongruity. I know. I see glittering incongruities. I see people on fire. Right there on the front page of newspaper, leaning against the gumball machine because it was raining so hard, I saw the girl on fire in the corner of the photo, crouching. Then I felt the panic like I do always when it's like that, like it's happening right now, like they're dying in front of me.

I turned to get help, to ask the man at the counter or the woman in back what had happened. They said it was just sports. Apparently there was a big game and some jocks set some stuff on fire. It happened days ago. Everyone is fine. But they're not. I can see from their faces. I can't speak Chinese but I can tell they are not fine.

Sports. Sports riot.

I took a few breaths and tried to calm down. Raina says nothing's ever really wrong it's just the story we tell ourselves. I think it's the other way around. But I tried anyway. I rewrote the events in the picture. The woman crouching in the smoke had pockets full of bobbleheads. The man and the young girl had just shared a hot dog and arena nachos. It wasn't the war. It was just a game. But of course it was the war, I could hear it breathing under the net.

Down the street I heard some kind of blast or crash. Following the Law of Superposition it should be: sound> association> meaning> rxn—but it isn't order because the meaning never changes and the sound can be anything. There was a rumble that I couldn't place—step out on to the broadening path! On even the brightest days when everyone is shining in the sun-flooded world what's wrong with a golden retriever playing with a pink child on a green field? A red Frisbee cutting through the blue sky under a white cloud? Nothing. It makes watching it all get blasted to tendons and fur so life-like. Sports riot. Terror is a chemical storm. The events are static, not the meaning. Sports. I left the box of fortunes by the register, said I'd get it later.

In front of the Asian market I could hear for a thousand miles. The rain was getting lighter and the streets shone. On the corner was a sports bar. I know because it had a poster of a rabid dog tearing some other animal apart and a co-ed with team color panties on the door. The parking lot was full of tanks and The Game reflected off their windshields...I dreamt one thousand basketball courts, nothing holier than sports...I'm going to make them feel what I feel. I went to a payphone by the bus stop. I mean what it's like to be fucking scared all the time and caught in the center of some big horrible thing you have no control over, that you can't even feel the edges of, a slideshow of species trauma.

I looked up the number of the sports bar and called in a bomb threat. I don't even know where the idea came from. When the bartender answered I told him they were all going to die in multiple explosions during the fourth quarter. Then I went and looked through the windows to see what would happen, but nothing did. They were pink and bored. The bartender finished a crossword puzzle. One guy near the TV yelled when a ball switched hands and slammed his fist down on the table knocking off a red plastic ashtray, which rattled in circles on its rim then stopped. They are untouchable.

I waited a little while then called Jimmy. I asked her to pick me up because I didn't want to call Annette. She showed up in her truck. I got in and put the box of fortunes between us on the seat.

"Are you okay?" she asked.

Sure. I love watching the ship timbers wash ashore in the tide.

"I'm tired."

We pulled out into traffic and sat there with the windows

down and water coming in everywhere because the defrost doesn't work and the windows fog up. Everyone was going under forty because it was rush hour and the rain was so hard. She turned on the radio and dialed it to a Mexican station but the engine hum cancelled out everything but the brass. Half a conversation. The trumpets were answering something inaudible. We didn't talk until we got out on the freeway.

Mirror had told me Jimmy was leaving. I think Credence said something about it too but I had put it out of my mind.

"I got my ticket today," Jimmy said.

"Costa Rica?"

"No, Honduras."

Cars sped up and fanned as a newly built fifth lane appeared on the left shoulder for half a mile then disappeared and drove us all back together.

"I got you a fan," I said. "As a going away gift."

Another pool of light.

"Yeah," Jimmy rolled the window up some, "I'm about done with all of this."

The traffic slowed near a huge billboard made of lights. It had a truck on it that spun in a circle and then exploded into yellow stars. Every time it happened Jimmy's face lit up and the fine brown hairs on top of her head turned gold. She looked like she had an aura and I thought, maybe that's how people see them. Maybe you have to know someone really well to see those things.

"It has a cherry tree on it," I said.

"What has?"

"The fan I got you. It's all white with a black cherry tree on it. I think it's winter. There aren't any blossoms."

Another burst of the billboard lights and Jimmy's hair was gold again. Even her eyelashes, when she turned her head, sparked then blackened. The traffic thinned and we started to move. The windows were still down far enough that the rain stung my cheeks as we picked up speed. She reached across and wiped fog from the windshield with her forearm and everything became clear. I didn't know it wasn't until she wiped it away and then it was so sharp it seemed ridiculous. Through the glass where the arc of Jimmy's arm had stopped and under the canopy of fog I saw a river of dark shadows glinting dully off each other. Steel and taillights poured into the valley then splashed up over the edge of a distant rise.

"Maybe I'll get a ticket too," I said.

A passing neon sign splashed vermillion on Jimmy's cheek. Again, I saw Grace, my mother, back before her hair turned dark and her eyes crawled the world like spiders. Suddenly, I got the idea that I wanted Jimmy to think about me when she was gone. I wanted her to say my name. I reached over and touched her face. She twitched so I pulled my hand back.

"What are you doing?"

"If it's not okay I won't."

She looked at me then back at the road. Cars coasted like blackbodies cooling in a sea of brakelights.

"Well," she said after a minute, "I guess it's okay. Just strange."

I touched her face again. I thought about telling Credence and how he would think it was funny. But it wasn't. Not really. It was as fucked up as everything else. Now? Is that too hard? No, it doesn't hurt. It's all about the breathing. It's about how much fear you hide in your cells: blue cells, green cells, red cells, sickle cells, sleeper cells, jail cells—people are shot through with it. But I don't hold my fear there. Everybody needs a place where they're fearless or they'd never survive, at least I wouldn't. Sometimes I hate this world. Especially when it's more beautiful than I can imagine.

The freeway lights stuttered and the valley sank. We ran with the rest of the traffic into a furrow lined with restaurant chains and competing gas prices. Jimmy's skin was light brown above her jeans and cream colored below like I thought it would be. And maybe I saw a garden beyond a gate. And maybe it wasn't a garden but a reflection of a garden. It was so clear to me now. I just somehow hadn't seen it. Everything had already erupted. There was nothing to save.

I had been kissing the hems of ghosts.

The morning light on Jimmy's face showed all the tiny scars she had from being alive. Above her eye was a small white scar that pulled when she squinted and next to that, another scar, thin as a wrinkle, from a car wreck. Under her chin was a ragged patch of raised tissue from wiping out on a skateboard. She wouldn't get it stitched because she didn't want to pay the ER bills.

I tried to move but her hair was tangled in my ring. I twisted it but couldn't get the ring off because my fingers were swollen from sleep. She was laughing the whole time, which made it harder. Finally, we had to cut the hair out with the scissors of her Swiss army knife, which was lying on the makeshift nightstand.

"Not like it matters," she said and threw the bleached orange lock behind her where it landed coiled and soundless.

The sheets were tangled. The white fan with the cherry branch lay open by the mattress. Jimmy reached over my body and picked up a photo that was lying face down on the floor.

"This is where I'm going," she said and handed the picture to me.

A colony of shacks sat unevenly on a clay hillside. Behind them, boxwood carpeted the mountain slopes, receding up into a distant cloud forest.

"The village is Indian."

Because the search for authenticity is a well without a bottom.

"Very beautiful," I said and handed the picture back.

Pale light filtered through the gauze window curtain, whitening the sheets and turning Jimmy's shoulder and hip the color of ivory.

"If you're going to tell Credence," she said, "I want to be warned."

"He'll just think it's funny."

"Funny because I'm a girl or funny because it's me?"

"Funny because it's you."

But Credence did not think it was funny. He called my having sex with Jimmy unscrupulous dabbling. Apparently, his time with her made him some kind of gender cowboy while mine just made me irresponsible. We got into an argument over which stance was more unenlightened, getting into bisexual relationships with lesbians (viewpoint Credence) or treating lesbians like incapable children who will automatically fall in love with you just because you are woman (viewpoint Della). I admit sleeping with Jimmy was lazy, though. Kind of like dating your cousin because you already know all the same people.

Annette didn't care. She just wanted to be the one to tell my parents. We all agreed the joy of my potential gayness would kill them. First, black grandchildren and now the fantasy of two women on the couch at family gatherings (entwined and laughing as if it were all going to be okay). Yes, they would finally be dead from politically informed glee. And, most importantly, the Bobbsey Twins of Labor Unrest though unable to rescue the PUBLIC from the slander of BIG GOVERNMENT would be placed in an historical context where the primacy of class had naturally yielded to its more ornamental, if secondary features: race and gender.

Annette said the only thing better would be if one of us went to prison.

"But you know, the next time you date a boy Grace is going to accuse you of exercising heterosexual privilege."

"Jimmy will be in Honduras before I see them."

"The anniversary is next week."

The green fans of the katydids fluttered.

"She could come to that."

I looked at Credence. "I'm not going."

Annette turned and walked into the kitchen.

Every year I say I'm not going.

When I first got hired at the restaurant Mirror asked about my parents.

"So, Della," she said, swallowing a chunk of raw tofu the size of a golf ball, "Jimmy says your parents are pretty fringe. Were they like total hippies?"

"No. My parents blew up hippies."

"For fucking real?" she threw the rest of the tofu into the trash. "Did they really blow up hippies?"

"No. But they would have if they thought it was necessary for the revolution."

She thought about it for a second.

"Wow. That's intense. What are they like now?"

"Pretty much the same."

"That's cool," she said, wiping her hands on her apron, "I'd blow up a hippy if I had to too."

Grace and Miro. The serrated edge of an ongoing revolution cutting its way through a thicket of injustice. Going out to their place once a year for the anniversary was the one thing asked of us. None of us ever said no, I'm not going. Which is what I told Credence that morning, which is why, without asking me, he called Jimmy and invited her to come. Being a good organizer is about manipulation after all. By the time Jimmy called me, Credence already had her committed to bring the vegan pineapple-lemon cake.

"Oh, Grace will love it," he told her.

Grace hates veganism. She calls it an elitist enclave for white people to lie to themselves about their role in the cycle of consumption. But that didn't matter. At the end of the day, Jimmy had taken the time off work, bought a book for Grace and Miro on permaculture, and wrapped it in re-plantable wildflower paper.

When I found out what Credence did, I slammed the door even though no one else was home. Way to drive turnout, Credence, you get a prize. What should it be? A papier-mâché head of John the Baptist? A tour map to the Rat Graveyard?

My cell phone buzzed and I didn't answer.

I stared at the white flags pinned on my wall where I'd been tracking a wave of immolations along the coast of France. I adjusted a pin. The flags bothered Credence, but not like talk of the box-mall-church. A few months ago I got lost in an industrial field behind there. I was trying to map the social events and boundaries that had turned our architectural vocabulary into drive-thru Christianity and free checking. More than that, I was trying to prove there is an end to it, but there isn't. It's endless. I had hoped to make an Aerial Map of the Carnage but it was beyond me. That night a bomb woke me up. Credence said it wasn't possible. That it was across the ocean and wasn't even ours. But everything's ours. The outside world is nothing anymore, just a franchise of nations.

I promised Credence I would never go to the box-mall-church again.

6   Aerial Map of the Carnage

On the bus out to the box-mall-church I counted rings of urban growth. Clouds burned off and new streets ticked by on my right, Car Parts Lane, Value Town Outlet Parkway, Pay Day Loan Road, Bank of Nations Plaza and Paul of Damascus Court. On my left was the long and windowless side of the box-mall-church. When it was built, a narrow road still ran between the mall and the church. But traffic bottlenecked so they built new roads and turned the old one into a covered pedestrian walkway connecting the buildings.

I was in school when the box-mall-church got finished. Which is part of why I worked on the Wal-Mart campaign. But Wal-Mart had already broken ground. Credence's strategy was to organize around traffic impact and slow down the permit process. Meanwhile, we were supposed to educate the community (70,000 ex-loggers watch as Credence and Della go door-to-door to force discussion of worker dignity and the price of neo-liberalism out of a traffic light). I had just defended my dissertation and my plans were shaky. I had been told to avoid anything stressful, to volunteer somewhere, get a dog. Credence decided my getting involved in a cause would be better. He thought Wal-Mart would be perfect but I didn't find the decimation of local economies all that relaxing. I tried to see the beauty in the flash of consciousness that passes over people's faces right before the total absence of light, but somehow I couldn't.

The bus pulled up to the first transit island by the service door of the box-mall-church. Russian and Vietnamese swing shift workers filled the aisles. Everyone else was staying for the round trip. Some had bus passes pinned to their shirts, wet brains and chatty paranoiacs talking about the gold standard. In the back row some high-functioning retarded teenagers were flirting with each other. I thought the one girl was going to take her dress off.

Walking into the box-mall-church always feels the same. Like something really bad has happened and no one inside knows. I entered on the side by the Cineplex. A kid ran in front of me pretending to be a commando. He hid behind a fake tree and took cover from an imaginary bomb blast. His parents were holding his ice cream and laughing while he ducked and dived through the indoor jungle. Chocolate ice cream trickled down in between his mother's fingers and she licked the back of her hand.

"Have you signed up for our raffle?"

It was a girl with lip gloss. I could smell the alcohol in her perfume. She turned and pointed to a shiny red truck about forty yards away. Big as a tank, raised dais and penned in by velvet ropes. Under its great wheels, long plastic fronds of coastal grass were matted flat.

I decided to start in the parking lot. It might be the center of the formation and the box-mall-church, or only a calcification or a reef built up on all sides of a cement lake. It may also have been that I couldn't take the glossy-lipped girls with the clipboards, the graduating class of None of Us Are Getting There Anyway, milling and spraying themselves with tester bottles off the cosmetic counters because nothing masks the blood and fear like Jubilant Day and Rapture, each with proprietary blends of torrential oils and myrrh. I went straight out the side door into the west lot and started mapping it in my field journal, walking it in ten-foot sections.

Map of Carnage

Notes on the Geomorphology of the West Parking Lot

The west parking lot stretches from the foothills of the box-mall-church to the edge of the Batholith, Wal-Mart. It is an arid basin shaped like a T and dotted with express banks. Across from the basin is a range of ancillary sub-malls. The cultural micro-ecology of the lot itself is clear: mobility through the social isolation of cars—oil wars, climate control, our primary method of civic discourse, the bumper sticker—are all factors in its evolution.

Lithography of the West Lot Basin: An Analysis of Sections

1) *What Would Scooby Do?*

A social-cultural laccolith of sanitized pot-smoking van kids, intruding laterally and prying apart two planes—a narrative mythologizing California beach life in the wake of the pill (below) and the Jesus freak movement the early 70s (above), which trended toward communism and anti-war sentiment as an example of first-century Christianity.

2) *Sure You Can Trust the Government, Just Ask An Indian:*

The statement then refers to a revised history that aligns "The Land / Noble Savage" with the values of the "Frontier / Frontiersman" creating a platform from which to promote the sale of semi-automatic weapons and assault rifles.

I tore out a sheet of paper and started over.

Notes for Further Consideration

1) Maybe the box-mall-church is the Piazza?

2) Maybe that road to Wal-Mart is the grand avenue leading to the gates of the castle. A new city set upon a new hill.

At that exact moment, a bomb went off downtown. A real bomb, in real time, that everybody heard. It destroyed the executive bathroom of the New Land Trust building. The whole area was evacuated. First responders surrounded the New Land Trust. There were no casualties but security measures were being implemented. Public transit switched to snow routes and on every TV screen in the country smoke from the executive bathroom curled up and out of the frame.

I heard about the bombing on the bus ride home. When the man told me about it, I thought he was lying. Then I knew he wasn't. My spine felt like a seismograph. I couldn't breathe. I might have screamed something. Someone handed me an inhaler. Someone else told me to shut up. I took deep breaths and thought of marine deposits. Everything falls silently to the seafloor. It's nothing personal at all.

Only the day before I'd been to the yoga studio and taken my place in the realm of rising home equity. It was so full I could barely move. The flower of gentrification, lotus spinning downstream. Raina walked to the front of the room.

She stood for a second by the window with the sun coming in on her, turning her face gold and her hair auburn. And in that stream of light I watched a million particles of fiber unwoven and unmeshed, freed from what we'd made of them—cars, rubber bands, backpacks, bombs and baby teeth—a gilded dust in a quiet room, they floated weightless. She reached behind her head, twisted her hair into a bun and clipped it at the nape of her neck.

"Let's take a moment to come into our bodies," she said.

She seated herself and took several deep breaths.

"Breathing out the day as we've known it until now and creating space for something new to arise. I invite you to let go of the expectations you came with and open to the experience of your body on the mat. Imagine a golden light coming in through the crown of your head with each breath, drawing it deeper into you and letting it go on the out breath."

My shoulders quivered. I saw Credence sitting in a field surrounded by katydids. They looked like leaves but when I ran over to him they all flew away. I thought this must be how it feels to speak in tongues. Right before, when no one knew you were about to.

"Letting it fill up each place that speaks to you."

Like abandoned airfields broken by weeds and baking in the sun.

"And bring special attention to those areas that may need noticing. Your hips, or your belly, or maybe a part of you that needs forgiving, that part of you that needs gentleness. And create a space for that gentleness to come in with your breath."

Mom used to say you have to look sadness right in the eye but I'm done with that. My body came alive. My fingers tingled and I could taste the salt in the air. I held my arm up and where once a sharp outline delineated me from the rest of the world there was a gradation. I was still myself, but my edges faded and when I moved I felt the Black Ocean give.

Everyone at Rise Up Singing knew who had bombed the New Land Trust building. Mr. Tofu Scramble said it was an intra-governmental squabble. Ed, Logic's Only Son said it was immigrants.

"They got their own radio station with fucking tubas and everything."

Mirror said she had a friend who applied for an admin job with New Land Trust and was denied an interview for refusing to claim a gender on the application.

"She could have totally done it."

Mitch, the cook, thought it was eco-terrorists for sure. Kelly, the fill-in dishwasher, agreed but then they split over whether it was an anarcho-primitivist cell or the Redwood Action Collective. That's how the betting pool got started. Mirror put each theory up on the "Specials" board as it came in and collected the money. By dinner she had erased the board twice, each time, writing smaller so it would all fit. As the list grew, I began to notice something. Everyone had a pretty good reason to blow up a building. I agreed with most of them. The names on the board might seem disconnected but there was a structural logic if you knew how to look.

We listened on the kitchen radio. A whole cast of heroes emerged. The janitor who could have been killed in the blast and wasn't. The junior executive who said he would continue to use the bathroom when it was rebuilt. The woman who was the first to see the smoke. Each of them, a bright star.

Meanwhile, customers congregated by the cash register, laughing as more possible terrorist groups went up on the board. Martyrs, bullies and causes in demographic filigree entwined in unpredictable ways. And where others saw fragmentation, I saw a terrible unity. The truth was that anybody could have done it. I could have done it if I didn't shake every time someone slammed a car trunk shut or think the birds were children screaming and garbage trucks were tanks. If I wasn't that way, I could have blown it up. It's not like I hadn't seen blast coronas paint the sky orange, devouring walls of flame. I see it in my sleep and sometimes behind the heads of people I love like a B movie backdrop. I was glad in a way that other people had to see what I'd been seeing. Even if the New Land Trust bombing was so much smaller than what was in my head, I was glad. They should have to see. In any case, it was another good reason to leave the country. If you were the type. I wish I were.

Credence says it's like leaving the scene of the crime.

"So have you ever thought about leaving?"

"No. Never," I lied.

"Good," he slaps my shoulder, "there's been enough of that," and with jail solidarity reconfirmed, Credence sets his coffee cup in the sink where it turns into a silk moth, flies into a light fixture, and rains down in a cascade of ash.

That evening I got a text message from Jimmy asking me to meet her at a party in the industrial district down by the water. I don't know if it was her idea or if Credence asked her to keep an eye on me. He probably thought a warehouse full of dystopic urban hippies was safer than any padded room. Nothing but the dull thud of zero contact.

"Come on," said Jimmy. "You'll meet people. It'll be good."

Because meeting people is always good.

The Glass House was a single-story factory between grain elevators where they used to make art glass in the 40s. Two summers ago when I was home from school I'd gone to a bunch of parties there. Mostly noise bands. It was down by the water where all the roads were industrial gullies and loading zones. Most of the windows of the Glass House were blown out and the electrical was badly patched because the copper wire got scavenged from the boxes every few months and sold. Someone told me there was a fleet of meth-heads in homemade boats crossing the river at night, sailing right up under the docks and stripping copper from the conduits. A Dunkirk of tweakers. I imagined them building a penny-colored palace in the hills with exploding processing plants and Guitar Hero going all the time.

I chained my bike to the side rail. Music came through the windows, some brown Goth thing with cellos and keyboards. By the door was a girl in a pink dress with a vintage apron tied around her waist. Her arm was tattooed with cherry blossoms and her hand was on a glass vase full of dollar bills. I didn't see Jimmy's truck anywhere. I asked the door girl if she knew Jimmy but she didn't.

Inside, sheets of colored glass hung from ceiling like guillotines and I could hear the words "New Land Trust" pattering through the room.

The event was a benefit for a media collective that taught underprivileged kids how to make chapbooks. On a table next to me were some of the books the kids made. I looked through them. They were full of basketball stars with guns and Spiderman cars, kids with blood drawn like tears. Slanted houses and sagging rainbows buckling in the blue sky. I couldn't take it. Everyone was eating almond pâté.

Jimmy said on the phone that she was bringing vegan cupcakes so I went over to the food table but it was all nut paste and tabouli. Behind me someone was talking about leaving the country and I glanced behind me. It was some neo-tribal Goth chick with thick silver jewelry and henna tattoos. She had a ticket to Mexico. A man with a thin beard spreading nut paste on a

cracker asked her where she was flying into—Mexico City—
and they compared notes. I thought about Jimmy in Honduras
and an aching swell like nausea hit me. I wanted to go. I wanted
to go and never come back. Honduras, Mexico, Bali, anywhere,
I don't care.

"I'll start in the north and work my way down to Chiapas,"
the girl said.

Her Nepalese bracelets clanked together as she reached for
the tabouli.

Another woman laughed.

"It won't matter where you go," she said, "it's all going to
happen here."

The woman who spoke was older than me, not by much,
maybe in her thirties. Most of her hair was dirty blonde but the
hair closest to her face was lavender.

"It's already started," she said and leaned across me to put
some tabouli on her plate. "Look at the New Land Trust building. You knew someone was going to try to take that thing
down. It was just a matter of time."

She put a forkful of tabouli in her mouth and chewed.

"So what," the other girl said, "They can blow up all the
buildings. It's still going to be the same stupid people walking
around."

The woman with the lavender hair put her fork down, staring blankly across the crowd. Her eyes were bright blue and she
had on gray glitter eye shadow that was creased and rubbing off.
Faint streaks of it sparkled under her eyes and across her cheekbones. Swallowing, she turned slightly and looked up at me.

"Well," she said, "What do you think? I'm taking a poll."

"About what?"

"Should we all just become eco-tourists until the sun shines
down?"

She reminded me of someone. I couldn't think of who it
was. I wasn't sure it was someone I liked.

"People should do what they want," I said.

My voice sounded thin and she caught it.

"Oh come on!" she laughed, "You can barely even get the words out."

"I'm just saying that, a lot of times when people leave, it's no loss."

"Like?"

Like me.

"Like I went to a party at an anarchist house with some Food Not Bombs guy. They had an old-time band in the basement and like six hundred crusty punks square dancing. I figure they can do that just about anywhere. There are a lot of islands in Micronesia."

The woman laughed abruptly. For a second I saw her real intelligence blaze out over the world like something that had escaped. It hit me again, that feeling that I knew her. She took another bite of tabouli.

"What about the New Land Trust building? Would you have blown it up?"

A couple of people smearing pâté on their seed crackers stopped. Everyone likes a bomb, I guess.

"No."

"No one got killed."

"Could have."

"What if no one got hurt?"

"Maybe," I said. "In theory."

"What if one person got hurt?"

"Then no."

"What if they just hurt? Time off with pay."

"And I was a psychic and knew for sure? Maybe."

"And he was an asshole. Like he beat his wife or molested kids?"

"I wouldn't be sad but I wouldn't do it."

"Oh," she said smiling, "so it's a matter of degree. Injuries are fine. And if an asshole gets killed you don't really mind as long as you don't have to do it yourself."

Some guy getting cashew butter laughed and the woman with the blonde and lavender hair grinned.

"They blew up a bathroom," I said, a little too loudly. "Not the fucking space station. They'll probably build the new one out of 800-year old cedar and elephant tusks. Blowing it up was fucking pointless."

Apparently you can be a terrorist as long as you don't raise your voice because everyone started looking at the ground, which is code for "You're dead to us now."

"So what's your great plan?" I said.

"To begin with I'm not leaving."

"I might," I snapped.

"Yeah, that will really change things for people."

"It'll change things for me."

My cheeks were on fire. If didn't get away I was going to start crying tears of hateful rage all over myself. Across the room by the door I saw Jimmy. She waved. The woman with the lavender hair glanced over her shoulder then put some more tabouli on her plate.

"I hear Goa has nice beaches," she said.

Jimmy came up, mild and oblivious. She'd dyed her hair tangerine and was holding a tray of pink frosted cupcakes.

"I put Red Hots on them. Want to help me frost the rest?"

"Well," said the woman, "I guess you can do what you're doing just about anywhere."

Jimmy handed me a cupcake. I wanted to throw it at the wall. The Goth chick wanted to know if Red Hots were vegan.

Outside they started setting off fireworks. I could feel them in my spleen. People pressed against the windows. Jimmy went over too. Explosion after explosion in a cascade of storylines, spiders and chrysanthemums, cakes and candles, beautiful showers of green and fuchsia rained down and all I saw was war.

Across the room I saw a guy who was the homeless boy-friend of a girl I used to know. Someone said he wrote a banjo retelling of the *Divine Comedy*. It was supposed to be good but I never heard it. What I did know was, if he was there, everyone else I knew for the past ten years was going to show up too. I went outside, told Jimmy I needed air.

Smoke from the fireworks drifted between the wheels of biodiesel trucks. On the other side of the water tiny campfires glowed. Abandoned cars parked along the frontage road with people crouched inside. Every now and then a lighter flared and car windows flashed like fireflies on the banks. On our side of the river were dancehalls and lit windows flickering like a net of stars. But it wasn't going to stay like that. The whole area was about to get a huge development grant. We were only there because we were cheaper than security. And, look! An art district! A cobbled bohemia between the packed earth and the leathered sole of the descending boot, a chapel of freedom.

I helped Jimmy frost cupcakes and stayed in the kitchen for most of the party. Jimmy offered to give me a ride home.

"I have to drop these trays off at the restaurant first but it won't take long. We can throw your bike in the back of my truck."

In the truck we talked about Honduras.

"I'm going miss this," she said gesturing vaguely at the warehouse behind us as we crossed the train tracks and lurched up onto to another frontage road, "but I'm not going to miss the rest."

We rolled up onto a newly paved street, which ran along the edge of a small park with rusted swings and a slide. Then we turned and drove up a hill until we came to a Catholic church and a coffee shop, the gateway to our neighborhood, and passed between them.

The world outside is only as big as a small island, I thought, a thin spit of sand. On one end they speak Spanish and on the other end Lao. I saw everything anew. We were already in Honduras. New Honduras. My problem was the language barrier. The streets weren't a record of community decimation. They were filled with merry peasants. Look! There's a bike shop. My neighborhood was filled with happy people. So much better since all that land reform went through. During the day young paisanos lingered by the food co-ops unloading trucks, glad to be helping farmers bring their groceries to urban markets.

"Hola!" I call.

"Hola!" they call back.

New Honduras.

Jimmy pulled up by Rise Up Singing and we dropped off the trays. When we were locking up I thought, why not leave?

"I might come," I said. "To where you are, I mean. For a little while."

There wasn't any moon, just an emergency light at the other end of the block. I couldn't see Jimmy's expression but I felt her body relax. Because that's the way it is when a possibility opens up; the body doesn't know any better. It reaches for the glittering incongruity.

The alarm went off and Jimmy jumped up to get it then walked into the kitchen. I heard dishes clank as she pulled cups from the full sink. She called out asking if I wanted tea. Her voice echoed on the wood floorboards and in the short hallways.

I braided my hair naked in bed. I couldn't find my rubber bands so I made two pigtails and tied them together at the base of my neck. My red corduroy dress was across the room under a book on historic churches of Honduras. I pulled it out and slapped it against the carpet to get the wrinkles out. There were little pink bleach stains all over the front, which I hadn't noticed before. They started at my ribcage and went all the way to the bottom edge just above my knee.

I put it on and went into the kitchen. The sky was white through the windows. Rows of green seedlings and starts lined the windowsills, which dipped unevenly and had rounded edges from too many layers of paint. Jimmy pulled a kettle off the stove. A ladder of silk now spanned between us. Jimmy set a Japanese teacup in front of me. With the windows full of the blank white sky and everything in the kitchen so clear and sharp, it looked like an unfinished painting, as if someone had meticulously filled in the details of the room but forgotten to draw the world outside.

"The anniversary is Saturday, right?" she asked, sitting down across from me.

"Anniversary?"

"Grace and Miro's. We're still going out, right?"

"God, I don't know."

Jimmy flushed slightly.

"I just don't want to think about it right now."

"Are you really thinking about leaving?"

"Maybe. Don't know where I'd go."

"You could stay with me in Honduras if you want."

I must have flinched because her chest tightened.

"I'm not saying we should get a dog or anything," she said, "I'm fine with however this goes. Just know you're welcome."

Jimmy's kitchen table was made of salvaged boat planks and I ran my hand across the bowed wood and tried to imagine what the Black Ocean would actually feel like.

She sliced some zucchini bread and poured green tea into a blue-glazed cup in front of me. I looked around like I had been born into that moment. Like I had been somewhere else all along. I saw the glittering incongruity. I was right in the center of it. It's simple when you're not clenching up and I was before but didn't know it. At some point that morning the clenching stopped. There was really no reason I couldn't leave.

Rise Up Singing was empty but the tables were full of dirty dishes. Mirror was throwing them into a black bus tub.

"There was a fucking bike messenger convention here. It was the annual race and Franklin forgot to schedule a dishwasher. It totally sucked. They all wanted smoothies and like ten plates of nachos each. We're out of rice. Rice."

"Are the checks in?"

"In the back. Franklin changed the work meeting. There's a sign up."

Above the time cards was a large piece of peach construction paper.

OUT OF RESPECT FOR MIRROR'S UPCOMING EVENT
AND CONCERNS ABOUT ATTENDENCE AT THE

WORK MEETING I HAVE CHOSEN TO RESCHEDULE.
WE WILL CLOSE EARLY THIS SATURDAY INSTEAD AND
MEET FOLLOWING BRUNCH. ALCOHOL AND VEGAN
CUPCAKES PROVIDED.

—FRANKLIN

Coworker Franklin had taken the time to draw fleur-de-lis and devil heads around the edge of the paper. I went back out. Mirror had a look of great satisfaction.

"Good for the sex party?"

"Good for fucking Franklin," she said and threw a heavy white dinner plate into a tub where it broke a pint glass. "I don't know what he was thinking by scheduling the day after the party. There was totally going to be nobody there. Birds chirping. I'm not even sure we'd be done."

Someone came in the front door, looked around and left.

"Good. I fucking hate people," she said.

Mirror grabbed a spoon and started eating lentils off the line.

"Franklin's changing the food policy," she said with her mouth full of food, "He says we should pay for salmon because it's so expensive. I told him he should pay for it by going to hell for serving it and that I hope a two-thousand pound Coho haunts his fucking elder years."

She dug around in a plastic container for some avocado slices.

My paycheck was nowhere near enough for a ticket. The prices were skyrocketing. Everyone with retirement was cashing out and there were 401(k) fare specials everywhere with slogans like "Why rollover when you can do-over?" Pictures of dilapidated colonial mansions. Beaches of beautiful children. Exotic sodas in Brahmi script. I passed them daily.

But while my money was limited, my credit was not. There was a world of predatory lending to explore. Mail had been piling up for months at my PO box. There had to be credit card offers. I picked up two tubs of personal history from the postmaster, lugged them home, and dumped them on the floor of my room. Letters from the geology department at UC Davis fanned across the carpet. There was one from my advisor urging me to apply for a position and another from an ex-boyfriend who'd read my dissertation, thought it was hot and wanted my number. There were the journals—paleographic, astrobiological, geospheric and a receipt for a six-volume set on brachiopods. Complimentary calendars, notes of congratulation, letters of concern, etc.... I threw anything that wasn't money-related back into a tub and wrote "Head of John the Baptist" on the side of it with a Sharpie. I picked out a credit card application from the Geological Society of America. 1-888-BUY-COAL.

I called them up.

"Star Bank Plaza One Visa, how may I help you?"

"I'd like to take advantage of a recent credit card offer."

I told them I was a full tenured professor with no kids. They loved me. I could have bought a plane.

"Would you prefer igneous, metamorphic or sedimentary rock structures on your card, ma'am?"

"Do you have the Deccan Traps? 'Cause I'd like the Deccan Traps if you have it. They're in India. You know, a lot of people believe that eruption caused the extinction of fifty percent of life on earth."

"No, ma'am. We have the Grand Canyon, one with some jewels on it and a Hawaiian volcano."

"Or if you have a comet smashing into the planet. I'd like that too."

"Canyon, jewels, volcano."

"Rim of Fire?"

While on the phone I drafted a speech to Credence and Annette:

Fellow Travelers and Attending Bellyfish,

> While I have walked this road with you, led mostly by
> your courage and commitment, it is now time for me to depart
> and cut my way through the jungle alone. May we all meet under
> the bright arc of social revolution one day as The Public and
> celebrate our re-emergence as citizens and lovers.
> Until then, I will set up web-based email and make sure you
> all have it before I leave.

Yours endlessly,
Friend of the Tiny Liver Hearts/Pool of Light

I took the bus downtown. I wanted to go to an actual travel agency because I thought that would make it feel more real but the buildings looked like cutouts and I felt like a paper doll. Annette gave me a white dress with little bluebells on it that belonged to her grandmother. I was wearing that but I could have been wearing anything else. I could have been dressed like a prom queen or for a day at the beach with a bucket and shovel. The background was fixed but I could have been stuck anywhere, made to lie flat on the lakes, hover above intersections, or placed askance on the painted ground.

I got off the bus at a plaza. It was paved with manufactured rock carved to look like flagstones. I thought they were real at first but then I saw the gutters between stones were too even to be actual masonry and that they weren't real and never had been, just like all of this.

The travel agency was on the other side of the plaza. I walked across the fake red rock and the sound of air brakes and wheelchair ramps faded. The air was dense. A boy threw a handful of pennies at some pigeons and they scattered to the skies.

He laughed and ran after the rolling coins. When he found all the pennies he put them back into a Styrofoam cup, waited for the pigeons to land and threw them again. Beating wings fluttered by my head.

I had come there as a kid when it was still called Redbird Square. My earliest memory is of being there with my mom. It was full of people and someone was speaking into a microphone. Every few minutes the crowd broke into cheering. Their voices rose and turned to a wild chant. I could feel the ground shudder with the rhythm of the words. It scared me and I leaned into a fold of my mama's red wool coat and squeezed her hand tighter. I put my cheek on it. It was as if the world came into me through her fingertips alone. No one's called it Redbird Square for years. They renamed it after the bank that paid for all the fake rock.

The travel agency stood before me. The window was full of fake snow, palm trees and sombreros. On a large white board, fares were listed:

Athens	$759
Belize	$386
Istanbul	$399
Mexico City	$284
Paris	$438
Panama City	$512
Phnom Penh	$

I saw my body reflected as a faint outline on the glass. Some of the cities were outside of me and others were inside. Two were divided and started in me but streamed out in lines of letters and numbers. Belize was over my eyes. Mexico City began in my heart and over my abdomen was Phnom Penh, but most people probably wouldn't have seen that one. "Get away. You deserve it!" floated backwards over my head in the white sky.

Inside the agency, a woman with frosted hair and terra cotta skin sat at a desk next to a large rubber plant. She was on the phone and typing but waved me over to the seat opposite her. She wore coral lipstick and a diamond solitaire on a thin chain that rolled back and forth across her breastbone when she talked.

I looked through a brochure while I waited. There was one with a collage of jungle and rice paddies behind an old man's brown face. He was smiling like nothing had ever been wrong. I wondered if he liked macaroni and cheese.

"So," the travel agent said, "what can I help you with?"

Her eyelids were slightly wrinkled and weighed down by pink shimmer.

"Travel," I said.

"Well, that's what we're here for. Where would you like to go? We have a great special on Southeast Asia right now. Four nights in three capitals and two bonus days on the beach. There are six to choose from. I went last year and had a blast. Do you like spicy food?"

I saw tiny liver hearts hanging like peppers, bound and bunched in doorways and storefronts.

"Yes, I like spicy food."

"Good, 'cause boy they have it! I can take it in Mexican but it was a little much for me there. My boyfriend loved it, though. Couldn't get enough."

The diamond bounced against her chest.

"I like beautiful places," I said.

"Well, it's about perfect for you then. I recommend Thailand or Vietnam."

She took the brochure from my hands, opened it to a page and pushed it across the desk.

IN AN ANCIENT LAND…(Women in cowry shell hats enjoying re-colonization on green) BEAUTY IS ETERNAL…

The travel agent held her breath. The diamond lay still. There were small snapping sounds and I saw a vision. I saw origami Buddhas and Popsicle stick palaces burning like hay and ashes blowing over manufactured stone flags, carved to look real. I saw a bamboo parliament of patio furniture lulled by the sound of quiet blackberries.

"It's green," I said and she started breathing again.

She pulled out a list of destinations.

"I have to say, Bangkok is still my favorite. Vietnam is very nice too. They have those cute little bicycle taxis."

"Rickshaws?"

"Rickshaws—that's it! I love those things."

"What about Laos? Or Cambodia?" I asked.

"I don't know if they have rickshaws."

"They aren't on the list of fares."

"Well, yes, we do book trips there but they're still coming up."

"Aren't they beautiful?"

"Oh lovely, but with… more of a history if you know what I mean. You can't get to some of the prettiest places."

"Why?"

The travel agent played with a ring on her finger and glanced over at a wall clock.

"Landmines," she said.

"Landmines?"

"I mean it's not impossible, just inconvenient. You can get a guide. The children know those areas like their own backyard. They work cheap too. It just makes getting around that much harder. And when you're on vacation…"

She trailed off.

"…You don't need those kind of hassles."

"What about Central America?" I asked and she bloomed.

"Oh! Now that is the place. I recommend Costa Rica. It's progressive, eco-tourist friendly and has some of the best beaches in the world. Do you like yoga?"

I looked at the brochures under the leaning rubber plant. Central America, the Atlantis of my people. In the end I bought a one-way ticket to Tegucigalpa. The travel agent saw me to the door and locked it behind me.

"Good luck," she said through the glass, the diamond rolling across her chest.

Della Mylinak
Get away. You deserve it
000000799.99

All night long I dreamt of the Black Ocean.

The next day I practiced telling people I was leaving. At the yoga studio—

Devadatta: Namaste!

Me: I'm leaving.

Devadatta: Oh well, we'll sure miss you here. Where are you going?

Me: Central America.

(Devadatta unravels a Guatemalan scarf from her hair. There were tiny people woven into in the pattern, each carrying a yellow cross-stitch crucifix.)

Devadatta: I studied yoga in Costa Rica. That's where I got this scarf.

She laid the scarf twisted and purplish like tangled seaweed on the counter between us.

Me: I like the little people. Are they slaves?

Devadatta: God no! They're indigenous.

And at work—

Me: I'm leaving.

Mr. Tofu Scramble: Well, Della, you know in the end we're really only citizens of Gaia, aren't we?

Ed, Logic's Only Son: I'm a citizen of the United fucking States.

Mr. Tofu Scramble: I'd think about Southeast Asia.

Ed, Logic's Only Son: You should all go to Cuba and get shot by Fidel.

No matter how I said it, I felt like a coward. The voice of the lavender-haired girl at the party sang in my head, something from childhood I couldn't pinpoint, that tone of disgust, and I was a kid all over again with nothing to back me up but a bellyful of *Kimba* reruns—Run, Kimba! A mother constellated of stars. Kimba! There is supernatural help. Your father is still alive in the forest—

"Right!" I said to myself aloud. "I should stay here. Publish a manifesto calling on all of us to dress our scarecrows from the community free-box so it'll fool the giant crows making nest out of hemp and third party candidates."

I went to find Credence. To tell him I was leaving, tell him why and make him understand. I charged up the front steps and began looking through rooms until I found him. He and Annette were scraping paint off the doorframe of the upstairs bathroom.

"Hey," I called, breaching the landing, "I wanted to tell you something."

—I am leaving. I don't want to watch anymore. I can't stop the bus from running off the cliff and the sea is already filled with lights. I don't know why I can't be one. I'm going to try. If I stay here I won't be anything the Bellyfish could lean on, I'll just be something they have to prop up—

"How was the benefit?" asked Credence.

"The benefit?"

"At the Glass House."

Again, the girl with the lavender hair.

"Fine."

Annette stepped through the doorway. "Are you and Jimmy going to drive up to the anniversary in her truck?"

I couldn't tell them, not in that moment.

"In the truck."

"Lesbians in a truck!" laughed Annette, "Grace will love it,"

60

and, grinning like a dingo, she walked down the hallway, swaying and humming with the Bellyfish darting and snapping inside her.

Credence handed me a chisel.

"See if you can get the stuff off by the lock without gouging
the wood."

I would tell them tomorrow. I would say: I am a pool of
light, then flicker like sun on a swimming pool. I would say: It
has already erupted. And then, dancing through the braided
shadows on the basin, wait for the foliage to land in the pool
water and make galleons and cutters out of oak leaves and elm.
Then they would have to understand.

The next day a second bomb went off at an auto shop down
the street from Rise Up Singing. Everyone was running. But you
can't outrun it. I know. I've tried. You just come to the same
place again and again. The return is so fast now for me that from
the outside it looks like stillness. Like nothing is happening at
all. But beyond that stillness is an unmappable topography, an
endless stream of content.

I was at work when the bomb at the auto shop went off. At the time, everybody was focused on a different drama. That morning Mirror had come in, thrown her bag down on the counter, and said, "They've totally sold the restaurant."

The cook, Mitch, came out of the kitchen. She was wearing a t-shirt of a pregnant woman carrying an assault rifle and her face was red from working the grill.

"No way. Franklin would never sell without giving us chance to buy it."

"I am so fucking serious it's not even funny," said Mirror. "It's a done deal. Everyone in the neighborhood already knows. That's what that stupid work meeting's about."

Mitch shook her head. "It's a rumor."

"Actually," said Mr. Tofu Scramble with his mouth full of potatoes, "I heard about it last week. A real shame. Well," he swallowed, "I guess things have to change. One less thing to miss about this country, right? Hey Mitch, tell Franklin thanks for getting the spelt. Can I get another order when you have a chance?"

Mitch's cheeks ticked. A pancake started to smoke on the grill.

"I just don't think he would."

"The new owners have been in here twice," said Mirror. "Kelly waited on them. They're from California. They're not even vegetarian."

Mitch stared at the toast crumbs on Mr. Tofu Scramble's plate. Then she went to the walk-in, pulled out a bottle of wine, and stomped back into the kitchen. Seconds later a two-pound whisk hit the corkboard with the minimum wage standards.

Word of the sale spread and took over the New Land Trust bombing as the favored topic. Everyone had an opinion:

Ed, Logic's Only Son: You're all going to get fired.

Mr. Tofu Scramble: Change often leads to transformation. Who would have thought I'd end up on one of the most beautiful beaches in the world?

Ed, Logic's Only Son: None of you are getting welfare either.

Mr. Tofu Scramble: You know the Balinese women are so graceful because they balance things on their heads.

It turned out Coworker Franklin had already put most of the kitchen equipment and all the decorative art pieces up on eBay. Half the neighborhood had been bidding on the Indonesian garden lattices for a week. Every time the outrage died out and Mitch calmed down, someone new walked through the door.

"Did Franklin really sell the restaurant?"

A loud crash in the kitchen as a heavy colander hit a row of hanging pots.

"Hey, can I see the Javanese batik screens? They look small on the computer."

Glasses smashing against the metal rim of a trashcan.

"You know, I always thought this place would make a nice tapas bar."

Mitch pours a bottle of wine into a pan and a huge fireball engulfs the stove.

As the shift progressed Mitch got more and more liberal with the portions until she was slicing a whole salmon or vegan chocolate cake into quarters and dropping them randomly on tables as gifts. Mirror made everyone free mimosas. By 4 PM we were all drunk and Mirror was raiding the lost and found box for clothes. She pocketed a couple of cell phones and put on a sparkly, red mesh top. Mitch asked her to get some things out of the shed but she refused, "I'm sick of burying rats." She walked over to a table of her friends and sat down. They were talking about the upcoming sex party and Mirror started to draw plans, "We'll put the stage over here, the DJ over there and upstairs…" But Mitch needed rice to plug the drains and cups for the free wine so I said I'd get them.

The shed has a padlock but no one ever uses it. That's how the animals get in. I opened the doors and stepped back to give them a chance. Nothing happened so I went in. Franklin orders rice from an Indonesian catalog and they come in these forty-pound canvas bags with red script and third eyes all over them. I grabbed one for Mitch. Everything had been eaten into. Egg noodles, salt crackers and buckwheat pancake mix. I found a bag of marshmallows cut open lengthwise. I pulled down a sack of paper cups. Behind it was a folded red bandana.

Carrying the trash to the dumpster, I passed the Rat Grave-yard. Most of the twig crosses had been stepped on and what was left leaned sharply and dipped towards ground. Someone tied the Buzz Lightyear doll to a new cross, the cross of the pregnant rat. Under Buzz Lightyear's dangling feet were blue marbles and around the mound a circle of pennies. I stopped and sat on the half-tilled soil. The sun was low and across Buzz Lightyear's helmet tawny light fell. Water soaked into my underwear. On the grave itself someone had pressed beads into the dirt. Hundreds of them sprinkled, set and flashing like pyrite in a creek. It must be a Rat Queen, I thought, what else? A Rat Queen, the natural symbol of New Honduras. Basta! I saw flags. Basta! On a field of red and yellow she towered over the computer-generated superhero, her belly full with the earth and at her feet pennies, marbles and beads like a thousand broken necklaces thrown in her path. Basta! I took the red bandana I found in the shed and tied it around Buzz Lightyear's plastic feet. Then I opened the front of his space helmet and left him there to die. A final act before the Black Ocean. I brought the bag of rice and the cups back to the kitchen.

Seconds later a large blast shook the building.

"What the fuck was that?" shouted Mitch.

Another blast came and I heard breaking glass. Everyone got down. The street filled with black smoke and people were running out of shops. We ran too. The guy who owned the vintage clothing store next to us was dialing frantically on his cell phone and there was a dog freaking out and barking at everyone.

The explosions came from the auto shop on the corner. It was on fire. We ran towards the end of the block where people were gathering. The blast had come from a truck in the center of the auto shop lot. By the time we got there it was nothing but a charred skeleton. A huge, bright tongue of flame had swallowed it. Reaching up into the sky it bellowed and snapped.

"That garage is going to go," said a woman next to us.

She worked at the salon across the street and still had hair clips in her hand. The orange light from the blaze reflected faintly on her cheeks and sweat cut fine pathways in her foundation.

"It's going to hit the kiosk first," said another man. "See how the wind's blowing?"

He was right. The paint on the side of the kiosk was bubbling and the blaze mirrored in the windows splashed like lava. A large gust of wind came up and blew it all back the other way and the sky opened before us. Stars pricked the approaching night, clear and cloudless over our heads. Then it all went black and the fire roared to new life devouring the kiosk. It exploded and pieces of the flaming roof rained down like comets. They landed on cars and sidewalks. A piece landed right in front of me, burning and vivid. I could hear the tar cracking.

"That auto shop was the last black-owned business on the street," said the man.

Everyone watched like they had somehow done it. More pieces fell hissing to the ground. People moved back as the great blaze shot sparks and embers into the sky. I saw the Rat Queen rise behind the gutted kiosk, her fur glistening with beads, and wearing a crown of broken marbles. Before me Old Honduras burned and New Honduras rose. Where once an old auto shop stood, now was raised a Popsicle stick palace, barely visible but there all the same. From one angle it was a bistro, from another a high-end knit shop. When I stood back it was a multi-use fa-cility with a tattoo parlor above and a naturopathic clinic be-low. The sirens came at last but they were far too late.

A policeman with a wide nose and an oily forehead grabbed my arm.

"No one is leaving this block.

The woman who ran the salon started crying because she had to pick-up her kids and there was no one else to do it and I don't know if the woman was tired or just scared but she went into hysterics, sat down on the curb, and wailed. Black tears poured down her face as her mascara ran. Thistles of kohl, briery eyes, she looked up and I saw the face of a saint martyred at the boundary of old and new. A patroness of New Honduras who would someday perform miracles for women stuck at work who could not pick up their kids from daycare in time.

"I can't just stay here," she sobbed.

"Nobody is leaving," said the cop and walked away.

The Rat Queen shook her head in a shower of pennies and beads and scratched at the cinders of Old Honduras looking for her children too.

Police set up a barricade at one end of the street and another several blocks down in the other direction. Mirror hauled the Saint with the Black Tears back to the restaurant. I followed a few minutes later, walking through gusts of smoke. Chips of flaming auto shop whizzed by my head, most of them no bigger than a quarter. There was still some pink on the horizon but mostly it was night now. Above us stars were hidden in the haze.

Rise Up Singing was packed. The whole block was standing around eating vegan doughnuts waiting for a chance at the landline. Gangs, they said. But not everyone agreed. Insurance, some thought. One guy said developers but nobody believed him because that would just be too obvious. Mitch was giving away more food. Mirror was taking advantage of the situation to drive turnout for the sex party. "I'm gonna need a warehouse," she said opening another bottle of champagne.

Jimmy called. I don't know how she got through. She said it was getting live coverage. We could see the news trucks but the police told us they would give the interviews. Jimmy said barricades were going up all over the north part of town. Time of the Crickets. I asked her to call Annette and let her know I was okay.

The cops weren't telling us anything and after a few more hours people had all kinds of dumb theories—bio-warfare testing site, elaborate casting call (we're all going to be in a movie!), or my favorite, foreign invasion. Like some kind of maquiladora Kindertransport had gone rogue and taken a beachhead. But around 2 AM the cops let us go. It happened all of a sudden. There was a radio communication and they packed their bullhorns and their sawhorses, took down the barricades and left. When we walked outside the auto shop was a cinder and everything had a film of greasy smoke on it. People wandered off drunk and stunned.

"Just leave the doors unlocked," said Mitch, "it doesn't matter anyway."

Mirror's friend Jolie showed up in a Ford Econoline and they started packing up the dry goods and what was left of the food in the walk-in. Mitch gave me some white wine and an untouched vegan pineapple-lemon cake, both of which I put in my bike basket.

Devadatta was asleep in a booth with her mouth open. She was wearing a t-shirt that said "Reincarnation—You Asked For

It." Her scarf was on the ground and the tips of her long red hair lay like wet paintbrushes in a puddle of beer.

"Someone's got to take her home," said Mirror and woke her up.

But she was too drunk to stand on her own.

"I'll take her," I said.

Mirror helped me get Devadatta on her feet and we left.

I rolled my bike down the sidewalk with one hand on the handlebars and the other on Devadatta. I had to sidestep debris that was still hot and smoking faintly. Every now and then a little piece would pop and crack open near us and we'd jump. After a few blocks she began to get more lucid.

"You know, Devadatta isn't my real name."

We passed under the emergency lamp near the post office and she stopped, swaying slightly.

"Really?"

"Really."

"Yeah, I picked it out when I was in high school," she stopped to pant then got it together again, "My real name is Galaxy."

"Galaxy?"

"Yeah. I wanted something less obvious. Devadatta was a disciple of Buddha."

"The one who slandered him and took over his monastery?"

"That's him," she said, and threw up on the leg of a mailbox, "He wasn't a very good disciple."

She tilted her face up and closed her eyes. The moon was thin and her skin was green. I saw vines and coins growing up around her. She smiled and started to walk again.

"So you just liked the sound of it?"

"No. I like Devadatta. Can you imagine fighting Buddha?"

She dug in her bag and pulled out something wrapped in a napkin. It was a chocolate doughnut.

"I think it was a punk rock thing," she said, taking a big bite, "I used to shave my head. Total straight-edge."

A minute later she threw up in a storm drain and sat down. I sat on the curb beside her and opened one of the bottles of white wine. Devadatta rocked back and forth on her haunches with her head hanging down.

"Malasana. Deep squat," she said, "Raina says it's good for the root chakra. I think it's helping."

"Have you ever washed your hair with wine?"

"Beer. And eggs."

"I'm going to try it," I said.

I hung my head over the gutter and poured wine on my head. I twisted my hair around my hands and wrung the excess out. I shook my head. Drops of Chateau Montaigut went everywhere.

"Oh my god. I'm gonna throw up," she said.

It was the smell of the wine, of course, but I had to get the dust of Old Honduras off of me otherwise I would never make it. I'd go extinct at the boundary like the rats and the blackberries and the blacks.

"Wait," she put her hand up, "I'm okay."

"Yeah," I said wiping wine out of my eyes, "me too."

Above us the night changed. Clouds from the south came in low. Devadatta pulled her sweater out of the bike basket and put it back on.

"Don't you think it's weird how the cops left like that?"

"It certainly wasn't a gang thing."

Devadatta looked down the street. The Roseway Bridge was about a mile off. Police cars were parked there. Something was going on. Spinning blue and red lights reflected off the girders and dark water. I felt like I could almost see it on her skin. Her eyes cleared and, for a second, I saw the diamonds in them just before a murky film shaded her irises.

She turned back to me. "Is Mercury retrograde?"

A hole in the clouds appeared right behind her and there were the stars bright as anything.

"Yes," I said, and why not?

"Thought so. Feels like it."

Devadatta stood. "I'll be fine the rest of the way on my own. I'd give you a hug but you smell like wine and I might barf."

It was 3 AM. The emergency lamps were behind us. Ahead was the next barricade. Devadatta started walking down the street singing something about blackout angels but I couldn't tell what it was because she was facing the other way. I turned back to the kaleidoscope of police lights down by the bridge.

Once, I asked Raina if she thought she could sit still on fire.

"I mean if you were trained to do it," I said, "like those monks."

"Well, I think if I were really convinced that I was done with this lifetime I could. But I think we make our own reality and that's just not the kind of reality I would make."

Yeah, well, I thought, the kind of reality I would make doesn't have people on fire in it either. Hey Raina! How do you say chardonnay in Sanskrit? I felt like a bullet in a gun. Like whatever was inside me was going to come out, like I had no control over it at all. I thought about the auto shop and the New Land Trust Building and all those people trying to figure out who bombed them. Not why, but who. Who exactly. As if by knowing, they would earn the right to forget about it. When I called the bomb threat into the sports bar near the Asian market, I did it because I wanted them to feel like I did, to cry over nothing and see bodies in the video aisles. It was only fair after their stupid silent wars, their reality shows and fake rock. They deserved some reflection on fear and the nature of impermanence. But it didn't work. It didn't work because they weren't already scared. If I had done it after the New Land Trust they would have been. Timing.

Walking home it occurred to me that the great thing about a bomb threat is how much it leaves to the imagination. Like your mom saying you're in trouble but not telling you why, you go over everything it could be in your mind. There were hidden rivers of guilt running underneath. There had to be.

In the morning I took a bus out to Four Points of Heaven Mall. We passed the smoking auto shop on the way. Brown figures wandered through the debris. They bent, turning over one object then another, before throwing them onto a pile in the center of the lot. The garage floor was strewn with flowers. Behold the shrine of the last black-owned business on the street! Scorched framing stuck out of the ground like whalebone and notes weighted with charred brick fragments fluttered in the morning breeze. The bus took a left at the light and it was gone. Beyond New Honduras, the avenues widened and bamboo blinds hung in the windows. Cats ran over welcoming porches. A woman trimmed a fuchsia in a light raincoat.

At a kiosk in an ancillary shopping park near Four Points of Heaven I bought nine prepaid cell phones. One for each child the Rat Queen might have had. I named them after the planets. In keeping with the inclusiveness of my new movement, I counted Pluto. I even got shared minutes. The lady at the kiosk called it the Hive Plan. The receipt had little bees all over it.

"The high school girls just love it," she said.

Because they need to coordinate their torture of each other? Or because it has bees?

"They just think the bees are adorable. And..."

They need to coordinate their torture of each other.

"And it comes in all these colors," she spread cell phones like cards on the counter. "Like lollipops."

And condoms.

"Or sweet tarts."

And handguns.

I paid for it all with cash pulled off my Grand Canyon Visa and spent the rest of the morning looking up FCC cell phone towers online and adding them to my maps. Little colored dots, like lollipops or condoms.

I got to the box-mall-church by late afternoon and the raffle hadn't started. The shiny red truck sat on the dais behind the velvet ropes like I'd seen it several days before, the coveted Aries Geo Killrover Conquistador. People gathered by its wheels and girls with clipboards circled the perimeter.

"Have you applied for a mall-wide Superland™ credit card yet? You're automatically entered."

I signed up the baby rats. Everyone deserves a chance.

The Piazza filled. I made a list of possible terrorist groups. I decided that it's only fair that with a personal savior you get a personal destroyer, niche terrorism being the obvious next step in identity politics. Narcissism meets the rest of the world. Hi! Howdy do? The market rallies. Satin-covered bullet cases? First-responder kits with your astrological sign etched on the front plate? I spent an hour in the food court by Mandarin Village watching a teenager serve fake rice and fantasizing about the Blackberry Apocalypse.

Just after 5 PM the Pastor of the box-mall-church stepped up on a riser next to the truck and took the microphone from the Human Resource Director who was making announcements. He jangled the key to the truck.

"Now, how come I haven't seen this many of you in church?"

Grace and Miro say fatherly admonishment is the sand in the cement of patriarchy.

The Pastor moved toward the huge glass barrel where the raffle entries tumbled. The crowd quieted. He put his hands down together in prayer and looked up. They burst into laughter.

I imagined his hand falling on a rat ticket, Venus Rodere. No single mother sobbing on stage about how she could now get to her second job. No honor student with gleaming eyes. No football star. No thankful soldiers whispering the prayers in Spanish.

She moved toward the tumbling barrel, a collective construction of fear and desire. A sexy black rat with vague family loyalties and an enhanced ability to survive on less? The sleek carrier of change and possible disease? The eldest daughter of the Rat Queen, a tall black woman with violet and copper extensions in a tight bronze miniskirt with a GPS in one hand and a machete in the other

Venus Rodere

You redeem others with your strength:

191292709.24

The backs of my hands quivered. I could feel the tiny hairs on my cheeks move like cilia.

It was about to start.

The Human Resources Director tumbled the barrel one final time and the Pastor reached in and pulled out the ticket. He cleared his throat and held it up.

A thousand people stopped moving but for the rustling of plastic bags.

I walked over to a pay phone, dug out a handful of change and called in a bomb threat. It was the easiest call I ever made. I told them I was with a group called Citizens for a Rabid Economy and that we were going to blow up the box-mall-church to stimulate local job growth. I also told them that we believed the creation of a media event would cause the increase in consumer spending necessary to economic expansion. And that they had twenty minutes to get everyone out of the building.

I hung up and sat down on a bench under some plastic palm trees. The Human Resources Director was making a short speech on the importance of community.

Two security officers ran past me. Then a voice came over the PA system: "This is an emergency. Please leave any shopping bags you have and move quickly to your nearest exit. This is not a test. Head to the nearest exit immediately. This is an emergency."

At first people were more annoyed than scared but after the second and third announcements, they began to rush the doors. I jumped in with the crowd. We were jammed through a side door and ended up out in the south parking lot. A couple of fat crickets with bullhorns ushered us toward a transit island in the center of the lot. People were asking them what was going on but they wouldn't say anything.

"I heard it's a bomb threat," I said.

"A bomb threat?" said the man next to me.

"Yeah, that's what I heard a cop say. Bomb threat."

And it bubbled through conversations, bomb threat, bomb threat, bomb threat, until it pattered out of earshot. Camera crews arrived in trucks and turned on the bright lights. All eyes on the box-mall-church. Police, reporters, shoppers—waiting, hanging on each tick of a second and nothing happened. Not a thing. People got restless. It was perfect. For the second time in an hour I snatched it from them.

Bomb squads were sent in to sweep the mall. Reporters went live with pictures of Rusty, the bomb-sniffing dog and asked viewers to pray for his safety. I didn't really think the day could get any better. But it did. Once it became clear that the police weren't going to let anybody back inside the mall and that it wasn't going to blow up, people began to leave. They got into their cars, thousands of them, but they couldn't get out of the parking lot. That took too much cooperation. They gridlocked themselves instantly.

I was laughing so hard my jaw hurt. Tears streamed down my face and every time I tried to get a handle on myself and calm down, I lost it again. It was better than being fourteen on mushrooms in a Denny's. At one point I actually had to sit down. Two hours into the fiasco they declared a city emergency and my ribs were so sore from convulsive laughter that I felt like I'd been beaten. I climbed up onto a ridge of new row housing that overlooked the city. Down below fire trucks and emergency vehicles flashed.

I lay down on my back in the lifeless dirt and stared at the sky. An hour later the first wave of street lamps went out in the valley. Under the new system they have to be off by 9 PM. I watched the neighborhoods go dark. From above with only the emergency lamps and chain stores visible, the grid system is gone and we are nothing but an aggregate of lights. Each gas station, fast food restaurant or all-night office supply store burns like an orange coal in the dark.

I started to walk. On either side of me were vacant, half-built houses. Their peaked roofs dipped with the angle of the road cut. Everything was wet from light rain but it was more like dew. I wandered through the new streets. I didn't know what I was doing. I did and I didn't. If I was really leaving I wanted there to be some kind of record showing exactly which side I was on, even if I was the only one who knew about it. The box-mall-church disappeared as I slipped over the backside of the rise. It had been a remarkable day and I was happy walking in that chilled, acid night.

By 10 PM I reached the old Asian business district. It had been shuttered and warehoused by developers. Cracked signs in Vietnamese, Korean and Mandarin hung unlit over vacant storefronts. There were no emergency lamps on the street at all. Light from the few apartments still occupied shone down in squares on the sidewalk. I felt like I was underwater. I wouldn't have been surprised if a cephalopod swam past.

The elation was dissipating. Currents of fear were starting to run through me but I couldn't place the source. No one had been hurt and I didn't care about their stupid traffic jam. Still, the fear was there, bordering on panic, flickering and then gone completely like a memory I could feel but not locate.

On the corner was a blinking sign with two neon Chinese children bowing to each other over a bowl of noodles. Underneath was some kind of bar. My legs hurt and I wanted to sit for a while. I walked down the wet stairs into the basement.

The restaurant was empty. I looked around, pink table-cloths, red carpets and video poker. On one side was a bar with a mounted television in the corner. A woman came out of the kitchen and walked up to the register. She set her hand down on the glass counter next to a fat jade Buddha and told me they were closing in half an hour. She was wide and unfriendly and when she brought my tea, she set the pot down so hard it splashed over the table. I watched the tea soak half the zodiac placemat. I read somewhere that the Buddha called all animals to enlightenment but only twelve showed up. The rat was first in line.

"What do you want?" she asked.

"Fortune cookies and a rum and coke."

She brought my drink and set down a black plastic tray with my bill and a white paper bag of fortune cookies next to it.

I turned my cell phone on to check the time and it rang immediately. It was Credence. I let it go to voicemail. He was calling about the anniversary. I was sure of it. It was tomorrow and the last thing I wanted to think about. A minute later the phone rang again. When he called the third time I sent him a text: CLIMBING RAT GOLGOTHA (GREAT VIEW). DON'T NEED ANY HELP. SEE YOU LATER, D. and turned the phone off.

I took the ticket to Tegucigalpa out of my bag and set it on the table. The cream envelope was getting worn and the corners were going, probably because I pulled the ticket out at least four times a day to make sure that nothing had changed—the dates of departure, the flight number, the destination, or my feelings about it. And three out of four was good enough. I held it for a minute then tucked back into the Velcro pocket of my bike messenger bag.

A few minutes later a man came out of the kitchen and sat at the far end of the bar with his back to me. He turned on the television. They were showing the box-mall-church and I felt that thrill return but only for a second because they cut away from it. Two, black faces appeared on the TV in split-screen. Yellow crime scene tape stretched behind a reporter at the base of the Roseway Bridge. The boys, who were wanted in connection with a robbery, had been shot by police near the Roseway Bridge the night before. A cricket with a face pink as a ham swore one had pulled a gun. It turned out to be some kind of robot or space doll, though. They showed the bridge again. It must have been going on while Devadatta and I sat by the storm drain. Can you cause something just by being near it? I let that thought vanish. The station went to a commercial and the man at the bar shouted something at the screen in Chinese. When they returned it was to a prerecorded show, Newscaster Barbie interviewing the head of the Church of Enlightened Capital, chatting intimately on studio couches. I'd seen him speak before down at Davis. It was pouring rain and the auditorium was packed with students, pressed heart to spine waiting for him to start. Steam rose from the audience.

"God is a broker!" he yelled. "We are his clients. We each have a role to play in this free market. Because the Lord Jesus gave us free will. We decide our destiny. How will we invest?" he shouted. "Who will we choose to be our broker?"

A guy next to me with a mohawk and a Celtic cross tattooed on his neck started crying like a little boy. The next week the cafeteria everyone was wearing t-shirts that said, "I'm a client." It was my first year at Davis. I hadn't made any friends yet and I didn't want to talk to anybody at school for months. All that felt like it had happened to someone else.

The head of the Church of Enlightened Capital looked exactly the same as he had nine years ago. Tan. Rolex crucifix as big as a human hand around his neck. Newscaster Barbie asked him questions on the couch. Numbers ran across the bottom of the screen and I couldn't tell if it was the Dow rising or the death toll or the temperature. I started thinking maybe I'd gone a little further out on the wire than I'd meant to and that it was time to inch my way back. Only a thin film separates God and commerce or environmentalism and colonialism, a film as thin as a cell wall, but that separation is everything and I could feel it dissolving.

The box-mall-church came on the TV again. Newscaster Ken's Black Friend Garth was interviewing the shoppers. Bringing a human face to the people trapped in the SUV line. A woman with red eyes was talking about how she'd gone to the mall to get a Pro-Life Penny Doll for her daughter, the one that comes with a little stack of blank birth certificates, and how she'd spent her yearly bonus on the doll and was going to surprise her daughter but it got lost in the panic.

I felt that horrible empathy again like a skin fever. I could feel the woman's grief at disappointing her daughter and her self-hatred at letting go of the shopping bag because she didn't have any money and it was a hard choice to buy the thing in the first place. And I could feel her daughter's desire for the doll and her attempts to hide that desire so it wouldn't make things worse and her overwhelming guilt for having mentioned it in the first place. I could feel it all. It was all suffering, all torque, a seamless garment of misery. Everything started to turn into little dots and I felt myself slipping. But it passed. My head cleared and I could see the wood of the bar in front of me. I looked at the woman crying over the doll and felt something else. I was sick of people acting against their own interests. Mooing about how to refinance the slaughterhouse. Putting skylights in the killing pen and pretending the bolt in the brain was a pathway to a better field. I paid my bill. Save your fucking pennies for a gun and a history book, I thought. But I knew I didn't mean it about the gun. I know I'd never be able to shoot anyone. I wish I could. I wish I could blow up things for real. Not really, but I do. Then the Roseway Bridge with the crime scene tape came back on and I got up and paid. After all, two black boys from Heritage Avenue getting shot by cops is the kind of thing that happens all the time. If I gave it one second of real attention, I would be lost.

I walked straight up the hill back to New Honduras where the simple natives were building cornhusk huts and hoping parasols would keep them safe in the catastrophic hurricane. Paradise under the emergency lamps. The box-mall-church, the boys, and the impending anniversary swirled around me. I tried to shut it out but couldn't.

Colony of the Elect Boulevard. I reached it at last. Rise Up Singing on my right, galleries and vegan sushi. It's a riverbed and there are two banks. One is green and the other is brown.

The way the current goes the trash all washes to one side. Broken wheels with bent rims gleaming, white cardboard boxes stained with grease and filled with crumbs, thirty-two-ounce Princess of the World drink containers, all strewn upon a single shore. And, on the other, side ghost mothers roll armies of IVF twins down the street. Carefully, wheeling their strollers around the mud and straw bricks of a pyramid that lie scattered and dissolving in the lapping water.

I passed by the storm drain where Devadatta had thrown up the night before and remembered the police lights down by the bridge. The shootings must have happened around then, right when we were talking about Mercury going retrograde. I thought about the dead boys and I thought about the box-mall-church. I put the image of the woman crying in the parking lot, the one with the daughter who lost the doll at Superland™, I put her face next to that of the two dead boys. They looked the same to me. The more I tried to see them as separate, the more they blended into a single face. The image came to me like a sending: a light-skinned black man with large red freckles and a bad perm crying for his lost doll while he bled to death from a gunshot wound. Behind him was the faint outline of a woman in a bronze miniskirt, a machete glinted in her hand, and over them all the Rat Queen stood, sniffing the air. Who cares? In three weeks I would be gone. This was all someone else's karma, the five zillion people before me who fucked everything up. It had nothing to do with me.

I was two blocks away from Jimmy's and there was one more thing I had to do that night. It's not fair to let someone you care about walk into all that history unprepared. When I got to her place the door of her apartment building was propped open with a brick. I heard katydids in the bushes as the door swung closed and I stepped into the black hallway. The carpet smelled like smoke. I crept up the creaking stairs to her apartment. There was no light under her door but that didn't mean anything. Jimmy doesn't like to use electricity. She says all this is just a war for resources and she doesn't want any part of it. I listened. It was silent. Amber light from the lamps came through the window at the other end of the hall. I pulled a sheet of paper out of my notebook.

Dear Jimmy:

My mom and dad have always believed that you should face hard things head on. That's how they taught the three of us, Credence, Cady and me. In case you didn't know, Cady and Credence were twins. She was the one holding my mother's other hand that day in Redbird Square when the people were chanting and I was scared and wrapped myself in Mom's wool coat. (Have I ever told you that when you smile you remind me of her?) Credence was on Dad's shoulders.

On the anniversary of her death, Mom decorates the house with pictures of Cady and drawings she made. She makes Cady's favorite food, Frito pie, and we tell stories about how she was. Do you still want to come?

Let me know,
Della

There had been a big debate and we held a family council about it when I was twelve. Should we celebrate Cady on her birthday or on the day of her death? The argument split along these lines:

Celebrating Cady on her birthday—All the obvious reasons.

Celebrating Cady on the anniversary of her death—People hide the sad things in the world from their sight. Bury their grief and, not facing the pain of their loss, devalue everything around them. They act like there's just one piece missing when what is missing was a part of everything. That's what it was like when

Cady was gone and we decided to mark the day she left us because that's when it all changed. For me, it could have been any day.

I folded the note for Jimmy and slipped it under the door.

There was a whirr of trees when the bus went off the cliff. I put my hand against the glass and green blurry streaks raced beneath my fingers. I imagine her in the thorny arms of wild blackberries singing. Mom used to say that we should look sadness right in the eye. I look Cady right in the eye, my older sister, thirteen, crying, tangled in metal, shining. I cannot turn away.

Cady Elizabeth Mylinek
You are always welcome at any gathering:
019791993.13

I lay back on the carpet in front of Jimmy's door. The wind was pressing against the windows. I was thinking it's like a castle. Outside it's so dark that even armies sleep next to each other, all dreaming of tomorrow's war. I was sure if I got up and went back down to the street I would hear nothing but owls and the breath of soldiers.

"How did they meet?" Jimmy asked me once. "Your parents."

"Dad came here on an academic visa. He'd been in the Paris student movement before that. They met at the library."

"Right. Credence told me that once."

"She was in there every day researching the history of regional water rights. It was very romantic."

"I'm sure it was," she laughed.

"No. Really. It was. Miroslav and Grace. They were the hot couple of the underground New Left. No doubt about it."

Grace would think what I had done at the box-mall-church was stupid. She wouldn't have said it. That's not how you educate through organizing.

Lying in the hallway that night I saw my mother like she was there. Her hair was the color of honey and her eyes were the color of rich earth. Grace. She was wearing a blue cotton blouse and on it were land use maps, hearing dates and statistics from the Water Bureau. Across her body, rivers flowed. They poured over property lines and carved canyons from unclaimed lands. I traced those waters with my fingertips from source to delta making circles in the air and slept that night in the hallway with all of us together, Grace, Cady and me, safe in some part of an old castle that only we knew about.

Light coming through the hallway window woke me up. My left cheek was pressed into the carpet and I smelled like cigarettes. Jimmy was moving on the other side of the door. I got up and left before she could find me.

On the way home I passed a newspaper stand and saw the headlines. My favorite was: CITIZENS FOR A RABID ECON-OMY THREATENS SUPERLAND™. A shock of joy hit me just like the night before. Fuck the anniversary! I thought. I'm mak-ing a new one. I flung open the door to our house, a victor.

Annette was in the living room with the shades drawn. Her eyes were dilated from sitting in the dark. She picked up an empty cereal bowl with one hand and raised the blind with the other. Sun came through the window and made the white cur-tains glow. Her cheeks were red and puffy. She retied her blue satin robe.

"No one needs this shit right now," she said. "That baby. I remember his first day of school."

Annette had been on the phone with the family of one of the boys who had been shot. She had dated the younger boy's brother when they were teenagers. Two rivers. The radio in the kitchen was on loud. They were deepening their coverage of the bomb threat at box-mall-church. Would it affect shopping? An-nette walked into the kitchen and yanked the plug.

"Who cares about that damn mall," she said and went back up into her room.

Grace wanted everyone out at their place by early afternoon. It soon became clear that we'd be lucky to make it by dinner. Because of the bomb threat and some unrelated concerns about rioting, large sections of the city were cordoned off and there were checkpoints on all the major roads out of town. We followed the traffic advisories all morning. Everything was backed-up. Jimmy called and wanted to know what time she should come.

"You don't have to do this," I said.

"What time?"

And my heart, like a sea anemone touched once, curled.

"Whenever. I'm not in a rush to get there."

I was standing on the sidewalk when Jimmy pulled up fresh-faced and rested with a freshly baked vegan pineapple-lemon cake on the seat beside her. Apparently her response to potential riots, bomb threats and dead sisters was to bake and talk about Honduran pottery collectives.

"I'm really interested in the way cooperative micro-economies…blah, blah, community kiln fire…regional glazing techniques…the hue comes from wood smoke…"

—Good. We'll need potshards. That way it'll be easier for future archeologists to reconstruct our civilization—

"By the way, I found a book on Honduran geology."

She smiled brightly and handed it to me then went on about a friend she had in Tegucigalpa who said he could meet me and how cheap it was to get around now because of all the hurricanes. Through the jungle vine I saw her, Queen of the Jaguars, twirling in a ball gown sewn by harpy eagles and howler monkeys.

It was after noon before we got on the road. The first checkpoint was easy. We told them we were going shopping and they waved us on. At the second checkpoint they made us kill the engine and show identification. They opened up our cooler and poked around in the ice but that was it.

Past the security rings, traffic flowed evenly through a colony of gas stations, day labor agencies and fast food drive-thrus on the other side. Kids sold flowers out of white plastic buckets and flagpoles went by like jail bars.

The original plan was to stay on the phones with Credence and Annette and hook up at a rest area outside of town but the cell reception was already sticky and it didn't look like that was going to happen. We were out of range before they left.

Driving through the barricades and idling vehicles of my own deathless Rapture I felt like a kid, back before I knew anything, back when sleeping sunburned in a pup tent or running barefoot through the dewy grass was still reality. That old feeling came and went. Jimmy picked up speed on the interstate and the truck rattled. The speedometer was broken and she could only tell how fast we're going by sound. On the outskirts of town and buildings, mini-malls and franchises went from a stream to a stutter with flashes of field in between. I rolled down the window. A crop of satellite dishes went by all facing the same way like sunflowers. We passed a warehouse with a thirty-foot spinning cell phone on top of it. After that, it was nothing but grassland.

I curled up on the vibrating seat with my arm around the pineapple-lemon cake and slept. When Jimmy woke me I thought for a second that I was fourteen and that she was Credence and I'd passed out again.

"Which exit do I need?"

"This one."

We turned west and the sun cut across Jimmy's cheek and thigh. Climbing into the wooded foothills the road dipped and curved under a belt of blue sky. We came into a part of the forest that had been logged several times and replanted in rows. The trees were all the same age, each the size of a telephone pole; they made avenues of filtered light, which appeared and disappeared as we drove. On the left was a gravel service road and we took it. A tall thin waterfall and a hazy valley flickered by then there was nothing but trees, green ditches and fallen branches on either side of us. Jimmy hit a pothole and we lurched forward.

"Go ahead and park," I said, "let's go the back way."

Jimmy pulled over. I got out the cake and we started walking. Ahead in a clearing was an abandoned cabin that had been wiped out in an avalanche in the 30s. The back half of the roof was caved in and the front door lay rotting in the weeds.

"Credence and I used to hang out here when we were kids. I'll show you the cabin. The trail is behind it."

I led her up onto the porch and through the doorway. The floor was covered with dry leaves and when a breeze came they scraped across the pine. I could feel her breath on my shoulder. A strip of light where the roof had caved fell diagonally across the kitchen counter. A forgotten glass bowl sparked in the sun.

"It's going to be strange to leave," Jimmy said. "Are you going to talk to tell them tonight?"

Intentions blowing everywhere like dandelion seeds.

"Probably not."

"What do you think they'll say?"

Through the hole in the roof I saw a hawk dive.

"See the hawk?"

She looked up. Her face was half shadowed and half lit. Tiny golden hairs played on upper lip. I slid right behind her while she was watching the hawk, put my mouth to her ear and whispered, "Let's leave after midnight when they're all asleep."

She thought I was joking but I meant it. Everything was already so messed up.

We hiked up the trail behind the avalanche cabin. The forest changed as we went. It aged and became dense. Deer's head orchids and fairy slippers slept all around and soon we could no longer see the cabin or the clearing or the rest of the trail down behind us. The trees grew irregular and roots twisted under our feet. At the top of the ridge the land leveled but was still wet. We walked on a pathway made of 2x8 planks lain over the black sucking mud. Mushrooms and wildflowers lined the soil and grew out of rotting tree trunks. All around rag lichen hung like lace.

"I'm really looking forward to seeing Grace again," said Jimmy, almost chipper.

The house was before us. There was a wind chime on the porch I had never seen. I reached up to touch it and just before I did, Grace opened the door. Her dark hair streaming over her shoulders and down her dress, which was a Mediterranean blue. In her hand she held a spiral notebook and from each strong and facile finger, a tiny creek flowed.

"Della," she said.

Her face was inches from mine and I could smell her skin. She had cocoa butter on her lips. When she kissed me I felt the print. She touched my head.

"And Jimmy," she shifted and her eyes turned yellow in the sun. "It's wonderful to have you here."

I saw Jimmy on the edge of a circling current.

"Miro will be back soon. Annette called. They just left."

"They were giving him a hard time about taking the day off," I said.

"Oh, whatever," Grace laughed, taking Jimmy's hand. "That union wants to be a vanguard so bad it just keeps leaching the life out of people."

She passed through the front door and, once through, let Jimmy's hand drop. She pulled a rubber band off the back of the knob and put her hair in a loose ponytail, tobacco brown strands playing by her cheeks.

"I mean they're willing to create a dialogue on class but..."

We walked into the kitchen and Grace stepped into a flood of sunlight. Leaning against the butcher's block counter, she unbuttoned the top of her blue dress and pulled the rubber band back out of her hair. A plane scratched a path in the sky and she watched it through the window then threw her head forward and shook her hair which, streaked with copper, cascaded around her ears until she wound it back into a ponytail and stood up. Her face was flushed and there was sweat on her forehead and under her eyes.

"They're too orchestrated. Too mired in Party structure."

She wiped her temple with the inside of her wrist and smiled.

"Jimmy, Credence tells me you're going to Honduras."

"Come see the garden," I said.

Grace uncorked the wine, "Where is it you're going?"

I grabbed Jimmy's hand.

Jimmy yanked her hand back and settled in. Clearly, she thought this was an opportunity to soften Grace up on the subject of expatriatism. But Grace doesn't soften.

"I'm flying into Tegucigalpa then on to the mountains."

Grace handed her a glass of white wine.

"Really? What made you decide to leave?"

"Well, I don't feel like there's much more I can do here and I don't really want to be a part of what's going on."

Grace brushed hair out of her face, paused, and then wiped the sink. When there was no response Jimmy went on, chattering about native cultures, indigenous medicine and artisan craft movements. And, maybe because it was the anniversary, or maybe because Jimmy's gay, I don't know, either way, Jimmy got a pass. I saw Grace make that decision. The faintest exhale, the smallest movement of an eyelid. Jimmy saw nothing and yet Grace watched her as if she were a pretty tangerine bird, waiting for her to finish, all the time with her flaming eyes dancing over the feathers until they caught fire.

"So then you won't be staying for the rise of the proletariat?" she said when Jimmy was done.

Jimmy laughed, "I'd only be cooking for rich white people anyway."

"You could always industrialize," she refilled Jimmy's wine glass. "You know, get a job stunning chickens in a factory to earn the trust of the working class."

Jimmy laughed again and accidentally spat Chablis on my legs.

"It's a pretty silly idea, isn't it?" said Grace, getting a rag. "Leaping out of the closet in a crisis?" She lowered her voice, "Don't worry, sir. I'm a revolutionary socialist. Everything's going to be okay."

Jimmy covered her mouth with her arm so she wouldn't spit on me again. Grace smiled. That's how I love her. My fearless Grace, my Broken Shield.

"Anyway, it's stupid. Who is going to run the healthcare system if everyone's picking grapes or on a tractor?"

She hung the rag over the faucet.

"That's why, in the end, I always thought what Della did was smart. Deciding to stay in school."

"Yes," I said, "because everybody needs an invertebrate paleontologist on the inside when the time comes."

Grace looked at me and I felt like she could see it all—the box-mall-church, the ticket in my pocket, even the seeds of new ideas that I couldn't yet see myself.

"I thought that went well," Jimmy said later. "I think she'll understand."

"Watch your head."

We were climbing the ladder into the attic. Grace waited below.

"Don't forget the Rainbow Brite dolls!"

I pointed to a stack of boxes in the corner.

"They're behind that."

Grace keeps all of Cady's things in a crib so that no one ever forgets to whom she really belonged. Stuffed rabbits, snap-on black leather bracelets with metal studs, half-used hair dye— Enchanted Forest and Electric Lava—black nail polish, a plastic record player, Mutant Ninja Turtle stickers, jewelry boxes, candles, incense, a Bauhaus poster, a walkman, cassettes. If you glued it all together it wouldn't look like Cady, though. Like when you look at fossils and think the world must have been nothing but seashells but it wasn't. It was filled with all sorts of things that didn't preserve.

"What's going to happen now?" Jimmy asked.

"We'll put some of Cady's stuff up, play her music. Make some toasts. We'll be out of here by midnight. I promise."

From the rafters, dried Indian corn hung.

"When we were little we used to play Battle of Wounded Knee," I handed Jimmy a box. "I never got to be a warrior, though. Cady and Credence were always the warriors and I got stuck being one of the babies left to die on the hillside."

Cady would make speeches of vengeance over my body and Credence would draw plans for a counterattack. If I moved, Cady would kick me. Hard. I broke some ribs once doing fieldwork at grad school and what struck me was how familiar the feeling was. I remember thinking it was lucky Cady didn't puncture a lung 'cause if I'd ratted her out she would have had me shot. That's how it was. We were all in training.

Through the window I saw Credence and Annette walking up the path.

"We should probably just take the whole thing downstairs," I said.

We dragged the crib into the dining room. Grace set out chips and guacamole while Credence and Annette caught her up on the shootings. Riots had started and were getting worse. Organizers were holed up at Higher Ground of Africa Baptist negotiating with the city and that's why Credence was late. He'd been trying to get the unions to pressure the mayor but the unions were trying to get the mayor reelected and didn't want him chastised over police accountability. Community leaders split—What solution was to be had? What mystical action could convey both rage and passivity? Candlelight vigil! Credence was trying to act excited but Annette's disgust was clear.

"Those boys were fourteen and sixteen years old. That baby was holding a goddamned robot toy when they shot him."

Just then Miro came in. The lost fish of the Morava, he swam muscled and aging, his scales like silver coins fell and glinted between the rocks. Something was wrong. His frayed fins beat the water. He laid a newspaper down in front of Grace. "They're tightening the borders. Soon people aren't just going to be able to leave."

Grace glanced at headlines then poured some salsa into a bowl.

"Sounds like you're going to get out just in time, Jimmy," she said.

I could feel Jimmy's eyes boring a hole in the side of my skull.

Annette asked her to help out in the kitchen.

Grace flipped through the newspaper.

"Let's get the stuff up," said Credence and walked into the living room.

Every year we each choose something of Cady's to decorate the house with. Some things always get used. The dried wildflowers she collected the summer before eighth grade and ironed between sheets of wax paper, her tape deck and the cassettes with her name written in nail polish on the plastic shells. I found a copy of *Pretty Hate Machine* missing its cover. Cady and I were singing "Head Like a Hole" on the bus the day she died. She said it was "got money" and I said it was "god money" and she called me an idiot and went to sit with some friends up front. Then she ran back crying because Jeremy Sokolov called her fat and she had a big crush on him. So I ran up and whacked him with my knapsack. Then we went off the cliff. All three kids in the very back were killed. I remember Cady like a magical animal with sharp lines and multicolored fur. I knew she would call me a coward for even thinking about leaving.

Miro looked over at me and held up a clay dog.

"She made this at camp, right?"

"Yep. She used to tell me it came to life at night and that the only reason it hadn't ripped my throat out was because she had asked it not too. Goddamned death hound."

Miro smiled, "I think it's exactly that."

Credence unrolled a huge Bauhaus poster. We spread it out on the floor and put books on the corners to hold it flat. Cady's face, soft with her baby fat, floated up before me. She had thick black eye make-up smeared just above her freckled cheeks.

Credence grabbed some of Cady's black nail polish out of the crib and Grace took the plastic record player. I picked out a drawing Cady made as a kid. It had a row of burning apartment buildings and everyone standing over a little dead bird. On the bottom of the picture it says "Africa" but I know it was Philadelphia. Cady drew herself too, big as a skyscraper, right next to the little bird. I laid it next to the clay demon dog.

Jimmy came back in. She wasn't saying much anymore. I didn't blame her. What do you say at a funeral? Or wear to a hanging? Or a bus crash or a school bombing? Nikes? A flak jacket woven from pieces of the true cross?

"How bad is this going to get?" she whispered.

"Maybe not so bad."

Grace put Rainbow Brite dolls on the shelves and tables. She tried to balance a couple over the door but the molding was too narrow and they fell off.

"Cady would kill you if she knew you were putting those dolls up," I said.

"I know," said Grace, "it helps me to see her face."

I heard the sea shift in her voice.

Miro taped the Bauhaus poster to the door and put the little clay dog on my dinner plate. I threw a napkin over it. Credence painted his nails black in the doorway. I propped my drawing up between some glasses. We used the turntable on the plastic record player like a lazy Susan and put the salsa and sour cream on it. Annette put the Frito pie on the table and Miro poured the wine. Then we all sat down. Credence blew on his nails to dry the polish. Annette looked like she'd rather be chained to a fence. Jimmy shifted in her seat and bowed her head slightly. The windows were open and outside the woods were filled with small sounds, sparrows and quivering tree needles. We always start with silence. It's my favorite part because it feels like Cady's there, like she's upstairs and lost track of time and might come down to dinner any minute. Grace rose from the table like a tsunami. With her breath she washed away the debris of the past until we were all floating in her massive sorrow and buoyed by her absolute conviction in life, vibrant and wild on the shores, she carried us forward and that's how we landed, all of us on this strange beach.

"It is a wonderful thing," Grace said with her glass high, "to raise a free child. To Cady!"

She drank then slammed the glass down. The wine splashed out on all sides and reddened the tablecloth.

"To Cady!" we yelled and drank and slammed our glasses down like Grace.

I stood.

"To my wild sister!" I shouted, "to Cady!" and slammed my glass down.

Jimmy jumped up to get some rags from the kitchen. I saw her minutes later in the doorway with her hands full of surgical gauze. Credence made his toast and she started laying down the dishtowels. Miro went and Jimmy scrambled to sop the wine that was pooling under the plastic record player. Then Grace went again and on and on until the tablecloth was a field of crimson flowers and Jimmy could find no more towels and we were all hoarse. Cady the bold. Cady the poet. Cady the fighter. Cady the argumentative. Cady the strident. Cady the gentle. Cady the unsure. Cady the secret crier. Cady the awkward. Cady the valiant. Cady the private. Finally no words, but there aren't any really. Jimmy was crying. And even though it was silent, I knew my parents were talking because they never stop. Grace is a tsunami and Miro is radio signal and they speak in waves punctuated by dolphins and sea glass.

Miro brought out an orange guitar with hummingbirds and brushed the back of his hand down the strings. It came to me again as I watched him that Miro is a radio signal. He arpeggiated a chord with his leathered hands and I thought—these sounds have traveled across a galaxy to get to me. My last thought was—the singer's been gone for years. He started to sing and Miro, the lost fish of the Morava, snapped his torn tail and bubbles filled with strains of Czech lullabies shot upwards, each for Cady.

We all have our mother's mouth and our father's cheekbones, sharp and high. I have my grandmother's lighter hair. It turns blonde in the sun and when I was at Davis nobody believed it had ever been brown. Credence has dark hair and dusky skin just like Cady did. Even now, in the end of September, there's rose on his cheeks. They both had blue eyes but Credence has a dark spot in his left iris. Someone told me that those are trauma scars and not genetic. I don't know if that's true. Eyes change over time though just like rivers and it would make sense if every place we'd been, everywhere that counted, we left behind a meander scar.

Mom cut the Frito pie.

"It's nothing but meat and cheese," I whispered to Jimmy.

"Shut up," she hissed.

The skin under her eyes was swollen.

Grace came over and tucked a piece of Jimmy's hair behind her ear.

"How are you doing with all this?"

"It's pretty sad, Grace."

"Yes. It is sad," Grace put her hand lightly on the back of Jimmy's head, "but it is important to remember that we have always had our political martyrs."

Grace reached across and pulled two grapes off a dense cluster in the center of the table.

"What do you mean?" Jimmy asked.

A veil came down between Credence and the world, thin, shimmering and nearly invisible and Miro, like a man waving in the distance at a passing ship, smiled. He set a piece of buttered bread on the edge of Grace's plate.

Grace squinted her eyes.

"It was a failure on my part, " she said, "Cady never really did understand the role that gender played."

She sat back down and took a bite out of the buttered bread.

"I don't understand," said Jimmy.

"You see, Cady understood class and race. She was very good on those points. She had a wonderful critical mind but she did not understand gender. Her grasp of feminism was tentative and that's where I slipped. You see she didn't have the tools to protect herself from gender-based criticism—she didn't know how to let what that boy said, calling her fat, roll off her. If she had had those tools, she wouldn't have run to the back of the bus."

Annette looked down at her plate and shook her head. Jimmy put her fork down.

"We have to learn from our mistakes," she continued. "I know you more than anyone at the table must understand the importance of gender. Della's always been pretty clear on that too. But I underestimated it. We are nothing if we can't face our own past with clear eyes, no matter how much it hurts. I take full responsibility for what happened to Cady."

Then Grace picked up the empty bowl and walked into the kitchen to get more salsa, trailing behind her the harpoons and tangled rigging of a terrible storm.

As I got into the truck to go home my hands were shaking. I felt like something was finally becoming clear but I wasn't sure what. Something had failed, something big and now there was a vast plain before us on which I could build anything. Jimmy spun us around on the trail rock and out onto the road.

We drove under the night sky with the windows rolled down and the cold air rushing around us. The broken speedometer bounced frantically between numbers as we barreled down the mountain. Capricorn blinked through a lattice of radio towers in the distance.

It was like the world had broken open and nothing was hidden anymore, like we were crawling all over it like salamanders. I felt my own life, a minnow in a brook silvered and fleet. I was alive for no reason at all, finally unindentured. Miro told me that he swam the Morava when it was flooding. All the landmarks he had counted on were sunken beneath the water, which just kept rising. He dove into the current and when he came up he was surrounded by sticks and card tables, shoes and bottles. He said it was as if the river had swollen with debris of his country, like it had done it on purpose to keep him from leaving. I felt that way saying goodnight to Grace.

We were on the porch and the light was broken. She hooked my fingers with hers and I felt the dark woods, filled with birthday trees, shudder. The whites of her eyes flickered like stars on the sea when she moved.

"Della…" she said and took my head in her hands, "Della."

Her breath wet my cheek. She leaned in and said something to me in a sharp whisper. It must have been important because it seemed like she said it twice but her palms were over my ears and I couldn't understand what it was. All I could hear was the ocean. And I thought, it's only going to get worse. Leave. Down below this mountain the borders are tightening, the nations are shifting and through all the dangling black branches I see Grace and Cady dancing in circles. If I look down for a second, I will never go. Grace, my Broken Shield, will hold me forever. And Cady? My Clay Dog Master, my Torturer? My Brave Indian Chief? She will certainly kick me if I move and shoot me if I talk.

Tapping Jimmy's windshield, I pointed to the rim of the valley.

"See that? Capricorn? That's the tail of the Sea Goat."

She didn't raise her eyes.

"Over there," I pointed, "Capricorn. By the towers."

"I don't want to talk about constellations. I don't want to talk about anything."

"But it's Babylonian."

"Della, that was the most fucked-up, masochistic fucking thing I have ever fucking witnessed. I felt like I was being asked to watch your mom slice herself to ribbons."

She had a point. If you look at Grace too long everything turns into scary little splinters but I didn't want to get into it and lose my own momentum.

"I thought it was really sweet of you to eat the Frito pie."

"Fuck the Frito pie!" she screamed. "Fuck the fucking Frito pie!"

The spinning cell phone whizzed by on my left and parking lots on my right.

Jimmy rolled her window up. I started to say something and she turned on the radio. There wasn't a clear station and several different ones came in and out of the static. A blast of Christianity, the stammering Mexican brass then nothing but free bandwidth. We turned off the freeway and eventually came to a barricade. There were packs of crickets everywhere and a large chirper sidled over.

"Where are you girls going?" he asked.

"Home," Jimmy said,

"Where have you been?"

"At a family gathering."

"Oh yeah, what kind?"

The kind where you celebrate the day a bus crash killed your thirteen-year-old sister because your mom believes that it is important to re-experience pain as a political construct. An anniversary?

"An anniversary," I said.

"I'm not talking to you," snapped the officer.

"At an anniversary," Jimmy said.

"Look," said Jimmy when we were through, "I need a few days."

"Sure."

I asked her to drop me off at an all-night Safeway. She pulled up to the curb by the sliding doors. I got out and started to say goodnight but she was already driving away. I didn't really blame her. It just wasn't what she thought it was going to be, being out there with them. I could have said, charisma is violence, but she wouldn't have understood. I could have told her, there is no haven, but it's hard to look those things in the eye. It's hard to see Grace as she really is. She's just too close to what you need her to be. Up until that moment I think Jimmy really believed that there was sanctuary somewhere. And not just driftwood shacks filled with sorrow, lit with oil lamps.

I stood in front of the Safeway for a few moments then went in. I have my own traditions. They have nothing to do with anyone else.

The store was empty. The meat glowed and a steel drum version of "Eleanor Rigby" echoed on the Congoleum. I went over to the customer service desk. A checker with fine brown hair, hoop earrings and tracheotomy scar walked up to me. She had a button pinned to her chest, big as a can lid, with a photo of a German shepherd puppy on it.

"Can I help you?"

"I want have my sister paged. We came in together and I can't find her."

"Have you looked around?"

"Yes, I've looked everywhere."

I went back to the table and waited.

"Cady Elizabeth…"

The checker's voice cracked shrill through the overhead PA.

A teenage boy unpacking a palette of potato chips looked up. That's right, I thought, you should be looking for her, my scary Indian sister, it's only smart. She'd slit your throat in your sleep you big sell-out. You're lucky it's just me here.

I waited a few minutes and walked back over and asked her to page Cady again.

"I don't think your sister is here," she said.

"Maybe she was in the bathroom," I said.

"Maybe she went outside to use the phone," she said, "there's a pay phone on the corner."

Maybe she's turned into minerals that got ground into soil and line the tanks of goldfish.

"Maybe your sister will come back later…"

As a gila monster or a grass spider.

Raina believes in reincarnation.

"What about birds?" I'd asked her. "Will they all be birds again? Do sparrows become starlings, or does it go the other way? What happens after you're a blackberry bush?"

"Well," she said, "I think we're here for a reason and that whatever we haven't learned before we get to learn now. Some of us won't have to come back."

I'm learning how to bury rats in the back of a restaurant without tipping off the health department. Do I have to come back?

"The point is to not to get too attached," she said.

Mirror believes in reincarnation too.

"Dude, I am totally coming back as a black chick."

"Why?"

"Cause they're hot."

"You don't get to pick. That's the whole idea."

"Right, you earn it. And I totally deserve to be a hot black chick."

"What about the black chicks? What do they become?"

"Nothing. That's it. They're done. They're the head of the line. Unless they shoot someone or run over a kid or something like that."

"Yeah," she said, "I'm going to be as black as a Nigerian with a huge fucking pink Afro. It'll be totally hot."

I think I should be a coral reef and Credence should be a dog salmon. All those kids they blew up in that school last year should get to be silk moths or new planets.

Thinking that, I left the commercial lighting of the Safeway behind and wandered through darker and darker streets until I came again to the edge of New Honduras. Ten blocks up an emergency lamp reddened the blackness.

It was just after 2 AM when I got in and I turned on the kitchen light. I was restless. On the counter was a letter from the Department of Geology at UC Davis propped up against a Rice Krispies box. I didn't need to open it to see what was inside. It was a copy of my article, soon to appear the *Journal of Paleobiology*. I flipped it over. My work. Years of academic torque folded in three and stuffed into an envelope. As pointless as anything under the sun. What to make of it? Origami swans? A fleet of paper airplanes?

Upstairs, the mail tub I'd named "the head of John the Baptist" overflowed, my own personal Lagerstätte, my quiet lake, silt-bottomed and still, to catch all the falling things and press them like wildflowers into the earth. I put down the letter. I didn't want to talk about geology with anyone ever again. I dumped the mail on the bed.

I hadn't done papier-mâché since sixth grade but that night I made wheat paste and tore my mail to shreds. All the scraps of my education went in, all for the greater glory of the head of John the Baptist. I formed the skull out of academic accolades and the ears from peer review. The hair was shredded junk mail. I couldn't bring myself to destroy the *Paleobiology* article but everything else got used. Paste and bits of paper stuck to my hands like barnacles. I want the head of John the Baptist to be as big as the head of a Minotaur, I thought. That's the problem with symbolic gestures. People never take them far enough. They don't see them as a system. They blow up something right in front of them, like the bathroom of the New Land Trust building, and then caper around like monkeys. They might as well throw bananas at it. When I was little Grace used to say we were a ship with a broken mast. She said we needed to be careful or we'd sink. And now I think she was right. But there's something new, I know because I stay up and listen to the world at night. We are on a ship, only we're not sinking. We're moving again, cutting fast through the sea with a crucifix mast, plastic bag sails and a hull made of disposable razors and straw.

I spread my field notes on the floor of my room. All the sketches and lists, the formations and fossils and indexing of trends, I laid them out.

It already was one big map.

I knelt by a series of Vietnamese nail salons and white suburban fitness centers. They were marked as a braided stream. At the mouth of the waterway was an enormous Asian market called Transcontinental. It never closes and inside huge HDL screens play karaoke videos with Filipinos running around Scottish castles. I marked it with a large red "U."

I put another "U" by the box-mall-church and looked at the map again. Transcontinental, The New Land Trust Building, the box-mall-church—they were all unconformities, non sequiturs. I put a "U" by a cluster mall that ran a free bus service back and forth to the high schools. I put a "U" by Redbird Square for appropriating a public space as a billboard for a bank. I put a "U" by the central library, which was half empty of books and had black birds in the rafters. Such hollow hopes should be punished, shown for what they were. Biodiesel fueling station with an armored vehicle bay? Large red "U."

I grabbed a copy of Vermeij's *Nature: An Economic History* off the shelf, unfolded the cover and tossed the book aside. Spreading the dust jacket on the coffee table I wrote "Della's Flag" across the top in red marker. At the bottom of my flag I drew a little Rat Queen Betsy Ross. The head of John the Baptist was drying on the coffee table and the nine rat cell phones lay on the bed unopened. It was now morning in the imaginary territory of New Honduras and I heard Annette and Credence come in downstairs. Opening my door, I leaned over the banister. She went into the bedroom and he went into the shower. I waited until I heard the water run then stuffed the maps and phones in my bag and left.

Outside, the dry bushes rattled and everything was tense like something hanging heavy was about to drop. The pressure was falling and the sky was the color of cement. I was halfway down Heritage Avenue before I realized that the windows of the neighborhood were black. Some were covered with cloth, some with construction paper. Some had coats strung across the panes on twine. It took me a second to realize that it was for the boys. Grace crossed my mind with her endless wake and I thought about texting Jimmy an apology but what was I to apologize for? Grace in general? The Great Onslaught itself? I tried to warn her. She signed up. Over the next few hours, funeral services would be arranged. Community groups would meet. Credence would try to get the unions to join the demonstrations. But whatever they came up with—an army of shiny jackets marching in phalanx and covered with buttons, a black rainbow invoking the mountaintop—it wasn't going to work. It never does. It was just adding color to the sand painting. Oh look! I really like that streak of brown, so bold where you put it next to all that red. In early springtime a man was hanged off the Roseway Bridge. Someone saw the body on the way to work dangling like a blackened branch over the river. They had meetings then too.

I took the bus out to Four Points of Heaven mall and got off a stop early. In the parking lot of the Village of Light Towne Square I activated the nine baby rat cell phones. I was calling in bomb threats by noon. First, with the tangerine cell that belonged to Venus Rodere. She got the cluster mall and the biodiesel fueling station (with clever armored vehicle bay) and the Asian behemoth, Transcontinental—all of which deserved to be blasted to atoms, the terrible little minerals. I ditched the tangerine phone in some lush industrial landscaping and went on to the next.

On the lime cell phone I called Better Gods and Gardens, the New Land Trust building (as a reminder) and the yoga studio:

Yoga on the Hill, Devadatta speaking.

Get everyone out of the building—

Hold please—

Typing. Online trying to befriend the entire country of Nepal.

—Sorry about that, how can I help you?

This is a bomb threat.

I think you have the wrong number.

I don't.

Well, I can't think of anyone who would want to blow us up.

I can.

Okay, well, I'll let people know but there's class going on right now and I think they're all in Shavasana.

Perfect.

Then I called Naught, a raw food tapas bar, because the bathroom sink counter had the name of a different god/prophet painted on every fourth tile and "ALL IS ONE" inlaid around the basin. Then I called all the strip joints that charged a stage fee. Then after that, the human resources department of a popular Vietnamese restaurant chain, demanding an end to bubble tea as the hyper modern equivalent to absinthe and a barrier to real revolution because the equation Bubble Tea = Something to Look Forward To depressurizes the misery of capitalism and is a Hello Kitty band-aid on the festering wound of Neo-Liberalism.

I threw that phone in the trash and boarded the Number 22 to Pretty Little Hopes.

Eartha Rodere
When the heart opens, the hands follow:
191292309.24

Up ahead was Brass Ring Employment Solution, a temp agency shaped like a refrigerator and built out of concrete and torque. Their motto was "Every little bit helps." Flocks of men in white shirts, crisp sleeves rolled down over their tattoos, kissed ass daily just to work for nothing. Hostages taking each other hostage. Jazz hands. Out of respect for the relationship between war and commerce and the necessity of cheap labor for both to thrive, I let Aries Rodere make the call.

Good Afternoon! Brass Ring, where we know that every little bit helps…(maintain wage slavery).

How may I direct your call?

Bombs, I told them, blast coronas the size of Texas. Bone fragments like chalk dust staining the sidewalk and washing away in the rain.

I heard building alarms. The bus driver closed the doors. I got off at the next stop, leaving the raspberry cell phone under my seat pinging towers all the way to Pretty Little Hopes.

I was only halfway through my list. There were so many facets. Redbird Square for being named after a bank and recasting cultural geography as a proprietary object. The central library for being a defunded sham, a gutted shell, a hope crime. The Cine-Tower for having 20 theaters, 10 levels of parking and playing Christmas music year round. The golden oldies station KGOD for being a mask of Christianity formed from revisionist musical portraits of the past. And for sending nostalgia into the valleys of the scurrying poor to get them through the work day then giving them a god to go to at night when they're tired. Me, third. 8, 8 and 8. The FM repeaters chattering like cats, selling bobbleheads, pushing mad cow meat and formula on babies so their mothers don't have to keep up enough body weight to nurse. The Happy Day Corporate Charity Center? O let me count the ways... IKEA monkeys, urban yogis with real estate kriyas, manifest class destiny—each target was a jewel on the web, a dewy gem reflecting the Grand Ravage back to itself.

When it got dark I stopped to organize my notes and get food. It was raining by then and I was in line at a falafel stand with a newspaper folded over my head. A small radio was playing Egyptian disco. Suddenly it stopped and the emergency broadcast signal came on. The falafel man turned up the volume. Crackling, competing with the slap of raindrops on the tiny tarp, the words "explosion," "dog track" and "panic" emerged. The woman next to me turned gray. The falafel man started packing up and dumping fry oil trays into the gutter. A bomb had gone off at the dog track and another at a parking garage downtown.

But I saw satellites in the terrorsphere and put my list away. No one had claimed the New Land Trust bombing. Superland™ was still generating bumper text even though nothing had happened. Is it safe to shop? And now with the new threats? If there was one thing I learned from Credence, it was how to redirect messages—the New Land Trust building, the dog track, the parking garage—their violence, reframed with a new message. Talking points for the Blackberry Massacre.

I was close to the cemetery on the border of New Honduras and that's where I went, deep into the acres and tall trees, past the new gravestones in Chinese, Cyrillic and Tagalog, and into the oldest part where it's nothing but flu babies and second sons by the statue of a mermaid. Under her bronze arms, I called in and claimed the real bombs as mine.

"Cultural obsolescence impeding the flow of fresh commerce," I told the police operator, "that's why we blew up the dog track."

I gave different reasons for the other bombs because Citizens for a Rabid Economy only described part of the ugliness.

I needed a name for the unseen hand behind it all and I found it. When I dropped the lemon cell phone among the leaves at the base of the bronze mermaid the name of my new movement was spelled out on the LCD screen: MANIFESTATION. It glowed phosphorescent on the face of the phone, a little pool of light. Then went black on the forest floor.

Above me were ribbons of stars. I no longer knew what time it was. The trees there are the oldest in the cemetery and their branches form a canopy under which it is always night. I went out through the iron gates to the east and cut across the lower part of the hill, walking parallel to Colony of the Elect. Several blocks from Credence's someone yelled my name.

"Della!"

I looked up. It was Mirror. She was sitting on the fire escape of a newly renovated building smoking a cigarette.

"What are you doing?"

"Cat-sitting but the cat ran away. Come have a drink."

I was nowhere near sleep, and so why not? She buzzed me in.

"We're in the back," she called down the stairs.

The apartment was spotless with white couches and white carpets and at least two Tom of Finland prints in every room.

"They're originals," said Mirror, "The guy's dying of cancer and he won't sell one of them. Not one. That's some fucking principles."

Sitting behind Mirror on one of the couches was the woman with the lavender hair from the party at the Glass House. She was winding a red ribbon around her wrist, unwinding it and winding it again.

"Della, this is Tamara. She thinks she's only in town for a few days but she's going to change her mind and stay for my party."

"Maybe," Tamara said.

"Shut up, Mara!" Mirror threw a towel at her, "You are so staying."

"We'll see. Either way I'd have to go back soon."

"Mara lives on a collective farm out near Breaker's Rise," Mirror said, "They have chickens, goats—all sorts of shit. She's pretending to be some neo-hippy chick but she's just a big old faggot and…" she threw something else at Tamara, "she's definitely coming to my party."

"Will you be there?" Tamara asked, "or will you already be in Goa?"

She grinned and I saw that one of her incisors was partially broken off.

"Honduras."

"That's right, Honduras."

Her eyelids were thin and this time she was wearing green glitter shadow. She was shorter than me and had on a dark gray t-shirt. They must have just dyed her hair because her fingertips were pale blue.

"So, Mirror says you're a scientist."

"I'm a waitress."

"What do you study?"

"Patterns of extinction."

"Important things to understand."

I felt my pride burn and resented it.

Mirror got out some hummus and made Greyhounds.

"That stupid cat better come back on its own," she dropped a bag of carrots on the coffee table, "I'm not making flyers. I already have to go to that stupid work meeting tomorrow. By the way, when can you get the van?"

Tamara shrugged, "I'll ask when I get back to the Cycle."

The Cycle was a squat turned urban farm collective on the other side of the river. Once a year police made a show of trying to close it down, anarchists threw bricks at them, and they left. Mostly because anarchist squatters are cheaper than fences and developers weren't ready. I'm waiting for the headline that reads: HOWLING MAW ACCIDENTALLY SWALLOWS SQUATTERS LIKE PLANKTON IN PURSUIT OF REAL MEAT.

"More hummus?"

Yes, because a last meal should be vegetarian.

"So what are you going to do with all that education?" Tamara asked.

"My brother says education is what you make of it. I made a papier-mâché head of John the Baptist out of my school papers."

She laughed.

"It's a piñata."

I started to smile slowly then I laughed. I couldn't remember the last time I had. It felt like something was being lifted out of me.

We spent the next few hours talking about the bombs.

"I think the bomb threats are far more interesting than the actual attacks," Tamara said, "I mean, Citizens for a Rabid Economy? It's fucking brilliant."

We made Greyhounds until we ran out of vodka. Tamara asked if I wanted to go out for more and I said yes. We left Mirror sewing some kind of bronze lamé shroud for the sex party.

On the corner in front of the liquor store I pulled out the fortune cookies I got at the Chinese restaurant. I offered some to Tamara.

"Sweet!" she said and grabbed a few.

"What do your fortunes say?" I asked.

"This one says…" she squinted, *"You were never closer to reconstructing the world than you are now."*

"It does not say that!" I howled.

"You're right," she said, "but I do."

Tamara ate the rest of her cookies without looking at a single fortune.

Daylight crossed the couch. Tamara and Mirror were both asleep when I left and stepped outside, still drunk. I unbraided my hair. Brown and crimped, it fell around me. I shook my head. A car started. I turned. Steam rose from the windshield as it warmed. It was Sunday. The street with its shuttered bistros and gated shops was half in shadow and where light struck the road, gray vapor shimmered. I walked out and set my feet upon the centerline and headed home.

I saw a group of pregnant women by the yoga studio. They rubbed their goldfish-bowl and snow-globe bellies. I could have gone around them but I walked until I was deep in the abyss of that winter aquarium. Annette and Jimmy. The Black Ocean and the baby rats. Credence, Grace and Miro. Everything, all of it, was on fire. The only thing to do was pass through cleanly. Everything would still burn. My cheeks would still blister and my hands blacken. The only thing that made any sense was the bomb threat because that's where instinct met action, clarity.

I turned onto our street and leaves blew across my path and skittered sideways like crabs, rattling up the sidewalk and settling on the grass. They were all over our porch. I put some in my pocket walking up the steps.

Annette was hanging a black lace shawl over a mirror in the entryway. The rayon fringe angled down leaving a corner of the glass, splattered with yellow paint, exposed. She hung then re-hung the shawl but there was always one part of the mirror uncovered.

"It's a Jewish thing anyway," she said and let the shawl drape like a sash across the frame.

She sat down in a chair by the door. In her hand was a cordless phone. I stayed back because I smelled like vodka and didn't want her to think I was out partying while she and everyone else she knew were getting ready for the funeral and police riots that were certain to follow. I tried to tack the shawl up again and finally got it to stay. Annette watched me the whole time but I wasn't on her mind. I was just another thing in the distance. She wandered into the kitchen.

On my way up the stairs I thought about something Tamara said. She said the black community is our Lord Brahma and that every time we try to escape their gaze another head grows and looks down at what we've done. Then the conversation had descended into debates about exoticizing minorities and ended up somewhere on the banks with the rest of the mud bricks of the pyramid. I went to sleep and dreamt of tidal waves. When I woke, the world was washed clean and the streets empty of water. But then I realized it wasn't over. It was only the drag of a great wave calling all of itself to itself, gathering. I looked at the dry road and knew that I was between moments.

Annette left a black dress that belonged to her grandmother draped over my computer chair and I put it on. The funeral for the boys would start at the church around 3 PM and be followed by a procession to the cemetery. After the eulogy some community leaders were going to speak. Then everyone was supposed to march to the Roseway Bridge and throw flowers in the river near where they found the boys. There had been chaos earlier in the morning when the city revoked the permit to march. They said it was because of all the bombings and the threats still hanging and that it was a matter of public safety. My plan was to go but leave early. I didn't know how much I could take, all that sorrow just spinning out into nowhere.

On my way out the door Jimmy called to say that the staff meeting at Rise Up Singing was still on as scheduled. Apparently, Coworker Franklin had meditated on the idea of cancelling (due to the massive funeral) but his inner coin flip had come up Capitalism and he wanted to re-open as soon as possible.

"As a victim myself…"

—Coworker Franklin tries to equivocate the looting of Rise Up Singing with the slaughter of children—

"…I think the most important thing for the community is that we get back on our feet."

A defiant cheek to the wind, cannon to the right, vegan sushi bar to the left—as an olive branch Coworker Franklin said we could talk about the shootings "as a family." The first fifteen minutes of the agenda was set aside for that process.

"I was wondering if maybe we could talk," I said.

"Maybe later. I just wanted to let you know the meeting was still happening in case you wanted to go."

"Can we meet there?"

"I'm not going."

"Isn't it mandatory?"

"Fuck him, I'm leaving anyway. What's he going to do, fire me?"

Right. Queen of the Jaguars.

The streets around Higher Ground of Africa Baptist were packed with people. It took me twenty minutes to make it through a block. About halfway into the thickest part of the crowd, I saw Credence. He was jammed up against a side door of the church, which had been opened to let air into the building. A group of twenty or so, mostly younger men, stood next to him looking in. I worked my way there. He saw me and held out his hand and when I was in range pulled me through the crowd. He was about to say something when a chorus of shouts deafened us. Over the shoulders of the congregation I saw a man with stained-glass light on his face gesturing at the ceiling. He waved his arm across the crowd and then brought it back to his heart. I thought for sure he would catch fire. I almost heard the hissing of wet wood. Another cheer went up for Jesus but everyone near me was silent. They rustled impatiently in their suits and leaned in closer. The crowd inside began to move and the choir started up. People by the doors were telling us to get back, get back, and ushers lined up on either side of the main entrance. Through the side door, I could see them carrying out the coffins. People gathered around the pallbearers in front of the church. The coffins looked like driftwood in an eddy and I thought the crowd wasn't going to let them through, but then two hearses drove slowly through the mass of people and the crowd parted, still, while the pallbearers slid the caskets into the backs of the cars, and silent until each door had slammed shut. Then a roar went up and the hearses began to roll down the street. People closed in around us. We passed the church in a torrent of bodies and poured out onto Heritage Avenue. At the cemetery the crowd split in two columns and peeled off to the side so that the hearses could drive through. I could see the statue of the mermaid and the garden by the older graves where I'd called in bomb threats only the night before. Someone next to me was talking about the latest police reports and how—a concussion grenade went off behind me. Something was wrong. People with the bullhorns trying to keep the crowd together but the roar was building. Riot cops were coming down the hill in formation. A bottle sailed over the divide between them and us and shattered. Then another. And the shiny black birds, they beat their plastic wings. Clattering, they hit their shields. Faster and faster, until they broke and charged the crowd and the march exploded into slivers under the impact. It was more than a riot and more than a funeral. It was the conjunction of those two, grief and fear, fueled by the bombs and media cycling, combusting all around us. People were getting pushed down toward the promenade by the river. I saw more bottles come down near some cops. One got hit and the bird-crickets fell like a pack on a person running up the hill. Tear gas was fired randomly into the crowd. A concussion grenade went off right beside me. When I got up, I couldn't hear anything out of my left ear. A man who had been talking to Credence earlier stopped to see if I was okay. I asked him if he'd seen them. He said they had stayed up by the church and were probably still there. Then he picked up a forty-ounce bottle that was near my feet and hurled it. Run, he said and I did. Rubber bullets whistled by and blasted the bark off a tree. As I ran I could feel my blood vessels swell and my heart beat like it was underwater. I was halfway back up the hill before I realized no one was following me.

I was alone. My lungs hurt and I still couldn't hear anything out of my left ear. I pulled out my phone. There was no reception. I couldn't get back home without crossing the riot so I decided to try to make it to Rise Up Singing and call Credence and Annette from a landline. Concussion grenades still went off in the distance but only three blocks from the cemetery the day was filled with normal Sunday sounds. A little boy played in the yard of a partially remodeled house, balancing a rock on a can of Jasco and knocking it off again. Everywhere on Colony of the Elect were kids, sun wheels spinning in the breeze and hearty blonde neighbors helping each other out. The Dawn of Compassion had come. Suffering had ended. There were traffic circles and recycling bins. At one point the trees broke and I could see the river again. Puffs of tear gas like a gentle mist appeared then dissipated along the promenade.

Duct-taped to the door of Rise Up Singing was a proclamation from Coworker Franklin. It expressed regret at the recent bombing of the auto shop and begged people not to steal from COWORKER FRANKLIN because he was a PARTNER and a FRIEND of the COMMUNITY and often made them MACARONI AND CHEESE. At the bottom was a stick figure with open arms.

The meeting was in the garden. When I came through the gate the entire staff except Jimmy was standing around a table full of donuts and shots of Cuervo. Coworker Franklin looked nervous. No one was drinking or eating and sun made the glaze on the doughnuts shine.

I asked Mirror if I missed anything.

"Just fucking Franklin admitting he's a sellout who should die, which we already knew. What time did you leave?"

"Around dawn. You were both asleep."

"You know, that stupid cat never came back. I spent the whole morning shaking a bowl of Meow Mix like a fucking shaman."

Coworker Franklin was talking about the sale of the restaurant, assuring everyone that a great new era was coming. That the people who bought the restaurant were enlightened. That there would be lotus chairs made by Real Tibetans and distressed wood platters of hewn hemp. The latest in neo-colonial fusion cuisine. A patio. Orchids. A bocce court and a koi pond where now there was only a rat graveyard.

"In this time of change," Coworker Franklin waved vaguely at the world of bombs, malls and riots outside the garden, "it's all the more important that we stay together, even if we've chosen to walk in different directions."

Mirror passed me a folded up sheet of paper. Inside was her rendering of the figure from Franklin's sign. Next to it was a huge salmon about to tear it in half over which she'd written "Stick-Franklin in the Afterlife." Mitch took it and drew a four-panel strip of Stick-Franklin dissolving in lye.

"But like any birth process," said Coworker Franklin, "it's going to be hardest during the transition. There are going to be some new rules," he looked around anxiously. "To start with you are all going to have to get your food handler's cards."

Mirror rolled her eyes, "No way, dude, waiting in that line sucks."

"And..." said Franklin, "just so you know, they're going to shorten the name to 'Rise.' Which I think is really very cool. I saw it on the new menus. They look great. Copperplate. It's a nice font."

I was the first to hear it. Tiny popping sounds in the distance, a quiet siren. Some dim chirping and a ripple of adrenaline went through the staff. What was it? One or two people glanced over the garden fence. More sirens and then I could feel the lift in energy. There wasn't any fear, only excitement. Again I saw two rivers, each flowing through the same place, irreconcilable geographies. Reaching deeper, though, I found a third, cutting ever downward and pooling beneath the mermaid garden.

Coworker Franklin was talking about the schedule.

Police cars pulled around the corner and raced down the side street. Their blue and red lights reflected off the windows of the apartment buildings nearby and I saw it all differently. I saw the scene as it would be on another night. The same blue and red lights dancing on the koi pond, turning to rose and violet the white arbor trellis with its bending boughs to come. Occasional explosions like fireworks and the sky.

Coworker Franklin was talking about the robbery on the night of the shootings. How he got to the restaurant around 3 AM, and had seen a man by the shed, probably someone from the neighborhood who knew we didn't lock the side gate. And how the man was wearing a red bandana, and had something in his hand, probably a gun. And how he had called... My breath started to slow and I couldn't feel my hands because it seemed like the whole world was dipped in nitrogen and the slightest shift could shatter it...with all the gang stuff going on, and given the police a description of the man.

My eyes moved over to Mitch, who was standing between me and the Rat Graveyard. Don't move, I thought, stay. Stay right there. But Mitch moved and behind her I saw the beaten sunflowers and the trampled graves. The Buzz Lightyear and the red bandana tying him to the twig cross were gone.

"Truthfully," said Coworker Franklin, "I don't expect much will come of it..."—but of course something had—"and as you know, I'm not big on consequences..."—like what happens when you tie a toy to a twig cross? Or call in a description of a black man with a red bandana and a gun?

Or when you walk down an empty street drunk and wash your hair with stolen wine? Or tie a Buzz Lightyear to a cross? I didn't say it. I didn't say: The red bandana you found hidden in the shed belonged to the boy who was shot.

Or, the Buzz Lightyear you tied to the cross got him killed. Or, the reason Coworker Franklin called in the description of the boy in the first place was because the restaurant had been looted and he thought the boy was involved, but it was only we. I looked at the faces around me, the sweating doughnuts and the Cuervo, and I thought, these are charnel grounds and even though I hate it, I am as entangled as everyone else and part of how one thing led to another. Pollen, butterfly wings, I tried but you can't see it. You can't round off the small numbers because there are universes inside them. I thought I could stay above it, walk cleanly through, but you can't. Even my bomb threats, which I'd thought of as commentary, weren't. They were also universes. I had been lying to myself.

After the meeting I called Jimmy a couple of times but she didn't answer so I went over to her apartment. She was annoyed but let me in.

"So I heard there was a police riot."

"Sorry about all that stuff at Grace's. I didn't know what it would look like from the outside."

"You guys do that every year?"

"No. That was the last. I mean for me."

Another little spider crack because like the two rivers with the third hidden underneath, the bandana and the boy, I saw now that there wasn't a single move I could make that had no effect. There is a freedom in that too.

I stepped closer and put my hand against her ear. I still couldn't hear out of mine. She relaxed. More cracks lacing the ice. We talked about Honduras and what we could do there. She grew animated but I could feel it all coming apart in my hands. Let's get out of here, I said. Let's take a cab across the river and go somewhere where there aren't funerals and koi ponds, and she agreed. We went salsa dancing at a Latino bar near the old international district. We told them we were sisters so that they'd let us dance together. Then, when we were leaving, I kissed her in front of all of them outside on the street with the light of the Salvation Army sign falling down all around us.

On the way home I wondered how many chances we get. According to Devadatta the reason things are so fucked up is that so many people are human for the first time. I put my key in the door and turned it as quietly as I could. That's the problem with me. I want to believe in a world of endless second chances but I can't.

I have two recurring nightmares. In one, I am out of control on a river filled with Nikes, bulk tampons in twenty-pound bags and Indonesian patio furniture. In the other, I see the Statue herself gather her gowns and step off the island. Liberté! Liberté! Hairpins falling like cluster bombs in the harbor and a bustle of chattering soundbites—she wades in. And I think I could take having these dreams if I knew when they would stop. If someone said, you will have the first one two hundred and thirty nine more times and the second one six times, I could be okay and get used to it because I would know that it wasn't forever. The problem is that I will never know, not until the day I die and look back and say, oh! that was it. February 22, 20—that's when they stopped. Likewise, I don't know when all this will stop. It's a strange thing to be god of someone else's terror, even minor god, because I knew I was harmless. People were figuring that out but there was a shining moment in between, a strawberry on the cliff, passing, it still shimmered.

The phone rang. It was Tamara. She wanted to meet for brunch at Naught. I liked the idea of eating somewhere I had recently threatened to bomb. Besides, I heard they had an ice sculpture there of Leda and the Swan, but that was probably just wishful thinking. Tamara said she had a friend in the kitchen that could hook us up—cashew hummus, seed crackers and probiotic gin—whatever we wanted. I walked into the restaurant right before the rain started. The group of men that came in behind me turned when they heard the thunderclap.

"Just in time," said one of them as the door shut. No, you're not, I thought. Someone turned up the bossa nova.

Tamara was in the far corner with her face in a book. I walked over and sat down. Her hair was in short pigtails and she was wearing a green t-shirt with owls on it, light freckles over the bridge of her nose and her fair skin almost violet under her eyes.

"So, do they really make probiotic gin?" I asked.

"Yes. I always get it. It's disgusting."

She handed me a glass. It tasted like the bottom of a planter.

"Guess what I saw on the way down here?" I said. "'Superland. We will never forget!' sprayed right the a wall by the bus station."

Tamara picked up her menu, "Do you like nori?"

"Do I what?"

"Like nori. I like dulse."

"Did you hear what I said?"

"About what?"

"Superland. We will never forget?"

"That's the problem they already have," she flipped the menu over. "Do you know what makes something a sea lettuce?"

"Come on, it was cool. Citizens for a Rabid Economy? What was the other one, Manifestation?"

"All I'm saying is that it's a fucking lovely day to buy more IKEA. They're already out shopping."

"Two days ago you said it was brilliant."

"Yes," she shrugged, "but it was a wink, wasn't it? It didn't really change anything."

"Oh right, it would have been much more effective if they lit a trashcan on fire and spray-painted anarchy on the wall."

The waiter set a small glass dish of sprouted lentils on the table.

"Not saying that."

"So it doesn't count because no one torched the parking lot?"

"No one did anything. It was more like a joke, right? Just like all the other threats. And," she leaned across the table, "you're right, a lot of people claiming to be anarchists are pathetic suburban kids that just don't want to clean their rooms, but I'll give them one thing, they've got it right about property destruction. It isn't violence, war, poverty, now that's violence. Blowing up someone's SUV when no one's around it is just a good idea. Either way, don't lump me in with them."

Tamara's face was inches from mine. I could see gray lines in the blue of her iris, her cornflower fingertips on the gin glass. She was a bully but we were more alike than different. I might be too chicken to set an SUV on fire but I wasn't really against it. In fact I loved reading about things like that because I knew the people who did it were on the same side I was. Even if they didn't know about me, I knew about them and that made all the difference. I began to think that maybe what I viewed as sensitivity and compassion had just been squeamishness all along.

Tamara settled back and called the waiter over.

"I'm going to have the sea lettuce," she turned, "and you?"

"Nothing."

"My friend will have nothing."

Tamara handed him the menus. She sipped her green gin and read the local produce roster on the chalkboard by the bar.

"Squash, garlic, cilantro. Good, I like cilantro, kale, also very good."

"If you're such a revolutionary what's your suggestion?"

"Chard, apple... Don't know what I'd do. Have to think about it. Pretty sure it doesn't have anything to do with committees and talking points. Fingerling potatoes. Aren't they poisonous raw? You're a scientist, Della, you should know."

"Oh, you must be part of the underground no one's ever heard about."

"I don't belong to any group outside of my friends."

"That's a real bridge builder."

But it was a pretty hollow response. I wasn't part of any group either, and not just because my wiring was shot and I cried all the time, but because I had never met anyone in any political organization that I liked. "Eat with your hands like the African people," that's what this one girl I knew used to say. Someone told me she referred to a fork as fascist. And they were all like that, macrobiotic Belgian trust-fund junkies, park bench anarchists, mean white lesbians in canvas clothing and dreadlocks—each ready to denounce you as a cop at the slightest sign of dissent. My dirty little secret was that I only liked militants at a distance. Up close I couldn't stand them. Their targets were always the same, a cow path from the cell to the Great Reactionary Dawn. I wanted something more creative than dead clerks.

"So Della, on a similar note, what do you think will come from the demonstrations around the shootings? An editorial? An oversight committee? Constructive public outrage? 'Cause I'm betting on nothing."

She took a bite of the seaweed the waiter brought.

"This is the grossest thing I've ever had. Try some."

She pushed it toward me. I pushed it back.

Fucking Delphi of Gnostic Anarchism. Gatekeeper. Hey, I have to go now. I'm late for a hanging. Gonna celebrate the eight-hour day with some friends, you should totally come. Fucking elitist. Assuming I hadn't thought about these kinds of things. But inside me something quivered. It was a road I had never gone down. My family has no patience for anarchists. Grace sent me to a Marxist reading group when I was sixteen so that I wouldn't be tempted to become one. Credence didn't have to go, the little loyalist. I remember when I showed up, this really sweet, old communist thought I was part of a youth brigade that didn't exist. He'd talk for hours about revolutionary strategy. His analysis was flawless but it was like being forced to watch a starving polar bear clamber over breaking ice after a fat and agile sea lion. Nice left! Shame about all that saltwater. Ever thought about hunting in packs?

I was the polar bear. I got up.

"I told Mirror I'd help her move stuff for the party."

"Good. Me too. We can go together."

"Do what you want."

Outside, the rain had stopped for the moment. The sky was dark gray but there were bands of pale light on the horizon. Driven against the ground, they brightened under the compression and made everything slightly blue. A bald man's head went by, vivid as a robin's egg.

"We can walk from here," Tamara said.

It was raining heavily again by the time we got to the Cycle. We crossed a muddy inner courtyard. Wet chickens walked in jerky patterns through rows of vegetables and rainwater barrels. Mirror had everything stored in an uninhabited part of the squat and we walked into a common area that was once a lobby. Posters of bands and demonstrations, black silhouettes of raised fists and barbed wire, devil horns and drag races covered the walls. In the center of the room around a table two men and a woman sat rolling cigarettes and drinking coffee. One man introduced himself as Black Francis. The other, with ashen blond hair and pale skin, was Jules, and next to him was Britta, who had short henna-red hair, gray eyes, and a wide flat milky face. I knew a hundred people who looked like her.

"Come on!" yelled Mirror from the corridor ahead. "We only have the van for a few hours."

We loaded the van with props, tools and decorations at the Cycle then hopped in and drove to Mirror's place to get some boxes she had there. The whole way there Tamara couldn't stop going off about the bomb threats and how pathetic they were. We were coming down the stairs of Mirror's apartment when I finally yelled, "What the hell do you care about Manifestation anyway?"

"Nothing! I don't care about it at all. It was a hoax. There's nothing to care about."

I wanted to push her down the stairs but my arms were full of boxes. I'm a foot taller. If I hit her it would hurt. I thought about that going down the stairs.

"And how do you know it's a hoax?" I said. "Half the town is still blocked off."

"Because they haven't found a single bomb. They don't even think it's related to the parking garage or dog track."

"They don't know. It could be related."

"Well, do you believe it is?" She stepped in front of me to push open the front door. "Or do you think it's a hoax?"

The rain was so loud I could barely hear. I tried to go through but Tamara was holding the door and blocking it all at the same time.

"Well," I said jamming her against the doorframe as I passed, "I don't think it was a joke. I would have been scared if I was there. If someone called and said they were going to blow the place up. I would have been terrified."

Tamara grinned flashing her broken incisor and moved aside.

Mirror backed the van over the curb and honked. We ran the boxes in off the porch. It was a fucking downpour. I could see Mirror in the front of the cab talking to someone on the phone and eating a cupcake.

"In fact," I said throwing some boxes into the back, "I like what they're doing," I slammed the van door, "someone should be drawing those lines," I was shouting, "pointing that stuff out. People should have to think about their world and if no one gets killed, even better."

"Right," Tamara yelled, "think. Think about it. Not do anything about it. If you like that stupid group so much why don't you go join up. It couldn't be that hard. I'm sure they have a blog."

"Oh yeah it would have been much better if they actually blew up the dog track."

"So you don't believe they did it either," she laughed.

"I don't care who blew up the dog track! It wasn't exactly a call for class war, now was it? I mean who even goes to the dog track? Poor, stupid, white people. They need to be organized, not traumatized over the death of their favorite dumb fucking anorexic greyhound."

I stomped back up the stairs and was about to make another point, a really good one about vanguards as a sub-cultural delusion, when Mirror came in behind us, freaking out because the eyehooks at the warehouse weren't going to hold and she wanted slings and a trapeze.

"Hang plants," I said.

"It's supposed to be sexy," she screamed, "not some hippy soft porn garden scene. Nobody wants to look up and see ferns."

"And what you've got can't hold a person?"

"Not with the kind of torque we're going to be putting on it."

"Post a weight limit," I said.

"The fucking fat chicks would slay me. Slain. I would be dead. No more parties. Ever. I would actually have to slit my own throat to have an afterlife."

She kicked a box of glassware.

"This rain sucks and I'm totally going to get a yeast infection if I keep eating this much sugar."

She threw the half-eaten cupcake in the trash.

The phone rang and she asked me to get it. It was Devadatta.

"Turn on the TV."

"I don't think there is a TV."

Mirror made devil's horns with her fingers to signify television.

"No. No TV."

"Well, they blew up that temp agency. You know the one out by the malls, Brass Ring? They blew it up."

"That was a hoax," I said.

"I'm watching it now. The blast took out the whole front."

Once, I fell into a frozen river. It was like that. I held the phone away from my ear. Tamara saw my face and came around behind me so she could hear too.

"Were there others?"

My voice was so quiet I'm surprised she could understand what I said.

"Yeah, they found another bomb in the Olde Towne Mall. You know where all the high school kids hang out? But they got that one before it went off."

Tamara turned on the radio. There were two more, one by the loading dock of Transcontinental and the other in a small pho place that served over 100 kinds of bubble tea. I thought I heard one go off somewhere nearby but it was someone closing a door. Car engines sound like low-flying planes and the woman clapping for her dog to come like hand grenades. I was an atom. My electron cloud awareness charged everything around me. I could feel a part of myself, way, way beyond the universe. I had done something terrible.

"I guess I was wrong about that group," said Tamara quietly. "Maybe they are about something after all."

I didn't say anything. I was running over the list trying to figure out how many places I'd called.

We went to a bar with a TV and stared for an hour. Devadatta met us there. Bomb squads and cameras were trained on the New Land Trust building like it was a birthday cake with a stripper inside. Then they cut back to Brass Ring with its missing face.

"Man," Mirror said, "just look at that."

I couldn't stop. I saw the buildings burn in live time. People were crying. They were scared. High school girls huddled together waiting for their parents to come get them. A little Vietnamese boy wailed in his mother's arms. Oh god, I thought, oh god, oh god, oh god, oh god, oh god, oh god, oh god, oh god, oh god, oh god…and I ran my shaking hands through my hair. With short sharp fingernails I scratched at my chest until it was red with crosshatches. What had I done?

Newscaster Ken's Black Friend Garth was interviewing crickets.

"Chirp, chirp, rutuhtuhtuhtuhvrrrrrr… MANIFESTTION. Chirp, chirp, rrrhhhhhtuhtuhvrrrrrr…"

Mirror got up. "Everything is going to be fucking closed for days."

"Are you going to reschedule the party?" Devadatta asked.

"Fuck no! Letting the terrorists win and all."

Devadatta pulled out a scrap of paper with a phone number on it and handed it to Mirror. "Oh! I forgot. I talked to Raina and she's definitely coming. She's even talking about leading a class there, you know, like an intermission. That way everyone can stay grounded. She said to call her. Most people never get to practice yoga naked. I really think it will help keep people in their bodies more."

"Whatever," Mirror said, "just don't make it too granola. Focus on stretching the perineum. Mula Bandha, that's something people could use for sure. Remind me tonight and I'll get mats."

They left. I barely noticed. My eyes were on the Miracle Station. Every so often the feed went back to the news desk and anchors gave updates on some border skirmishes they were following. But I couldn't tell which border, or whose. Then they went back to the bombs and the fires here, where it was all burning and no one had been hurt, not yet. New ejecta glittered in the terrorsphere.

"Come on," Tamara said, "I'll walk you home."

She dragged me off the stool but I blocked traffic in the doorway because I couldn't stop watching and she had to pull me out.

"Everyone's fine, Della. Take a breath."

The people on the street said it was a miracle. Not one person hurt. Tamara thought it was a miracle too. I started thinking about it. It couldn't be an accident. Whoever did it must have been really careful. They must have meant for those other bombs to be found. It was my own flag waving back across the gulch. After walking a while, I saw the natural balance of cause and effect in play, karma created long before me. With every block, I grew confident. I hadn't bombed those places. They deserved it but I hadn't done it. I was sick of feeling responsible for other people's decisions. Paying for other people's wars. My muscles began to relax. And, instead of horror something else filtered through, the faint thrill of becoming. It was a miracle. The Saint with Black Tears passed me and waved, her children safe at home. Up the street I heard the jackhammers. They're building a supermarket made of mud. It's going to have valet parking, be completely organic and only fish that was inhabited by the souls of former rapists will be sold. Workers will get emergency room coupons and free coffee. I looked at the sky. Everything has a beginning, middle and end. The rain had stopped. Then it started again. It wasn't personal.

We got to my door. Nobody was home. Tamara said she wanted to see the head of John the Baptist and when I showed it to her she laughed so hard I thought she was going to choke.

"The cheeks are made of sought after recommendations."

My pride. Taking credit coming and going. Tamara was on her back, tears rolling down her face leaving little webs of eye makeup under her eyes. "What are we going to do with it?" she asked when she got breath.

"I was going to give it to my brother for his birthday zipped in a body bag with 'For the Fairest' written in Greek across the front and a My Pretty Pony inside."

She didn't know what I was talking about. I didn't know what I was talking about. It didn't matter. She sat up, flushed, looking about thirteen years old.

"Let's take it somewhere and let some kids bash the hell out of it!"

We put the head in a pillowcase and caught a bus to the Ukrainian neighborhood out near the suburb of Pretty Little Hopes. The rain had let up a little but the sky was still dark. On the way we got bags of candy, a cheap baseball bat and some twine. Everywhere around us people were glued to their televisions or on the phone. Sirens sounded intermittently. A couple of times I wanted to turn back but she wouldn't let me.

We found a tree near a middle school and strung it up. Kids started gathering even before we were done. I let a tall fat boy with an Ozzy patch on his jacket have the first go. We blindfolded him with his friend's bandana and spun him around. His first swing missed but his second cracked the cheek of John the Baptist. Next up was a girl with stringy hair and new breasts. She crushed the Prophet's chin. After her came two boys, one after another, each small and fast but neither of them left a mark on the head.

A sheet of sunlight came through the rainclouds and fell on the children, lighting up half a face, or the top of an ear. It made the gold crosses on their pale necks flash. Then it shifted and broke, streaming through the cracks in the dark gray sky, and played off the tips of reaching fingers. It turned the baseball bat white as it cut through the air.

A girl stepped into the pit and all the kids started yelling in Russian, trying to get her to swing one way or the other but she just stood there while the head of John the Baptist swayed above her. I swear to god she was listening to it move. She bent her knees slightly, wrapped her fingers around the bat and swung. The bat came down across his left eyebrow and split the head diagonally. Candy rained down around her and the kids started squealing.

"My kind of religion," said Tamara.

The tall fat boy with the Ozzy patch jumped at the battered

Prophet and got hold of an ear. He yanked and tore off the back of the head. A few more pieces of candy fell out and he dove for them leaving the papier-mâché skull shapeless on the ground. I walked over and picked up the piece. I recognized the handwriting on the inside of the brain case. It was a personal note from a council officer at the Paleontological Society asking me to attend an event. I threw it down and kicked it. I never felt so free in all my life.

Tamara and I began to walk. I folded the pillowcase up and stuck it in my bag. A large droplet of water splashed down on my scalp. Then another.

"Here it comes again," she said but we didn't walk any faster.

"That's something I'd remember," I wiped water out of my eyes, "if I was a kid. It would stay with me until the day I died. Do you think they knew whose head it was?"

"No. I don't think they cared."

"Would it have been better if I told them, do you think?"

"Probably not. By the way, I really liked the thumbtack eyes."

"Thanks, I enjoyed pushing them in."

"And the junk mail hair."

"That was fun too."

"Was your diploma in there?"

"No. I cut it up and gave it to a toddler who wanted to color."

When we got on the bus we were drenched. Tamara buried her chin in her coat, "You should come out to the farm. Stay with us for a while. It'd be good for you to get a break from the city."

"Yeah, I heard you got goats."

She laughed, "That too. But more importantly people, we have people who think like you do. There's a bunch of us out there. You should really come."

She got off at the next stop and I watched her shrink as the bus rumbled down Colony of the Elect Boulevard. All the way home I hummed a song Grace taught me about soldiers and sailors and the shining North Star.

The next morning I crossed the river lit by smaller fires. In my bag were the remaining rat family cell phones. I went to the Central Transit station, which was full of displaced workers thrown from their schedules by the bombings and scrambling to adjust. I sat down on a long bench in a crowd of people and pulled out the phones. Busses came and went on either side of me. I picked up the grape cell phone belonging to Jupiter Rodere and set it aside without turning it on. Saturn, Poseidon and Uranus I switched on and programmed to call-forward to their targets. Then I sent them off on different busses and walked two blocks north to a busy shopping plaza.

My whole life I had held back. But at that moment, I threw myself into the arms of an invisible collective and with all my heart, leapt for the sea lion.

I called in the Happy Day Corporate Charity Center first because I felt the hand of Jupiter should strike it dead directly. Lightning bolts of hate. Then I called the strawberry cell phone, Saturn, which call forwarded to the Oldies Station, KGOD and told them they were going to be bombed. I didn't explain past that. I figured that if they had to ask, they wouldn't have understood. Next was the blueberry cell, Poseidon. It forwarded to the Central Library. Then Uranus, which hit the Cine-Tower. I did it fast then threw the Jupiter phone into the flatbed of a passing truck.

I crossed back over the river. On the water, the city upon the hill wavered, an inverted reflection, and broke into scallops of stuttering light as the sun set. I went to a de-paving party once and watched people tear up a parking lot. I cried and cried because I'm a sap and it was so fucking hopeful I felt ashamed to even be there. I never let myself believe things like that can happen but I finally admitted that hidden in my scientist's mind was a dancehall that I had kept shuttered. I forgot the prettiest fossils are worthless. All the important material eaten by crystals. I felt like that was what was happening to me.

Two days went by and no new bombs went off. The security subsided and people fell back into their patterns. During that time I saw Jimmy twice. Both times it was awkward. She was somewhere else. I was someone else.

The first I heard of it was from a woman walking her dog. She said, stay away from downtown. Three more bombs had gone off. I asked her if anyone was hurt. She said no. It was a miracle.

Over the next twenty-four hours more fires started. Some of it was organized and some of it was just kids throwing Molotov cocktails. And no one was hurt. I know. I asked several times and not just the same person. They all said it, Milagro! Milagro! I broke open like a geode.

I know someone whose gratitude practice is centered on appreciating every object from the day it comes into his possession until the dystopic collapse of society. Vacations (soon nobody's going to be going anywhere, man), new cars (what the hell, we'll all be walking before long), guitars (how else are we going to have music without electricity)—the guy was a Zen master. I walked in the golden autumn light thinking he was more right than not.

I stopped by Rise Up Singing and listened for a while to the coverage with everyone else, huddled around the kitchen radio. The Happy Day Corporate Center was decimated. Boxes of irregular Nike shoes melting like butter. KGOD went down, a burning bush, a sign for all to see. Look! A new star in the heaven under which we shall find the baby—oh, maybe not. What's all this charred cinder block? The Cine-Tower, a lighthouse, a beacon on a hill.

The last thing I heard about were the two AM radio towers south of town. They exploded like timed fireworks, dancing around like sparklers on the Fourth of July. It was a beautiful thing about the towers but there was only one problem. I hadn't called them in. The AM radio towers were on my original target list, not on my working one. They were alone on the border of town near the spinning cell phone and I decided there was no point calling them in because there was no one there. I had crossed them off my list days before but they were burning all the same.

I called Tamara. She didn't answer.

Fires burned all the next day. Mid-afternoon Jimmy called. She said she'd had a change of plans. When I got to her apartment she was standing in the archway between the living room and the kitchen surrounded by boxes. There were white squares on her wall where pictures had hung.

"I'm leaving next week."

Her hair was dyed brown all over. She had cut off her cord necklaces and taken out her piercings. If had seen her in kindergarten, and then seen her now, I probably would have said she never changed. She leaned down and ran a strip of packing tape along a box of kitchen supplies.

"What do you want to do between now and then?"

"I'm actually heading out tonight."

"Tonight?"

"Yeah, as soon as I'm done with these boxes."

We talked about how things had moved too fast and how it was a hard time for anyone to know what they wanted. My favorite thing about Jimmy is her way of saying something she doesn't want to say. Like if she thinks something you are doing is wrong, or if she is sad about something she can't change, she'll just tell you. Simple and light as a silk parachute falling over everything, you will know. There is no hesitation in her and no violence. None at all. That's probably why Grace was so disturbing. Grace is all violence.

We talked and packed up kitchen supplies to take to a shelter. The rooms were empty. The plants were gone. On the floor was a Chinese calendar. She picked it up.

"Here," she handed it to me, "there's still three good months on it."

She smiled and shook her head then put her hand lightly on my shoulder. "I'll send you my address. You'll always be welcome."

"Mirror will kill you for leaving before her party."

"Yeah, I'm sure I'll get the lecture on a postcard."

Then she picked up the last box and asked me to hold the door. There wasn't anything else for me to do but load the truck.

Jimmy decided to spend the last few days with her family. They had a house out near Pretty Little Hopes in an adjacent suburb called Fair Prospect. That's where she went. Mirror asked me why she left before the party. I told her going to that thing would be like crashing your own wake and you just can't be in two places at once. I didn't blame Jimmy either. All this glory is too much glory. She needed to get away. From the smoke, the fires, the bomb threats, the bus crashes and me. I see her beyond the orange lights, twirling in a ball gown. Queen of the Jaguars.

Mirror said she'd pick up the dental dams and lube herself. She sounded annoyed. I was in the kitchen of Rise Up Singing listening to a new string of reported fires when she called. The radio was up loud so I couldn't tell what she was saying at first. She wanted to know if I had everything?

"Everything what?"

"Dams and lube."

I had vaguely promised to get them days earlier before everything was on fire.

"I forgot. Sorry."

"Dude, don't fuck up my party. Ben Hur Playland is going to close in half an hour."

"Right. If it hasn't already been gutted by a wall of roaring flame."

"Whatever—do me a favor at least, go outside and see what's happening."

I walked out of the back of the restaurant and around the corner. I leaned against the mural of the smiling black woman in the Pan-African headdress and looked down the hill.

"Okay, I'm there."

"What do you see?"

"Black smoke covering everything."

"Everything?"

"Well, mostly the south and southwest parts of town."

"What about east?"

"Clear."

"Fucking God loves me better than anyone. Call Ben Hur. Tell them not to close. I'm on my way."

Nobody knew where the party was going to be held. Just that it was in a warehouse somewhere, probably in the industrial district. It went this way: if you had an invitation it told you to go to a website where you logged on as a guest. You didn't need to give your name but you had to say who gave you the invite and write a few sentences about your current sexual fantasy. Once you were vetted, you entered a contact number. On the day of the party everyone would get three text messages. The first would say if the party was on or not. The next message would give a thirty-minute warning and the last would have where to go for the pick-up. There were four meeting points and you had to get there fast. The party was going to cap at 150 people. Not everyone was going. Common logic was that if you made it to a site within half an hour, you were going but anything after that was guesswork. The drivers who ferried people up to the party were all in contact with each other and kept a close head count.

I got the first message earlier in the day, around 2 PM. I was watching footage of bomb-sniffing dogs running through more pho places when it came in.

It said: YES LIKE YOKO…

I didn't want to go to the party necessarily but I wanted to find Tamara and thought she might be there. I'd called her cell phone but it was forwarding. She might already be back in Breaker's Rise. But Mirror said she might stay. If she had, I wanted to see her and ask her about my map and what the hell she thought she was doing.

Credence called about a candlelight march. They were going to retake media high ground with nightlights to prove how harmless they were. New fires were starting. The air was filled with static. Everything I touched shocked me and all I heard was crackling. Given these things, the sex party was like a reaction to a world that no longer existed, a Victorian ghost floating through the mustard gas. So I didn't call Ben Hur Playland like Mirror asked. Instead, I watched smoke rise over the southern part of the city. Down along the river where it bent towards the sea I stared at the coastline like some kind of mystical destruction was about to take place, like we could turn the corner on the Grand Ravage right then and take it by surprise. West, toward the Roseway Bridge, the candlelight marchers were gathering. With the cloud cover gone it was going to get colder. Soon they would cross the river. In my mind I saw them line up. I saw them light candles, one to another down the row, cupping their hands to keep them from going out. I felt the bird crickets perched on the grass hill waiting for the march to move, jerking and cocking their heads. When it got dark and the emergency lamps turned on, I headed toward the bridge thinking that I could catch up with the march. It was just over a mile away and they would be moving slowly. I began to run. Alongside me the molten pennies in the Rat Queen's fur radiated.

A quarter of a mile before the bridge the crickets had set up a barricade. I went south for a few blocks and saw that it stretched down to the cemetery. To the north it ran to the cement wall of the freeway. They had cordoned off the whole area. The marchers had no way to retreat and I couldn't get to them.

My phone beeped. It was the second message.

SOON IT ALL STARTS ANEW.

It was dark now and all throughout New Honduras people were dressing for the party. I wondered if Tamara really would be there. Jimmy wouldn't. I knew that. I tried to imagine her in Fair Prospect. She'd probably spent the afternoon in a lawn chair next to a bucket of fried chicken she wasn't going to eat while everybody pretended she was going on a spontaneous vacation. Now, Jimmy, how do you say T-E-G-U-CCI—I missed her, but more than that, I missed the idea that there was a way out of this.

Behind me I heard a bullhorn. There was a riot police sweep coming, about a block up. I saw bird crickets fanned out in full gear. I had the map and the last Hive phone, Pluto, in my bag. I looked around for a place to stash it but it was all houses with clipped yards and ugly little rock gardens. There was nothing that was overgrown. I began walking fast, first south again, then southeast, ducking through the side streets and listening for the rustles of riot gear. A couple of times beams of light fell across sidewalks I had just walked over. They were moving in a wide semi-circle and I could feel it start to close.

My phone beeped again. It was the third text message.

I KNOW A BANK WHERE THE WILD THYME BLOWS…
27 NE EVEREST / 988 SE MARKAN DR. / 1031 SW TORRENT /
2847 NW GILLAHAN

I was eleven blocks from NE Everest. I ran. The police lines hadn't closed yet and I made it through. Outside the perimeter it was dark and silent. There was no way for me to get home and no way for me to cross the river. If the Roseway Bridge was cut off, the South Bridge was too. I walked the remaining blocks to the pick-up site with my messenger bag pulled tight around me and my head and face down.

The pick-up site was a middle school playground. People were milling about under a covered basketball court. Maybe thirty or forty of them, all made of glass with flames dancing on their backs. I recognized some of them, a couple of neighborhood bike mechanics, some girls from the co-op, a guy that collected and sold scrap metal and his friend who was supposedly some big eco-terrorist. The woman who ran the tattoo shop was talking with two guys I knew from way back. One had gotten totally into urban biodynamic farming and I thought the other one was dead. Someone told me that, years ago. Meningitis.

The first driver pulled up and people surrounded his van. He said they were getting through. That the cops had closed off certain sections but didn't have the numbers to really lock everything down. Too many officers were still out on the fires.

A second van pulled up behind the first and a third behind that. Most of us went in that first run. Some waited behind for friends who were still coming. I got into the third van with the girls from the co-op and the guy I thought was dead and we took off. We drove with our windows down and the lights off listening and feeling the city surrounding us as we passed.

The party was held at a warehouse next to a huge old public utility building that had been abandoned for years. The land around it was so thoroughly poisoned by chemicals that the city had condemned it pending federal funds for cleanup. They couldn't even get crews to work on demolition there.

Mirror was standing in front of the main warehouse door in a pink and black striped top, go-go boots and fishnets with a cut out crotch. All pink to match. She waved the drivers over to a lot and went back inside.

We parked and as I got out the girls from the co-op pushed past me and ran laughing over the gravel and dust to the warehouse. I found Mirror right inside the huge hanger door talking with someone in a kitty collar. They were going to raise the cap. There were already about a hundred people there. I waited until she was done then stepped in close to Mirror.

"Have you seen Tamara?"

"That faggot isn't coming."

I felt the weight inside my body shift but I couldn't tell if I was lighter or heavier. I stared at an abandoned substation adjacent to the parking lot.

"You know this whole area is a roiling caldera of toxins, right?"

"Fuck Hazmat. It's not sexy."

"Neither is respiratory failure."

"Don't eat the dirt."

Mirror grabbed another girl in a kitty collar who was passing by, holding a basket full of bracelets.

"Pick a bracelet."

The girl with the collar held the basket up and Mirror began digging through it. "Red is all access, open to anything. Blue is hetero only. Pink is girl on girl—don't say it, I already gotten a rash of shit from the leather dykes—black is boy on boy, which doesn't apply…Safety Orange means you just want to watch and probably shouldn't be here anyway and you're not wearing that one because I would never speak to you again if you did and…I guess that's it. Red, blue or pink. Which is it?"

"Red," I said and slipped the bracelet she handed me onto my wrist.

"Good girl," Mirror nodded, "and if you get bored of being hit on by dudes you can always come back to the safe room and switch bracelets."

Mirror let the girl with the kitty collar go and walked off herself in a different direction. I didn't see her again for another two hours.

I walked into the safe room. It was filled with soft furniture low to the ground, worn out green couches and fraying velvet chairs. In the center was a dining table laid with tabouli, hummus, halvah, vegan cupcakes, tureens of carrot ginger soup, pomegranates, star fruit, bread, dark chocolate, raspberries, blueberries. Crystal punchbowls full of mango and papaya juices sat beside a decanter of cold mint tea and a pot of mulled cider on a camp stove. People were hanging out eating. Some were taking a break from the growing intensity of the party and others were just freaked out by the whole thing. A girl beside a wedge of brie was talking loudly about the other rooms and bragging about how she'd been out there several times already. Her hair was full of glitter and she looked like she had been crying.

Maybe this was the other Piazza. The other city upon a hill.

To the left of the safe room was a large alcove with a gauze curtain. I saw a woman go in and I walked over. More and more people were coming in through the front and the sound was growing. I pressed myself back against the wall near the alcove. It was pitch dark behind the gauze but I knew they could see us. I could hear bodies moving. Someone laughed.

I spent the first part of the party on the edge of the safe room but after an hour I gave in and left the safe room. I passed a place called the Den, which was set up like a rec room with board games and mattresses all over the floor. I looked in for a second but it was mostly hippy guys in skirts snuggling with their bi girlfriends. In the main room of the warehouse was a DJ. Mirror called it the Big Tent and had divided it into three rings, each reserved for serious BDSM play. Mirror warned me weeks ago that she was going to banish pretenders to the Den.

"Anybody wandering around PVC not doing anything is going to get it," she said. "It's not Stand and Model. I don't want to see sorority girls in pleather."

As far as I could tell, there weren't any. Mirror had painted the safe word, EXTREME on the cement floor of the warehouse, her own line in the sand, and it seemed to be working. In the first ring were five muscular gay men. A totally old school pornographic map—real leather, metal cock rings—everything. Two of them at least were over fifty and breaking out the canes. It was the kind of thing none of us had ever witnessed, something from old magazines, unassimilated pre-death sex. I saw Mirror walk by beaming.

The ring next to that was a gender mixed role-play. I recognized one of the bottoms, a boy from a camp I taught at once.

She was a girl then, Trina. Her parents were Christian hippies. They had a group house somewhere upriver and took in runaways. I knew some people who lived there for a while and said it was pretty cool, that they weren't bad. Trina was a neat kid too but I liked her better as a boy. It seemed more natural. He was part of a role-play involving a police officer and a bad storeowner. He was the kid caught shoplifting. It was pretty wild. People started to gather and everything got super electric, and with the audience getting into it so much, the players in the scene pushed more. Trina yelled for help and said he was innocent, but no one believed him.

In the last ring two men and a woman were doing Japanese rope torture. The woman moaned when the thin rope that ran between her legs was cinched tight and the top, a tall shirtless man who tied knots as delicately as if he were making lace, tugged on it again. The crowd surged.

Outside the rings, on one side of the main room was straight up orgy. There were some pillows thrown around and a rug but that was it. It was slow when I first came in but now it was really going. On the other side under a row of broken out windows the swings were set up. Mirror had painted sawhorses, a workbench and a rack bright primary colors so it would have a playground / construction site theme. Mitch was standing by the swings in a kitty collar with the liability paperwork.

The party was packed, easily closer to two hundred people and still more were coming. The synthetic hum of the music resonated in the huge warehouse and was absorbed by bodies. Ambient loops vibrated the aging and rippled windowpanes that remained. It was getting harder to move, harder to hear. I felt my way through the crowd, asking anyone I could find in a kitty collar where Mirror was. Finally I found her talking to a couple of sullen fetish model types near the punchbowl in the safe room. She saw me and came over.

"Dude, the swings have snapped twice, half of my tops flipped because this whole town is just a bunch of fucking slaves," she glared at the two girls by the punchbowl, "you better have some good news for me."

"Flipping roles can be sexy."

"No. It's not sexy when you have two totally passive bottoms trying to out-meek each other. Not sexy at all. If I wanted that kind of action I'd run a knitting café."

"I was wondering when Tamara left."

"That faggot! She split earlier today. If she hadn't painted the sawhorses I'd never speak to her again. Oh," she pulled an envelope out of a pink faux fur clutch, "She wanted me to give you this."

Just then Mirror saw a pack of Goth chicks heading for the alcove.

"I got to go. There's a No Bat Wings Allowed policy in that room. Someone got stabbed by a wire earlier. I need to tell them to hang the wings by the door."

She took several steps away then stopped.

"Della, you should check out the upstairs. You'd like it," she grinned. "It's called the Motel."

Mirror disappeared into the darkened alcove and seconds later a girl with bat wings emerged, sulking.

I opened the letter.

Dear Salome,

I wish I could have stayed for the party but I should have been home days ago. Come to the Farm. There's a place for you here. I think you would like it.

xoxo,
Mara

Inside the directions were folded up into a little swan. I turned it over. For that one moment there was no pull in any direction. I let out a breath. Nowhere for me to be this night but here. I unbraided my hair and shook it out. I had been waiting for something and not known what. Unpinned from all the things to which I was beholden—Grace in the hall of mirrors, Credence in the candlelight, Jimmy, the box-mall-church, the head of John the Baptist—I felt my body like I owed it to no one. Loosening the strap on my bag, it fell to the ground and for the first time in forever I let everything slip. Soon I might be in a foreign country, or maybe in jail, but right then I was under that broken slab of concrete with everyone else.

Steam rose from people in the Big Tent, condensed on the metal rafters and rained back down on the crowd. Raina was in the corner, her long auburn hair falling over her naked body, moving through her Vinyasa. Several people followed her and more were coming and going. She led the asanas, flowing through the warrior stances, lowering each time to the ground and arcing back then down again in a metered dance half time to the industrial buzzing of the DJ loops. I walked past them all and up a narrow, metal stairway. At the top was a door with the word MOTEL written in small black letters over the door handle. I opened it. A long carpeted hallway stretched ahead with rooms on either side. They must have been clerical offices a long time ago. Mirror had painted numbers on the doors. The one closest to the stairway was empty and I could see in. There was a ratty bed, a chair and an end table with a lamp that gave off yellow light. Mirror put a Bible next to the lamp and covered the window with a dark sheet to block any light from outside.

I took a few more steps in. It was cold in the Motel. I could hear beds creaking and soft moaning. It was full of people. Down the hallway a woman cried out and I heard the door slam shut. The hallway was dark. Some had kept their lights on and others had them off. At the end of the hallway there was a room with the door open and the light off. I went in.

A man was sitting in a chair.

"Claire?" he said and turned.

He couldn't see me. The end of the hallway was black.

"No. Not Claire."

He went back to looking out the covered window. Through the green flannel sheet the outline of Public Utility with its dormered windows and gabled roof could be seen. I walked over to him until the arm of the chair was pressed against the front of my thigh. His skin was pale and his chest smooth and I could see my breath under the dim light of the window. I wondered why he wasn't cold. His hair looked black in the room and the way he said Claire sounded like he was from somewhere else.

"Are you Russian?"

"Yes. Mostly."

After a few minutes he stood up. We were inches apart. His skin smelled like wood oil. I felt for his wrist and pulled it towards me. He laughed. I held it to the faint light. A red bracelet dangled.

I liked the sound of his voice. The shape of his hip and the way his hairline feathered at the nape of his neck. I liked that he was tall. I liked the combination of being cold and then too hot but never warm and never any one feeling all over. Sometimes I saw people in the doorway, standing shadows. Then later they would be gone, as if they had been looking for something and found it. Other people came in at one point and I bowed out for some of it. I took my turn in the chair staring out the green window and sat like he had, naked from the waist up, to see what it felt like and watched my breath dissolve in the muted light.

I stayed in there until daybreak. He was sleeping when I left. I wandered down the hallway and into another part of the building where there was a landing and a back staircase and down to the main floor. Gray light came through the high windows of the warehouse. There were people everywhere tangled and twisted like a photograph of a crash site. Behind hanging blankets, some lamps were still lit and I heard groans and the movement of bodies.

I found my things and walked down another hallway, constructed of corrugated tin, to a makeshift kitchen where a sink was. A staging room of some sort. Pallets of bottled water were stacked in the corner and towels and first aid kits sat on chairs beside them. I opened a bottle of water and walked out the back door down some rotted steps into a field of beaten yellow weeds. It was much colder than the day before but not raining.

There was a fire pit several yards in front of me and I watched gray ashes, bright as stars, get swept upwards by the wind and fall to the ground, settling on the trampled grass. I took a seat on some cinder blocks near the back steps and looked up into the white sky.

The Russian man I had spent the past few hours with came down the steps and sat beside me. He had a tin can full of water and some pliers. I helped him start a fire in the pit and we set the can in the middle of the flames on a brick. It felt like field camp. The air smelled of snow. There was a tree up against a fence and its limbs raked the sky. When the water was hot and the sides of the can were scorched black, the man took a plastic bag full of coffee and poured it into the water. He smiled like a soldier, the way you would at a stranger you passed. A tiny spider crack, infinitesimal, reminded me again that there was no clean way through this. My scientific training was all about prediction but there is no prediction. I had called in bombs and no one was hurt. I had tied a Buzz Lightyear to a twig and driftwood caskets swirled in eddies. Both were universes and there were millions more, smaller than anything I could imagine.

I kept looking at the sky. Then at the Russian's black hair, his gray sweater, the poisoned industrial field, trampled and soaked, then back at the white, white sky.

"What do you think about all the bombs?" I asked.

"Manifestation?" he laughed and pulled the coffee out of the fire then set the blackened can down on another brick. "Doesn't change much. More cute, I think. Meaningless, really."

He reached into his bag and pulled out a thick porcelain coffee cup. He dipped the cup into the boiled coffee and handed it to me, "The fires will go out. Something else will take its place."

I drank the coffee. The tree behind him had such fine leaves on it that they seemed to belong to another tree all together. They were crumpled and the color of dried roses. The man stood.

"I have to go. Do you have a pen?"

I found one that had slipped down into the torn lining of my coat. He squatted down in front of me and pulled my free hand toward him.

"This way, if you want, you can always claim it washed away," he said and wrote his number across my palm.

I looked at it several times that day. Each time I washed my hands, it faded more until it was only visible to me because I knew it had been there.

I was going to the Farm and I knew it.

Two days later I caught the bus to Breaker's Rise with Tamara's folded swan in my pocket. I didn't tell her I was coming. Creeping past my hidden desire for things not to be fucked, to belong somewhere, I made up other reasons for my trip—It's a lovely time of the year to see the coastal range; I heard they've got raw goat's milk kefir. It was as if I actually believed that none of my violated hopes were real if no one else knew about them, just like how someone's not dead until you say it on the phone.

The Blackberry Apocalypse was settling into a traffic menace and the maybe the Russian was right that not much had actually changed but I saw it differently. Over the digital streams and dammed expressways, my flag like gauze in front of the stars.

I packed like I was going to sea. I took my maps, my rock hammer, and the last Hive phone. In my PO box was the actual issue of *Paleobiology* featuring my name in black script on the yellow peach cover. Out of sentimentality I took that too.

Credence got the morning off and drove me up to a small town north of the city so I could catch the bus there and avoid the long security lines downtown, which was an all-around good idea. The rains started again but it was colder and I heard there was snow in the pass. We talked a lot about the candlelight march. They never even got across the bridge. The police came in from both sides and started arresting people. One girl got so scared she jumped. Broke her leg in three places. Before if I had said I was leaving town after something like that he would have called me a coward and accused me of exercising white privilege in the face of the real costs of gentrification. But when I told him I was going out to a friend's farm he seemed relieved. Lowering expectations being the secret to my success.

Credence bought me lunch in a Mexican restaurant near the Fallon City station and waited with me until the bus came. We talked about the babies. Annette had picked a birthing center and he had negotiated his time off with the union. They were going to go in for another ultrasound the following week.

"Got any good twin names?" he asked.

"Romulus and Remus?"

He smiled, ordered an horchata, and stared out the window, the parking lot reflected in his eyes.

It was raining harder when the bus came. An older man with matching luggage got off and they switched drivers. Two women who got out to smoke were complaining about being late. I was standing in the aisle when we pulled out and Credence flickered away. Dog salmon super 8. The bus moved north then east along a river. We stopped in a few other small towns before turning onto a long stretch of road that ran parallel to an old railway line. I looked at the bedding planes of the road cut. My mind ran between riots and Rat Queens. I'd remember the Russian man, stark in the green of the Motel, and suddenly see Grace, her dark hair streaming over an aquamarine dress and tiny creeks flowing from her fingers. There were no anchor points to my thoughts at all.

I laid my head on the glass. A wave of nausea swept through my body when I thought about the bombings and what I had done. But eventually, lulled by the vibrations of the bus and the passing geology of my childhood summers, my mind cleared. Nobody was dead. I didn't need to know what happened. And living in the center of that thought the vertigo and nauseous fear came and passed. Twice I had to stop looking out the window, fix my eyes on a single point.

The bus pulled sharply to the side and the engine made a

loud stuttering sound. People who were dozing woke up and looked around as the driver edged us onto the shoulder. We were there for about twenty minutes then the driver got back in and said we were going to have to find somewhere to stop for a while. He limped the bus a couple of miles ahead to a truck stop right off the main highway and tried to fix it there but he couldn't so we had get out and wait for a new bus. People started calling their friends and trying to get rides. The rest of us set up camp in the truck stop.

The Farm was only about four hours away but it was on the other side of the mountains and the woman behind the counter said the pass was getting worse and would probably close by nightfall. The cell reception was bad and I had an address not a landline number so I couldn't have called anyone at Breaker's Rise anyway. I found a place near the showers on the driver's side of the truck stop, a waiting room with black vinyl seats, a television and three courtesy phones. I curled up there near a window and watched as the rain turned to flurries, a white line moving down the mountain.

There were tanks on television rolling through the snow somewhere far away. It was night there and everything looked green on camera except the icy ridge they were climbing. Tanks disappeared over it like seals into water. Then there was an explosion. I could tell by the way the sky lit up. After that they just showed maps.

I got up and got a cup of coffee. The snow was falling thickly. I looked out at the bus parked at the far end of the lot. Soon the wheels would be buried. Already the roof and windows were covered. I sat back down and pulled out my notebook. A man with a belt buckle the size of a steak got up and switched the channel for a weather update. More snow. Early for this time of the year. Pictures of flooding roads in the valley. Pictures of giddy jocks on the slopes. A reporter in a pink fleece with a cup of hot chocolate. The trucker changed it back.

They were showing footage of the fires for anyone who missed it and then Newscaster Ken's Black Friend Garth interviewed the minister of Higher Ground of Africa Baptist, then back to the fires. For a second I couldn't tell if it was really happening or not. Like the first time I ever heard a bomb when I was four and I didn't know what it was. It was on TV but there was no screen between the fire and me. There were all these apartments burning and I couldn't understand where it was because the newscaster kept saying Philadelphia but then people talked about how they bombed Africa. I couldn't sleep. Grace and Miro stayed with me. I remember Grace talking. She walked back and forth trying to explain something. Some things she said again and again but it didn't get any clearer. We were in a war, but not really a war. Not everyone knew about it. Some people did but pretended they didn't. But it was going on all around us all the time and we must never forget or we'd lose. Everything depended on that. Miro sat on the bed while she talked with his heavy hand on my leg. I woke up in the afternoon. I'd been dreaming of dead birds.

A man nudged me.

"Hey, are you Della?"

Then I heard the page.

"Della Mylinek. Della Mylinek. Please come to the convenience store counter. Della Mylinek."

"Never mind," someone said, "I see her."

Tamara tromped in wearing a big green coat with a fuzzy hood. There was snow on her shoulders and boots.

"Come on, quick. The others are in the car. We're going to try to make it back through the pass before it closes."

She grabbed my bag and we ran out the back and climbed into the car. There was a guy in the front passenger seat and a girl in the back. We took off with the chains ticking as they dug into the snow.

"I called Mirror to see how the party went," Tamara yelled over the rattling engine, "she said you were coming," she looked back at me and grinned. "There aren't too many busses that go all the way out to Breaker's Rise."

In the car were two of the people I'd met at the Cycle. The man with the light hair, Jules, was in the front seat, and the woman, Britta, was in the back. Jules watched me get in but said nothing. I climbed in next to Britta. When I got settled, she handed me a thermos of yerba mate and we pulled out onto the highway, now a white alley where the sky and road met. Steering between the dark underbellies of trees shrouded in snow and the hazard lights of stranded trucks, we headed for the pass. Tamara's hands were the color of bone on the ochre steering wheel.

"I told them all about you," Tamara said when the pitch of the road lessened.

Jules glanced away. I could see freckles faint on his cheeks and his blond hair was ashen in the snowlight. Tamara slapped him in the stomach and he smiled. They had the same bone-colored hands. I wondered if they were related. Britta pointed to an abandoned DOT truck on the shoulder.

"That's a bad sign."

Jules rolled his window down to wipe more snow off the side mirror and I thought I heard a dog yelping but it was just a harmonic created by the wind and it went away when he rolled it up.

Closer to the pass were more parked state vehicles, ploughs and salters buried in the whiteness. I closed my eyes. Tamara was telling a story about some guy she knew who was so afraid of snakes that he broke up with his girlfriend because she got a snake tattoo.

"What a fucking coward!" Britta said.

I went to sleep wondering what tattoos scared me that much.

We came through the pass when I was only half-awake. It was dark and they were talking about what to do if we got stuck and had to make it through the night. I raised my head. The dashboard was a constellation of vectors and points and the view through the windshield was a gray parabola. Tamara said it would be fine as long as no one got out to go to the bathroom. Jules said it would be fine even if they did, just colder. Britta laughed and said she'd rather use the thermos. Their lips were teal. They might have been speaking Yupik or Estonian. That's how foreign I felt among them.

Grace once told me that the easiest way to radicalize someone is to isolate them and that I should make sure that never happened to me. It might be that what she said was true. But I didn't really mind being cut off from everything.

I woke up in a wooden bed under layers of quilts with the idea in my head that something was about to change. I sat up and looked out the window. Everything was covered by a thin layer of snow except for where the goats had beaten muddy paths into the ground. There were several outbuildings, rounded cob structures with embedded color tiles in geometric patterns. One looked like a woodshed and to the left of that was a brick structure with dark gray smoke curling up into the sky. I put on my clothes and went downstairs. The kitchen was empty. A bag of coffee sat on a large oak table and someone had been baking bread. There was a note from Tamara saying that she was out back and to come find her.

I set the note back down and got some water. I had been with Grace and Miro in a hundred kitchens like that. Everything was wood, metal, paper or glass; nothing was disposable. I knew where to look for cloth filters, tea, compost buckets and co-op containers of peanut butter, honey and tahini. I knew how the bread would taste, how the clay mugs would feel and how cold the kitchen would be until people came and it got warm from the bodies. I knew someone would have to boil the water for the dishes and someone would have to bury the trash at night so the bears didn't get it. And if you couldn't feel the despair that was in everything, if you were numb to the intense loss at the center of it all, it was like stepping right into a children's story. Fresh milk and cozy fires on the cusp of a wild wood.

I walked out back to where I had seen the cob buildings. A

goat bleated at me. Tamara was over by the smokehouse. She waved me towards her.

"Want some smoked fish?"

"I thought you were vegan."

"No, Mirror only speaks to me because she considers my conversion a life goal."

She handed me a pink strip of salmon jerky.

"She says you're a big old faggot and you're off the party list forever," I said.

Tamara smiled and blew into her hands.

"Good. I like Mirror. She's stubborn."

Tamara cut off a couple of bigger pieces of fish. A roll of wax paper was strung up on the door and she wrapped the salmon.

"Where is everybody?"

"They drove into Breaker's Rise to pick up Astrid, Britta's girlfriend. You'll meet her later," she closed the smokehouse door, "Astrid's kind of like Mirror, a little overzealous about details. She's okay. I think I like Mirror better."

There was a sharp, faint glare in the east but it didn't look like the sun was going to break. We came around the other side of the smokehouse. A cord of wood was covered with a blue tarp and tied with bright yellow twine. Tamara got down and cinched it tighter.

"Want to see something?" she said.

She took me around by the woodshed. Under a tin overhang next to some baskets of kindling was the beginning of an elaborate Nativity scene on a platform of baled hay. It had a cob manger with little tin foil solar panels and a computer chip star.

"We do something like this every year but this time it started early," she looked up at the sky and blinked. "I think it's the war. People feel it coming."

She flipped a switch and tiny white and red lights lit the crèche.

"Astrid wants to put the three kings up against the manger wall with a firing squad of PETA Barbies in orange faux fur bikinis. Can't you see Mirror doing something like that?"

"Why do you say it's the war?"

"Because that's what's driving everything right now."

"Yeah, but when I talk about the war people act like I'm delusional and just trying to ruin their 70s t-shirt glitter decal fantasy march."

She laughed and shook her head.

"That's because you talk about the war all like it's already happening. It's not happening for most people. Some of us, yes, but not for everyone."

"Because they're fucking desensitized automatons that reproduce through violence?"

"People are on their own learning curve and outrage is a personal thing. We're short on it already."

She pulled a box off a shelf.

"And," she said, "when people do figure it out, they need something on the other end that they can be a part of."

"Like a tableau of horrific understanding?"

She stopped.

"You know, Della, you're funny but you're like a switch that's stuck open."

A thousand answers went through my head but mostly I just wanted to leave. Turn around and walk off. But what was I going to do? Hide behind the nearest goat? I stood there on the verge of tears feeling like I wanted to punch a wall. Tamara plunked the box on the thatch next to the manger.

"Britta's mom sent these."

She opened the box. It was full of Barbie and Sailor Moon dolls.

"We're using them for the nativity scene. I originally envisioned the Virgin as some sort of homemade Valerie Solanis action figure but I got out-voted," she picked up an anime vampire in a biohazard suit. "I'm trying to adjust."

She waggled the doll at me.

"No gods! No masters!" she said in a toy voice. "Hi! I'm Della," she squeaked, "I like dinosaurs!"

"I hate dinosaurs," I mumbled.

The doll danced in front of me. I tried to ignore it.

"I like Pterosaurs!"

She was too stupid to look at.

"I'm an invertebrate paleontologist."

"No. You're a pussy who can't take criticism."

"Fuck this!" I said and shoved the box.

"Oh relax," she said, "we're all a little like that."

I felt that part of me that couldn't be moved, moving, a glacial shift in all my horrible pride.

Tamara put the doll back and turned off the manger light. I stepped out from under the tin roof. Two dog-sized goats wandered toward a covered stall. Tamara blew on her hands again. Her lavender hair was vibrant against the whitening sky.

"Come on," she said, "I'll show you around."

The temperature was dropping and the sounds were changing as the layer of snow crunching underfoot began to freeze. Barn swallows rushed the sky and their chattering calls echoed on the dormant landscape. Not all the people who lived on the Farm were there. Some were travelling and some were in the city. We passed empty bedrooms and I saw yurts and straw bale shelters tucked in the woods. I heard their names as I went: Coryn, Marco, Daria, Asher, Miranda, and the one I met at The Cycle, Black Francis.

We took a trail through the pine trees where a creek cut, jagged and half frozen through the new snow. Tamara pointed to a small hutch covered in tarp with lines running to it.

"Most of our power is solar and we pull the rest out of the creek. The batteries get charged there and we run it into the house."

She led me back up through the woods past where the yurts and tree houses were. We talked about being teenagers. She grew up near Los Angeles in some suburban corridor between a mall and a freeway. She got pregnant halfway through high school by some skater kid who bussed tables at the Olive Garden and had an abortion.

"I'm sure we did it just to have something to do," she said, "Nothing ever changed there, nothing ever happened. I swear time doesn't even fucking exist in those places."

We ran over the names of some of the bands that were around then and I knew some of them, they were mostly political hardcore.

"I was super vegetarian then and used to go to the Krishna house feeds all the time but I never believed in reincarnation."

She opened the wax paper took a piece of salmon, wrapped it in its metallic skin and ate it.

"I loved LA though," she said.

I hate LA. I'm all for the earthquake.

"It's nothing but cement and razor wire," I said.

"Right and I felt like if I could be alive there, nothing could kill me. It was exhausting though. I lived in a house with fifteen other people then. All the bands stayed with us when they came through on tour. A lot of Italian political hardcore bands, some Dutch. There were a lot of fights with the police then. They would come down to whatever demonstration we did in riot gear and we'd throw bottles at them. A few people would get arrested, a few would get stitches and everyone walked around the next day acting like heroes. It got pretty ridiculous sometimes. We had to fight the skinheads at the benefit shows and it would go on the news as a riot like we were all the same people. It seemed for a while, though, like something was coming to a head. Riot cops were shutting all the stores and marching through the streets in the thousands. I really thought that we were close to some big shift and that it was all about to happen but it didn't. That winter one of my best friends killed herself and like half the house started shooting dope. By spring there was nothing left of it and the bands coming through were more like jocks than anything else. It was like the whole thing dissipated worldwide at once. That's how I met Mirror. She was part of a younger set that was all into queer politics and being vegan."

Tamara put away the remaining salmon and smiled.

"You know, she would kill me for telling you this," she said, "but when I met Mirror she was a brown-haired runaway hippy chick who listened to Ani Difranco."

"I am so glad you told me that."

"You should definitely tell her."

Tamara pulled off a glove and shook it. There were small chunks of snow in the weave and she picked them out.

"I still can't imagine you with the Olive Garden skater boy but I can see you in Los Angeles."

"Yeah, when I came here it was shock, all the cold and gray. I went out to the coast and the water was freezing. The beaches were rocky, black and sharp and it seemed like everyplace I'd felt strong and free and alive was gone forever. I felt like someone else completely."

I also knew what it was like to be somewhere foreign, waiting for the person you used to be to show up. It was something that connected us.

We came out of the woods and followed the creek back down to where we started. She took me through the outbuildings near the smokehouse. Inside one were several fifty-five-gallon drums with lines running out the bottom into five-gallon containers. It looked like a still. There were small electric heaters on the ground. Clean white t-shirts hung on nails.

"This is where we store and filter the fryer oil to make the low-grade biodiesel. We pick it up from the restaurants and run it in the secondary tanks."

I followed her to the garage where another old Mercedes was being converted to run on fryer oil. The work areas were immaculate. Every tool had a place and every drawer was labeled.

We talked about the war and people we knew in common. Who was leaving and wasn't. She said if she had to go anywhere it would be Columbia or Chiapas. We decided that the general consensus in our demographic was Nepal or Costa Rica. I told her about Mr. Tofu Scramble and how he wanted Sri Lanka for the curry but couldn't take the monsoons.

"Yeah. I don't really mind people like that leaving. They're all born landlords anyway. I mean have you ever had a your rent raised more often than when a hippy owns the building? 'I'm sorry but I got to, man.' They should have it on their fucking tombstones."

We walked out onto the dirty snow in front of the garage.

"People like you, though, it's different," she said. "Are you really going to leave?"

"No."

I felt ashamed for even thinking about it.

"Well, if you are staying, you can't just be out alone or you'll go crazy. For instance," she paused, "one person could never have set off those bombs in town, not without casualties. It took lot of people working smart together to pull that off."

The air electrified. It was the closest she'd come to admitting involvement. I wasn't sure what to say because I realized then that I didn't actually want to know.

Tamara looked out over the gray and white land.

"It's just something you'll need to think about sometime," she said and started walking again. "For your own sanity."

We spent another hour going around the property and looking at all the stuff they built or were working on. They made their own beer, jam and goat cheese. There was a slaughterhouse several hundred yards away where the creek turned south, a one-room brick building flush with the horizon line. Tamara said they butchered and skinned whatever they shot hunting right on the property. Deer mostly, and used everything but the teeth, which they kept in Mason jars over the fireplace.

"Britta says she's going to do some big art project with them but I don't think she's going to get around to it for a while. Here."

Tamara held out a jar of grooved yellow teeth.

"No thanks."

She didn't move. I thought she was joking.

"No really, no thanks."

She didn't move. I couldn't figure out what she was doing or what she wanted from me. She just kept standing there with the deer teeth. Maybe I was tired, or just confused but I started to think that it might all be a test. Like she was the freaky homeless woman on the road with the magic charm that I don't know I'll need later but only get it if I do what she says now—TAKE THE DEER TEETH, DELLA! —And if I don't it all vanishes, the goats, the crèche, the idea that something different is possible, all of it—TAKE THE DEER TEETH, DELLA! —And I'll wake up in a convenience store parking lot. Blazing patio furniture on the traffic island and wearing nothing but my finest identity, a nosegay of slivered contrast unified by the ineffable mist of personhood. It was too much. In that moment I wanted to be on the farm and nowhere else. Tamara shook the jar at me.

I snatched the teeth out of her hands and opened it. They smelled like acrid leather. I think it was the iron in the blood.

Britta walked in. I felt instantly guilty. Like she was going to ask what I was doing with her deer teeth. But she didn't fucking care. No one does. I live in my own goddamned world. I screwed the lid back on the jar and stomped upstairs embarrassed. I grabbed my rock hammer and notebook and went out over the snowy field, walking towards the bitterbrush. I stopped at every ridge that might be exposed rock. Anything I found that looked like it wasn't mud I smashed with my hammer.

"All I know is I don't want to be part of it. Not their power, not their plastic, not their food—fucking gross slavery meat."

Astrid dropped her dishes into the soapy water. Her thin blonde hair was in pink plastic barrettes and she wiped her forehead on her upper arm.

Tamara laughed.

"Oh fuck primitivism!" she said, "Fuck Zerzan, Jensen and all those guys. I don't see them taking down elk with a spear or foraging the roadside between speaking engagements."

Britta turned into a blowfish and floated towards Astrid spiny and offended. Astrid sponged the back of a silver bowl.

"I don't want to be on their grid, that's all," she said.

"Well, that's fine but a lot of people do and we're going to have to stop pretending Hippy Easter is coming and everyone's going to just wander into the wild and live polyamorously."

Astrid darkened and her large freckles stood out.

"Yeah, well you know, when the shit comes down and their whole world's nothing but blowing ash, then they'll fucking 'wander into the wild,' as you put it."

Tamara slipped a stack of plates into the water.

"No," she whispered, "they'll wander over to the next town and they'll take whatever they can take through force until someone takes it from them."

The blowfish, Britta, floated away from the sink.

It was like watching a leftist soap opera. I liked the girl with the purple hair but she was kind of a bitch. I thought the blonde one might be up to no good and I didn't care about the other because she was part of a boring subplot. But it was no different than hanging out in the kitchen at Rise Up Singing and I no longer knew why I was there. I was beginning to think what Tamara meant by saying there were "people like me" in Breaker's Rise was no deeper than Barbie doll humor. We hadn't talked about the bombings at all and every time there was an opening in the conversation for it to come up naturally, she changed the subject. I felt lost at the Farm. They weren't interested in what I was interested in. I tried to open up new lanes of discussion, anything other than baking without yeast or how funny the strip mall chains would look with grass growing on them and beetles everywhere, but I failed. I could no longer see why they wanted me there at all.

On the fourth night it changed. Jules was setting up a Go game in the living room. Astrid and Britta had gone into town to do laundry. I was in the kitchen explaining the possible causes of the Permo-Triassic extinction to Tamara.

"Changes in glaciation, feasible but boring. Comets and supernovas, which I like better, but then I lean toward catastrophism, and my personal favorite—"

Britta walked in, excited.

"Someone tried to take out a transmission line going into the city."

"—killer methane bubbles the size of North America."

"It was stupid," said Astrid, coming in behind Britta. "They tried to drive a car into it."

I thought about saying it again but no one was listening.

"At least he tried," said Britta. "I remember when I was in high school a line went down in the river and the surge blew out like half the televisions in the city. It was fucking awesome!"

"Oh, come on," Astrid laughed, "it was stupid. He tried to

drive his car into the base of the tower and some dumb guard threw himself in front and he swerved. If you're going to do something that pointless with your life you should at least be willing to take out the stupid guy who jumps in front of you. Instead, he didn't hit the tower and still killed the guard."

"That's a shame," said Tamara.

I wasn't sure if she meant the guard or the transmission line. I was still looking for a polite way back to the Permian Extinction.

"Can you believe somebody would do that for minimum wage?" said Britta. "Hmmm… serve nachos at a fucking Mexi-kiosk? Or stand by a phallic symbol of resource enslavement waiting for someone to drive into it so you can leap in front of the car."

"Does anybody know the name of the guy in the car?" asked Tamara.

Astrid knelt by the wood stove. "Do you know how much power runs through the main lines going south?" she said. "About 4200 watts at full capacity. That's like, three nuclear power plants."

"Suicide by transmission line," said Jules.

Astrid put more wood in the stove belly, her cheeks fuchsia in the heat of the open firebox. She closed the latch. I wasn't paying that much attention to the conversation. It was the kind of talk you could get anywhere over spelt cookies and a micro-brew but Astrid was stuck on the idea.

"Yeah, but if you did take out some of those big lines out it would be a total mess."

"Well sure," said Jules, "but they're all gated now. You'd need a car or truck filled with explosives to get through."

"No, you wouldn't," I said.

I was thinking about Holocene deposits and how I had never really given the Cenozoic much of a fair chance. Mostly because I'm anti-mammal.

Jules was annoyed.

"Yes, you would," he said, "even if you jump out, a truck or a car is not going to get through the gate with enough momentum to knock the tower over. You'd need explosives."

The blaring subtext broke my train of thought… Hi, I'm Jules. I'm the Know-How Guy of the Group. Sitar music fades… It was just bunch of residual pre-feminist hat-doffing and it was irritating because I wanted to explain methane clathrates to Tamara.

"You don't want to take out multiple lines running south anyway," I said. "You'd want to take out one big line going south so the others lines stay open and carry the overload. That way you might even blow a substation if an HV fuse opened too slowly."

Tamara set a full kettle on the woodstove.

"So how would you do it?" she asked.

"I'm curious too," Jules said.

I hadn't thought about it but I hate being patronized. I'd defended my dissertation against some of the best scientists in the world. Real jerks, some of them, and I didn't feel like getting talked down to by some tinkering Robinson Crusoe of Anarchy Island.

"Well…" I said loudly, "I might start by looking at the soil those things are built on and when they were built. There's a lot of silt, sand and gravel along the river and compacting is expensive. They used to be far more carful about it than they are now. I'm sure they did as little as possible. I'd look at where the towers sit on non-cohesive soils."

Kimba swipes at the usurper.

"That just shows where it's less stable, not how you'd get to the base of the tower to set explosives," Jules said.

From the jungle, Kimba's spirit father yells out a warning—

"Fuck getting to the tower. Those gates are meant to slow

down someone stupid enough to drive a truck through them. I wouldn't bother with it at all."

—But his words of warning turn into fireflies and Kimba charges on.

"I'd find a spot on bad soil where the line crosses the river and set a bunch of charges to try to dunk it in the water."

"It wouldn't work," said Jules.

Methane bubbles popping as I followed my pride down a hole.

"It's called soil improvement," I said. "They tried to use it to build the Russian railroad in the 1930s. A guy at Davis was an expert in it. You set charges on unstable ground to cause liquefaction. Works like an earthquake and turns the ground to quicksand for a few seconds. Half this area is prone to mudslides and everyone builds on it like they're setting up a pup tent. Theoretically you could do a lot of stuff that way."

"Could you really?" Tamara asked.

"I have no fucking idea but it beats driving a Volvo into a transmission line."

The room was silent. Tamara's eyes were sharp small moons. She held a tea bag by the string between her fingers and it spun midair like a cat toy.

"Well," she dropped the bag into a cup and grabbed the kettle, "Coryn and Asher get back tonight. We can ask them if they know more about the guy who drove into the tower."

"Who?"

"Coryn and Asher."

I had forgotten about the others. The empty rooms of the farmhouse were integrated into my sense of the natural order. The idea that people were coming to fill them disturbed me. I knew nothing about them, just irrelevant details, that Marco and Daria shared a room but weren't together, that Asher was trans, that Coryn spent a year in Thailand with a begging bowl and Black Francis had a crush on Tamara, which she resented.

"I think you'd like Daria," Tamara said, "She was a biology major."

I hate biology majors. It's the chick squad for scientists.

Nothing more was said about transmission lines or the Permo-Triassic Extinction. After that conversation though, I began to sense the work going on beneath the seed-based cheeses and zines. An undercurrent of excitement bearing no relationship to anything on the surface and which ran through the most trivial interactions. I recognized the feeling from my childhood, the excitement that was there when people came to our house. Or when we went to theirs and slept over or drove back late. Credence, Cady and I would spend the whole day running around with all the other kids, chasing chickens or playing in the forest in our underwear, then get carried to bed half-asleep while the adults talked. There was nothing they said that I could pin the feeling to, but I knew it like a smell or a quality of air. It was so familiar that when I caught it again as an adult, it hurt. It was a ghost from a lost world and I was the only survivor, that's how it felt. When we were older the whole thing was less mysterious. It was the family-friendly side of the revolution. Later, we were taught the basics: a clampdown will come. When it does, don't talk in restaurants. Take your trash with you or shred it. Never say anything over a telephone line you wouldn't want read back to you in court. I spent my childhood waiting for a signal to go underground. And now, here it was.

Soon everyone who lived at the Farm was back. Tamara was right. I did like Daria. She was a substrate receptor geek who played drums and competed in Miss Leather contests. Coryn was all right too, a femmy redhead with cobras on her back who had wandered out of her high school Dianic coven into West Oakland and spent her twenties there. She said she didn't mind the drive-bys but couldn't take all the new white people. I told her they were here too.

I barely saw Marco and Asher because they spent all their time with Jules in the garage. Black Francis, however, was unavoidable. He followed Tamara everywhere. And when she told him to go away, he followed me.

Other people began to arrive as well. Three one night. Seven the following morning. More after that. There was an action coming up in the city to mark the anniversary of the formation of the New Land Trust and several collectives were involved. It seemed like every few hours somebody was showing up. Britta and a girl named Desiree got put in charge of sleeping arrangements and Astrid organized the grocery store runs and monitored power usage so that the lights stayed on.

The action was to be a coordinated lockdown. The idea was to block traffic all over the city while another group did a guerilla theater piece in front of the New Land Trust building. Tamara referred to it as Puppets of Rage.

"I'm sure the kids will be crying."

She wasn't much moved by the spectacle.

"Wake me when we move on to real people," she said.

Heads of giant puppets sat like boulders along the driveway.

Coryn was in charge of setting up the work groups and Tamara signed me up to make papier-mâché.

"From each according to his ability…" she said and walked off.

I found an outcrop of rock near the farm and crawled around on it. When anyone asked, I helped out. I got to make the puppet of Consumer Debt. Mostly though, I spent my time eating lentils, smashing open concretions with rock and hammer and listening to Radiohead. It was almost a vacation.

At night everybody hung out in the kitchen or in the hallways or stairs, having circular debates until near dawn. Ends versus means? Nature versus torture? Where to buy a thousand feet of rope? Someone suggested the six-month anniversary sale at the Wal-Mart near Superland ™. A fight almost broke out. Deal-breaker? Or using the enemy's greed against them? I was going to argue the position of changing the system from within but the conversation turned when someone said they'd gone to school with someone else's sister and everyone started tracing their histories back to the most fleeting intersections. You knew K—? My ex-stepfather's son recorded a keyboard track on an accordion side project he did for this compilation. Small world (destroyed by flames of gross misunderstanding). Wow. I think I had that CD. With the before and after shot of Dresden, right? But in it all, I saw my own granulated past. A friend in high school, a waitress, a lab partner's boyfriend. I didn't want to be connected to them but I was. Some part of me from a long time ago was returning.

From one of those talks, I got news of the city. There was a curfew and it was being obeyed. Marchers clashed again with the police at the Roseway Bridge but no one was seriously hurt. Organizers were trying to keep things from getting out of hand, at least for the moment. No one thought it was going to last.

"They still talk about Manifestation night and day," said Coryn.

Daria said the government made it up. "It's like those old Bolsheviks in your bathroom posters—Be on your guard! Manifestation is all around you," she giggled. "It's totally postmodern."

Coryn said eight cell phones had been found but that there was supposed to be one more, "The infamous death phone Pluto," she filled a water glass with beer and shook her head. "It's fucking great. Every time someone pulls out a cell phone on a bus, people dive."

"Oh, god!" Daria laughed. "They totally made that up too! Shameless terror-mongering fuckers."

"Technically, Pluto's not even a planet," I added.

"Oh, I'm totally sure the moons of Jupiter are next."

Daria got up to get a sweater. Coryn stretched. "Well, if there was another phone it probably got tossed."

She drank the glass of beer and did a sun salutation in the hallway. Jules looked at the shiny black windows. His face reflected back in waves on the undulating glass. His cheek line was almost vertical in profile and the lens of his eye, translucent. He looked at me several times but I ignored him. An understanding had grown up in the silence between us, that we don't talk about it. I was off the hook somehow now anyway. I went upstairs to bed with two sets of eyes, his and Tamara's, on my back. I felt the phone in my bag wrapped in an unworn t-shirt. It had only been turned on once when I activated it with the others in the parking lot of the Village of Light Towne Square. A souvenir? A genie's lamp? I wasn't sure myself why I still had it.

The next morning I walked out into the field and sat on an old carriage stone. Sleeping bags curled like maggots in the yard. I counted twenty-one. The wet fog was about to burn off and the back edge of the slaughterhouse roof was streaked with sunlight.

People worked late into the night filling beer cans with gravel and taping them shut, hundreds and hundreds of them. They were stacked in boxes by the garage door and beside them buckets full of pulleys, bandanas and carabiners. The giant puppets were covered with tarp and their nametags wrapped in cellophane. And all day long people practiced chaining themselves to things or getting dragged like egg noodles over the yard because it looks so bad when they beat you and you're all helpless and squishy like that.

"Future Christians," was all Tamara had to say about it.

They ran the play. A short piece in which the Oil Baron and the Water Baroness were married on a logged and desolate hillside by the Deacon of Capitalist Expansionism. At the end they were going to scatter Fair Trade rice over the crowd.

I suggested they use deer teeth instead and gave them my jar.

Tamara said she'd rather get bones set than do political theater.

"I saw the Specter of GMO Corn torn to shreds by police dogs though. That was pretty cool."

She stuck with organizing medical supplies.

"They're going to need it when they get the shit kicked out of them," she said flipping through an illustrated book on minor surgeries.

"I think I could do that," she said, pointing at an appendectomy.

Everything was intensifying. No one had slept well and everyone was cranky. Asher, who was newly trans, had been called Brianna one too many times and lashed out at some dumb college kid who'd followed his girlfriend there and made him cry. There were other things too, people throwing tools or yelling at someone for nothing. But it didn't stay that way. Half the crews were leaving the next morning to organize bike brigades in the city, so as the puppets got finished and the supplies staged, the atmosphere turned from a frantic and stressful panic into a fevered debauchery.

It started around dusk when Marco and Coryn ran power to the yard, which was strewn with disassembled puppet legs and arms. They organized the sound and began to DJ. Nets of speaker wire glinted between the outbuildings as the sun set. The last bit of work, sorting the medical supplies by affinity group, was finished in the dark.

"This way they'll at least have some gauze to staunch the flow," said Tamara after handing out the last package.

Britta dragged a keg into an empty goat stall and turned the space between the garage and shed into a homemade biergarten. People started changing clothes. From nowhere, out came the striped stockings, glitter, lace slips and hidden jewelry. Dressing again, they braided their hair or cut it for no reason with stiff hands in the cold. No one could see. Jules lifted the garage door and a trapezoid of thin light fell over the driveway. He stood there in a cloud of breath.

Coryn found a wedding dress stuffed in a bag. It was huge, size 26 with a train. It had been for the puppet bride but they didn't use it and she carried it to the garage and slipped it over her head. Jules cut a length of rope from some of the climbing supplies and tied it around her waist. She twirled, her cream hem rising and falling like a sin wave. Asher climbed into one of the Mercedes and flashed the headlights like a strobe while she danced.

"Black Francis!" yelled Asher. "Get the projector out!"

Francis hung sheets from the farmhouse windows and showed newsreels and industrial films. Lime and gypsum, the heart of our nation. A breadbasket of waving grain. A boy in pink vinyl pants and gumdrop hair danced with Josephine Baker, jerking on the southeast wall.

Tamara asked me to climb up on the roof on the garage with her and I did.

Coryn circled beneath us in the wedding dress.

"They could do without plumbing but not hair dye."

She twisted a piece of lavender hair around a finger. Her legs dangled off the roof. She zipped up her sweatshirt and pulled the sleeves down over her fingers. "I wish it were enough just to be alive."

I knew what she meant more than anything I had ever known.

A girl with tangerine hair who reminded me of Jimmy went by and I wondered where she was, if she was still in Fair Prospect with her parents or already on a plane. Someone put on Stayin' Alive and at first it was like a joke, then everyone went crazy. Francis jumped off a barrel onto the dirt, flailing like he'd been saved. Daria grabbed his hands and they swung each other around until they flew apart, then someone caught her and spun her the other way until she fell. Black Francis knocked over a stack of palettes and rolled onto his back laughing. I could hear him over the music, echoing on the tin siding of the garage.

People rushed the half-lit pit. But I saw the division like I always do. The axis of ironic response. Unfolding, the body of a butterfly. I fucking hate disco. What delicate wings. On one side, the actual impression. On the other a cunning replica. Jazz hands hooked at the thumbs, flapping across the driveway, a white bird. But I know what it means to crave what you're not. To want to sew up that rift because it's exhausting to hold it open. Sometimes you just need to be someone else, someone who doesn't care about anything at all. I know I do. I want emptiness but I can't have it. Marco turned the music up. Gumdrop hair stuttering in the high beams and flickering against the movie reels. Black Francis against the subsidized crop, wheat. Asher in the fields of rice. The stars, dusty above. Tamara asked me to help her and Jules take out some transmission lines heading south. I said yes. Every generation gets to decide its own relationship with the universe. And whether I liked it or not, this was my generation.

I started with FEMA maps.

"This is how they cost out earthquake damage."

I laid one on the drafting table so Jules could see.

"Sometimes people call them ground failure maps or hazard maps. They show you where the land is unstable and prone to liquefaction."

He leaned over. I traced a river gorge.

"Check that out."

Jules brought the arm light closer.

"And if you think that's bad, look at this."

I unfolded a second map.

"That's the city."

Jules shook his head.

"I can't believe you can just get these."

"Everybody has them. It's how they sell insurance."

But it's not like we were going to blow up a volcano or anything. Toppling a transmission tower was really a civil engineering problem. My job was just to figure out whether soil improvement techniques could be crudely adapted to destabilize land on a slope.

The transmission line inter-tie between where we were and all states south was only a few hours from Breaker's Rise. I began to map the lines running into it because they would be the ones to take out.

My initial research had to be done online so we needed to find a computer. There was an old desktop with dial-up at the

Farm, which Tamara kept for guests—"Weather reports and porn only," she said. It was her idea of hospitality. Not that I would have used it anyway. If I'd looked up charge density specs on something like that Grace would have disowned me. And she was everywhere in my thoughts.

Dear Grace,

> The land here reminds me of old summers.
> I have nothing safe to say. Aren't you proud?

Sending back the black dress,
Della

But we still needed a computer so we settled on the library one in Breaker's Rise. Mostly I would be looking at civil engineering websites and links off the Geological Society of America homepage, which was all pretty tame. As a precaution, on my first day there I spent forty-five minutes at the circulation desk talking to the librarian about sedimentary structures and grain size. After that she immediately went to shelve books when she saw me coming.

The library itself was an early 60s box of tan brick with a flag that specialized in books on tape and citizenship classes. Hey Juan, when you're done with those apples, remember to brush up on the Monroe Doctrine. It was also the turnaround spot for seniors on their daily walk and when I was working I'd take breaks and watch them make painstaking u-turns in the parking lot. I almost never saw anyone there that was under fifty who wasn't an immigrant or a visitor. They kept the computer in an alcove near an unused conference room and when I told them I was doing my thesis on a local radiation of paleobivalves, they practically wrote my name on the desk.

I found some PowerPoint presentations online that described how some engineers had tried to use underground explosives to resettle the soil. There were maps of an industrial park with notes all over them. I showed them to Jules.

"Those are blast patterns. That line is about sixty feet from the center of the park. The triangles represent the first round of charges and the circles the second. The squares are settlement platforms. Of course, we wouldn't be able to do it like that, but it's worth exploring. This one caused liquefaction down to forty meters."

I ate cheese sandwiches for lunch, usually in the car with Jules in the parking lot. Between bites I gave him a tour of the regional seismic record, mostly because I like reminding people that they live on the cusp of a geological catastrophe capable of changing worldwide weather patterns.

Jules reminded me of Credence, so convinced he was smarter than everyone that whatever he said came out like he was teaching you how to tie your shoes. Watching that habit slip, I saw how similar he and I really were. Only I had stopped trying to communicate with anyone at all, patronizingly or otherwise. My attitude was fuck you and your myopic mental laziness, tie your own fucking shoes. Under examination it wasn't a more enlightened stance.

Twice I used the payphone at the gas station. The first call I made was to Annette. She was worried about the air quality with the fires. Grace and Miro wanted them to go out there when the babies were born, just in case. Credence said he didn't want to take advantage of a privilege that other people didn't have, including anyone in Annette's family. Annette agreed, but not really. I could hear it her voice. She changed the subject.

I called Rise Up Singing to get Mirror to deposit my paycheck. I made sure to call during lunchtime so she would answer because she likes having relaxed, non-essential conversations when the restaurant is packed.

"Franklin says if you are on vacation, he needs to know. I told him since he doesn't really own the place after tomorrow it's none of his business. The new owners asked about you and I said you broke your foot at work and they should expect an L&I claim. I told them you tripped on the barista bar they're building. I thought that was pretty genius. They turned totally white, dude. Not that they could really be any whiter. What else…"

I heard the din of the restaurant in the background. Someone was saying excuse me over and over.

"Do you need to go?" I asked.

"No. It's just some fucking neon spandex biker who wants a medal for not driving his Porsche on the weekend. I hate those stupid helmets. Completely phallic. Hey! I'm a dick, get me a sandwich."

I could hear the kitchen bell dinging. Some glass broke behind her.

"Well, I should probably go," she said.

It all seemed very normal, talking to a coworker about bank hours and schedules, catching up on people we knew in common, but as I hung up the receiver it hit me, there would soon come a time when I could no longer call anyone at all, or write them for any reason.

Dear Jimmy,

The sky is white like in your apartment. The geological map of Honduras shows landmasses like fallen confetti. I would come but you are already in the Cloud Forest. I will burn this letter and think of you

—Della

The New Land Trust action in the city was still a week away and every few hours some new group came through, picked up friends or supplies and left. I bought a lot of stuff for it—chain, PVC pipes, long underwear, wheat paste and groceries—I put it all on my GSA Grand Canyon credit card. It wasn't like I was going to pay it off anyway. I thought of it as my contribution to the collapse of corporate serfdom.

Most of the time I was too busy to be part of the preparation because there are always two levels to any organization, the one you see and the one you don't. I was now in the latter. Everything went on as before, people worked, cooked, loaded cars, but there was a pane of glass between most of the guests and me. I knew there were other people involved too but I didn't know who they were. Every now and then I thought I did and would get confused. Sometime it was as simple as a look. Or the way someone was suddenly interested in all my thoughts. But nobody ever said anything outright. Half the time it was like being on acid and talking to someone not knowing what level the conversation really operating on. Are we actually talking about this stupid band? Or that dumb girl? Or are we having the real conversation? The one that never stops in the Subterranea.

I didn't see much of Tamara that week. Somebody had to maintain the public face of the host collective and Jules was with me. So she got stuck packing papier-mâché hands and bibles into cars, which she loved. Fucking waste of time and energy, she said. On her knees in the cold by a tarp helping to label and dismantle the ten-foot spine that was to be ceremoniously given to the mayor by the Puppet of Abused Labor.

"Hey Salome! You got anything you want to put in this run?"

I saw her across the muddy driveway, her lavender hair violet against the snow sky, and her expression reminded me of something I couldn't quite place but whenever I saw it I felt like anything could happen. A surprise victory? A terrible defeat? I didn't know what it would be but it was going to be different and that was enough. It was like a homecoming.

Jules and I drove the countryside in the afternoons looking at towers. There was an airbase just over the state border and it turned out what they really wanted was a power outage there, not in the city. Jules said there was an affinity group willing to sabotage a plane if given a chance. He thought that even trashing one would dramatically change things.

"We have to change what people think they're capable of," he said.

And I knew too, that movements could catch spontaneously, like Cuba, Elvis, the Velvet Revolution, or Tiananmen Square, without an observable precursor. My own training showed me this. Punctuated equilibrium. Or even more so, the flipping of poles when compasses suddenly spin off from the demagnetized north and point somewhere else entirely. The rock record is full of it and it happens all the time. A threshold is reached and they flip. I could see that we were at a threshold too, or close, and after all, what had I come out hoping to find but a brilliant insurgency?

Tamara said we needed to do it before the planes were mobilized.

"You know it's coming," she said. "Do you have a problem with that?"

Those ugly fucking birds that sound like the end of the world? Let's see…nope. The idea that I could stop one was thrilling. Way better than Wal-Mart or KGOD or talking to rats.

It was clear that we weren't going to be able to use a by-the-book version of the soil improvement methods. We needed to modify them and just get as close as we could. With dynamite and glorified shovels we couldn't drill to the water table or set charges deep enough with a camera or guard around—Excuse me, wage slave, I have to core the earth where you're standing—whatever we did was going to be a hack job.

Britta wanted to try to turn a guard. Tamara thought it was idiotic.

"What are you going to do? Buy him beer and tell him about Kropotkin?"

I envisioned the conversation:

Vanguard: Wage Slave, are you aware that you are but a wire nail in the toolbox of capitalism?

Wage Slave: I thought I was a chisel.

Vanguard: No, the petit bourgeois are the chisels.

Wage Slave: What about a washer set? Can I be a washer set?

Vanguard: No, my ferret, run free! For I have unlocked your collar with knowledge!

Wage Slave: I want to be a chisel.

Vanguard pushes screaming ferret through hole in fence cut by the clippers of noblesse oblige.

"Well, maybe we could bribe him," said Britta.

Tamara laughed. "With what? Health insurance?"

My scientific opinion was that it was going to come down to finding the right target on the right kind of land and blasting the shit out of it.

"It's going to have to be a tower with a camera, not a guard," I said.

"We're going to have to work with what we've got," Tamara said.

She poured a pot of boiling water into the sink for the dishes, the little Ulrike. I stood, which I do when I want to get a point across. In high school I had more fouls than anyone else on the basketball team.

Tamara stared up at me and retied a little purple braid.

"What?" she said. "You want an ends or means death match? Pick a side. I can argue both."

And so could I. I let it drop.

Tamara never talked directly about what happened in town with the bombs and fires. But several times in public she mentioned that the search for MANIFESTATION was getting more comprehensive. I said it's always like that. She laughed.

"Well, I'm just saying, whoever made those calls should be careful."

When the SWAT teams come over the hill I'll throw deer teeth at them. What did she expect me to do with that information? She certainly didn't want me to stop surveying transmission lines.

"Causes and conditions are the near enemy of capitalism," I told her.

"Right, let's just hope that last phone doesn't show up."

I heard the Rat Queen squeal, trapped as she was by the mountain range, penned by the great river.

"How close are you?"

Her children scurrying through the brambles.

"Very close."

Burning monks and art students line the path to the sea but I didn't feel the same way about it. Working on something tangible was a relief after all those years watching Grace and Miro leave rice on the altar... Oh Great Movement Icons!—each grain a carefully constructed insoluble conflict—Look upon my works, ye mighty, and despair! No wait... Presente! But of course they're not. Chavez, Debs, Huey and Bobby, the George Jackson naptime reading group. Compared with that, blowing up a plane, taking down a transmission line and having sex in a warehouse full of strangers was a fucking joy. A perfect expression of sentiment. Unmediated and sharp as a dart.

"That's right. Fuck creating the crisis," Tamara said.

She threw an orange peel into the compost.

"Take the opportunity and the crisis creates itself. All that shady bullshit about being ready to step in and lead when the time comes—we shouldn't be stepping in at all."

Her blue glitter fingernails on an orange wedge held before her mouth.

"Party politics is all about having the same three people on twenty committees. It doesn't foster proletariat 'ownership of the process,' it's elitist and self-defeating. Nobody should be protecting anyone from the results of their actions."

I twitched at the hardness of the stance but deep down I agreed. Anyway, there weren't enough feathers in the world to soften the landing we were all going to have. Steep curve? Nope. Sheer cliff.

I mapped every transmission line that crossed the river, how they were built and on what. I worked backwards. I studied everything I could about how to avoid harming "nearby structures during explosive compaction of saturated cohesionless soils," then planned the opposite. Pore water pressures, decks of horizontal blast dispersion, cyclic loading and shock wave statistics by grain size, but after several hours of soil mechanics I had to get out. Rolling through the back roads on two-lane highways cresting without vision and taking blind curves I could almost remember what it was like to feel like something good was coming. I fell asleep sometimes and dreamed of the war like a sea vine dragging me down then woke up and remembered that we weren't there yet, not quite.

Jules and I killed time when driving talking about ex-boyfriends and girlfriends and what kind of music we were into in high school. We agreed on collegiate communists and disagreed on the squatters' movement. He said it was a proto-revolutionary act and I said it was shock troops for real estate speculation. Scouts for the New Honduran army. Regarding food politics, we both thought that you should only eat meat if you thought you could kill it yourself and that the argument over honey was monastic and not organizational. When we talked about our families we both tended to get a little shakier in our opinions and didn't stay on the subject for too long.

Jules' parents were back-to-the-land hippies and his grandparents were Slovenian anarchists that escaped to Hungary after the First World War. I told him I knew a Hungarian prince.

"Great. I'm sure my family probably worked for his."

"I think they've been out of power for a while. He spends all his time listening to the Beach Boys and playing guitar through effects pedals."

"That's useful."

"Maybe not. But it's beautiful."

I could see him on an unlit stage, one arm raised the other resting on a laptop. Dark blue light around him.

Jules didn't say anything for a while. We drove along a ridge of short dried grass. I could see the wildfire line where it had come down the mountain and crossed the valley all the way up to the road. On the other side the land ran, tea green towards a wide and braided stream that sunk like a handprint into the reeds. I lay my head back on the seat. The towers passed, silver lattices casting shadows on the half burnt fields.

We found three potential sites, two by the river and one running along a cliff above it. The one on the cliff had a guard shack so we took it off the list. Tamara put it back on.

"We'll just get him out of there," she said, "tell him there's a sale on elk whistles down the street."

I didn't bother to argue. Further surveying showed it to be untenable.

"Now how did I know that was going to be the case?" Tamara said, smiling.

'Cause you're a psychic who should do road shows?

That left two towers, one on a mud cliff and another on a debris flow that had been converted into a ramshackle jetty. At first I liked the mud cliff because it seemed like it would take so little to cause a collapse and the cameras couldn't see over the edge so there was lots of cover, but the points where we would need to set charges were too high up and I couldn't figure out a way to get to them, which meant we were going to go after the tower on the jetty. It was a more critical line but carrying almost too much energy. I didn't want the high voltage fuses to close too quickly. I wanted the load carried as far as it could be and there was a substation across the river not far from the airbase that fed into the larger southbound lines.

Jules was very excited about it.

"It's like a sand trap surrounded by water. There's an eight-foot cement wall and three cameras but it looks like they can't see anything at the water level that's within twenty yards of the jetty wall."

The idea was to come up to the jetty by boat, drill whatever holes we could with small equipment, jam a ton of explosives into the rock and hope we could just blow enough chunks out of it to matter.

"Della, what do you think?"

Tamara and Astrid both looked at me. I noticed each of them had yellow plastic barrettes shaped like ears of corn in their hair and I wondered if they coordinated or it was just synchronicity. It made Tamara look like the Goddess of the Underworld and Astrid like a sullen three-year-old. I remember thinking then, as now, that it's funny how symbols work. They're just empty vessels. Swastikas and sun wheels. Broken up bits of thought.

"I think it will go in."

Later that night I looked at a Mercator map I'd printed it out at the library. It was fuzzy where the ink saturated the thin paper. I remember as an undergrad reading that what Mercator was after was a "new and augmented description of Earth corrected for the use of navigation." I was after that too.

I told Tamara I was glad I hadn't left with Jimmy, or gone into seclusion with Grace and Miro, and that for the first time my education made sense and I was grateful because it hadn't for so long, except as an excuse, well, whole populations have died before, and that I wanted her to know how much it meant to be there. Halfway through my speech she started to cry. I was totally unprepared for that. Do terrorists give each other friendship rings? Whatever remaining distance there was closed.

On my way to bed that night everything I touched was cold, the faucet, the ceramic sink, the bedpost, all like ice. To keep warm, I slept with my head under the covers and it seemed like there were three of us there, whispering about the net of possible futures that spanned between us.

We drove past the air base and Jules pointed to a line of gray planes.

"You can see some of them there. When we come around you'll see the rest."

The road arced as we climbed out of the rain-shadow-channeled scablands. From a distance I could see that the whole compound was in a depressed basin. I imagined it, a bowl of fire lighting the desert. Pink skies. Black smoke. It was getting dark and we turned around. The moon rose through the front windshield.

"There's not much more to do," said Jules.

He rolled the window down. The cold air was shrill in my ears.

When we walked into the farmhouse Tamara, Black Francis, Astrid and Britta were there. Everyone seemed to be waiting for me to say something. I got some water from the kitchen and drank it by the woodstove, listening to the embers crack inside.

"That's pretty much it," I said, "We're as ready as we're going to be."

Tamara was thrilled that it was finally moving forward. I wasn't. I saw the power grid, currents flowing in all directions, televisions and respirators, barracks and airstrips, all inseparable.

The New Land Trust action was only three days away. We decided to blow up the transmission tower at the same time to increase the level of distraction. We also wanted to associate the sabotaged tower with the New Land Trust demonstrations so that it would form a big arrow pointing toward the city and away from the airbase.

There was nothing left for me to do and I needed to get my things in order so Jules arranged a ride for me into the city. I would leave the night before the action and come back out the following week. When I got back we were going to prepare the Farm for winter and then figure out any future plans. Tamara thought it would be a good idea if we did something harmless and highly visible.

"Like host an underground film festival. You know, something with bad animation and comments on the postmodern body."

"I know a woman who does porn flicks in infrared," I said.

Britta got excited.

"I totally know that chick too! She's like the best grant writer on the planet."

"Great," said Tamara, "let's get her to curate. Maybe we can shoot video of a deer hunt and intercut it with an underage sex scene."

Britta laughed. "We should get Astrid to do it. She looks like she's fucking twelve anyway."

"Oh, god yes!" said Tamara. "Put her in a training bra and some cotton underwear. Surefire boycott. That would be fucking perfect."

From there, the conversation spun off into storyboarding tales of animal porn.

"No, no, wait!" yelped Tamara, her face red from laughing and tears running down her cheeks. "And after the goat scene, we have the subplot: he's a vegan. She's a Native American whale hunter. Can their love survive? I can see the final scene now: clashing communities brought together by a violent white trucker who shoots a kid."

Her blue eyes glittered and the feeling of familiarity was so strong I felt it in my body, an electromagnetic field between us.

We planned a whole six-month calendar of events. The film festival, a pie party, tutorials on butchering and canning—Tamara's idea was that we make the Farm famous for irrelevant and controversial happenings. It was a pretty smart tactic. Over the course of the night, she told me about two hundred times how glad she was we met and how cool it was going to be to work together. Any regrets I had vanished.

The next morning Tamara and I were driving around and she wanted me to survey the land by Wal-Mart that was out a little ways from Breaker's Rise.

"Wouldn't it be great if we could wait until they close and sink that thing about five feet into the ground?"

We were driving back from the hardware store. She had her feet up on the dash.

"I would fucking love that," she said, tapping the window in cadence, "it would be perfect."

"It's stupid, it wouldn't work. Those things are single-story flat-bottom boats."

I was in scientist mode and a little more dismissive than usual.

"Besides, it would take a zillion charges and wouldn't do nearly as much a trashcan fire inside. They're just like big tents. And even if you could figure out some way of doing it it wouldn't be worth it. It's just a symbolic target."

"Oh, you're one to talk about symbolic targets," she said sharply, "fucking yoga studios and bubble tea?"

"Fuck you! I drew a picture. I pointed out the features of the problem as I saw it. I wasn't planning to blow anything up for real. You did that. I didn't ask you to and you didn't have to."

"Yeah, well, you didn't mind claiming our bombs."

I pulled over on the snowy shoulder.

"Oh my fucking god!" I laughed. "You did not blow up the dog track! Did you? That's so fucking unbelievably stupid. And the bathroom? What was that? A strike against plumbing?"

"What do you care?" she screamed. "You were talking about leaving the country. And if you didn't want anyone to blow up stuff on your precious map then you shouldn't have left it around everywhere. You wanted someone to do it for you. That's why you're here. You want someone to do what you're too fucking chicken to do and then you want to pretend it wasn't your idea."

"Oh fuck this! I'm walking."

I opened the door and Tamara backhanded me in the ribs. I probably should have figured it out then, what really connected me to her, that invisible string. My sister, my torturer, my hero at Pine Ridge. But I didn't. I was distracted by what she said because it was true and I knew it. I did want someone to do something, and I didn't want it to be my fault. I wanted everything to be okay, everything to change, and no one to get hurt. I was ashamed of myself. I got out of the car and slammed the door. Tamara slid into the driver's seat and rolled down the window.

"You're such a friggin' pussy, Della."

She turned over the engine and pulled up beside me, idling.

"I don't care if you walk. I won't blame myself at all."

I kicked the driver's side door. She rolled her eyes.

"Oh why don't you just get in and stop being an ass?"

"Fuck off."

"You want to race?" she revved the engine. "Come on, John Henry, you can do it. Want to race?"

"Why are you so fucking stupid?" I screamed.

"Why are you so fucking sure you're the only one having a hard time?"

Kimba eats glass. Tears of hate fall. I glared at the frozen fields. Steam from the tailpipe billowed around the car. The road was empty for miles in either direction. I felt my pride like a prison.

Tamara killed the engine.

206

"Really," she said, "why do you think you're the only one who hates it? Do you think I want to spend the winter eating canned fruit and deer jerky on a fucking farm waiting every night to see what bad thing is going to happen next?"

She blew into her hands and squinted at me. It had never really occurred to me that she had a problem with any of this.

"I don't know what to do," I said.

Those were words I don't ever remember having said.

"None of us do and we're all trying to figure it out together because there's no other option."

I let my new feeling of ignorance radiate. It was a quiet and gentle freedom, utterly foreign.

Tamara opened the passenger door. "It's going to snow. Get in."

Right then, I think I would have gone anywhere with her.

We got back just after lunch and the snow started. It was light and blew in swirls. Everyone was napping or reading or packing. The silence was so complete that when someone dropped a knife in the kitchen, even though I was outside, I heard it ring like a shot. I didn't feel like sitting down or sleeping so I went to the garage to find something to do. The green Mercedes Jules had been working on was in there and he'd left the hood up so I closed it. I turned the heater on and the light and sat down at the bench. Bags of salvaged nails, screws and washers sat unsorted on the worktable and I went through them.

While I was doing that, I remembered Jules had been looking for registration paperwork on the yellow Mercedes. I thought it might have accidentally gotten put in with the slips on the green so I went through the glove box to see. Everything was in an envelope and I pulled it all out to look at it under the lamp. Old maintenance records, a receipt for an alternator, a mileage tracker, the registration for the green Mercedes, I put them on the worktable. There was a sheet of folded paper. I opened it up and the other registration fell out. I was about to fold it back up when I saw the letterhead. It was a receipt from a travel agency for two tickets to Paris leaving in four days. Jules Kraka and Tamara Byrne. Direct to Heathrow and then continuing on to Charles de Gaulle. I read the date again and again. They had been planning to leave all along.

I sat there for a while, then put the papers back and shut the glove box. When I stepped outside, snow powdered the driveway. The daylight hurt my eyes and I had to blink before they could focus. Astrid opened the kitchen door and saw me.

"Hey, we're making pizza. Come get some."

Blonde hair in tight pigtails. Britta was right. She did look twelve.

I nodded. She closed the door. Smoke curled from the chimney.

Credence says I jump to conclusions. He says I never wait to find out the whole story. Maybe that's what Tamara meant once when she said that we'd all made hard decisions. Maybe she'd given up her escape and that's why she was so hard on other people about it. I could understand that. I don't know why she wouldn't have told me, but I could understand that. I looked at the transaction date. They had bought the tickets only the week before. Right when we were choosing between the transmission towers.

I went to find Tamara.

Astrid was pulling two homemade pizzas out of the oven when I walked into the kitchen, which was warm and crowded.

"There's a vegan and a cheese," Astrid said and set the pizzas to cool on the stovetop.

I sat down to eat with everyone else. Tamara was telling the story of how she met Black Francis. He'd been hitchhiking around, living off pharmaceutical studies. He'd gotten kicked out of a big study for taking acid and was stranded in Arizona. Tamara ran into him at an all-ages punk show that he was trying to scam his way into.

"So Francis was whining to the guy, telling him he should get in free because he had been using his body for drug tests as a profound act of social giving. 'I'm fucking helping to cure cancer!' It was so incredibly pathetic that I had to pay his way."

Francis's cheeks were red but he didn't seem to mind. I looked at Tamara. She seemed relaxed. You can't be relaxed when you're lying to everyone and on the verge of fucking over all your friends.

After dinner Tamara stayed in the kitchen to do dishes. I stayed too. When they were done, she sat down.

"I wanted to talk to you about something," she said.

My hope rose.

"It's about this winter."

My eyes stung.

"We're going to have to work to frame the events so that people can take something real from them. There's no real point if we just let it feed a media storm unquestioned. Maybe we could train others on the methods we used, if it works. You and I could do it together. People know me."

Tamara reached across and grabbed the last pizza crust off my plate and ate it. The way she did it, like she didn't have to ask, was just like Cady. And that's when I got it, that buried wire. There were a million reasons why I was there, but only one I had never seen. I had been drugged by my own longing.

She picked up my plate and took it to the sink. I felt nauseous.

"Tamara, what's the hardest decision you ever made?"

"I don't know," she said with her back turned, "I haven't made it yet."

She poured some coffee and sat back down. I couldn't read anything in her expression.

"Well, did you ever think about leaving?"

She looked right at me, "No. I never did. I don't believe there's anywhere to go."

"Never?"

She stirred sugar into her coffee.

"Never."

Tamara looked through a newspaper on the table. I felt like there was no air left in the room. Everything around me sharpened. I could see the bevels inside the wooden sashes of the kitchen windows and the coffee grounds on the floor across the room by the compost bucket.

"Well," she said, closing the paper, "I better get back to it."

I watched her stand and finish her coffee by the sink.

Credence says I don't give anyone a real chance. He says I act like people are either good or bad and there's nothing in between and no point where they could take a turn. What I loved about Tamara was the way she would take anyone on. It didn't matter who or how many. She was fearless. Sit there twisting a hank of lavender of hair around her finger or painting her toes and suddenly say the smartest thing you ever heard. She had a brilliant natural mind. Just like my sister. But Cady was pitifully honest. A black rock in a bay. With her, you saw everything. Anyone could make her cry, but no one could get her to stop whatever she was doing. She'd tell you about it the whole way too, no matter how it cost her or what names she got called. That's how I knew her from all the others. A charcoal statue in the harbor. I guess we each have someone we don't see coming. Someone shaped like someone else we miss. I felt so stupid.

"I should go," she said.

She and Jules were driving Astrid and Britta to the bus station in Breaker's Rise. On the way back they were going to pick up some stuff we forgot earlier. I told her I wanted to take a walk and followed her out the kitchen door, heading out over the field, the flurries thickening around me.

I came to the slaughterhouse, the oldest structure still standing, and bent to tighten my bootlaces. My fingers were red and I was crying. I couldn't untie the knot. My nose got stuffed up and I sat. The car started in the driveway. I clawed at the knot and tore my thumbnail. Tiny red droplets speckled the snow as I shook my hand. I sat down on a rock next to the slaughterhouse door. Old red bricks littered the ground by my feet where part of the wall had collapsed a while back. That's where I was when they left. Tamara waved. I saw her get in the car smiling and almost threw a brick at her.

As I watched them drive away, I nearly threw up. They weren't about making things better at all. They fucking knew that blowing up planes was a game changer and they were going to Paris. I grabbed the biggest brick I could find and threw it. It landed twenty yards away and disappeared in the snow. I grabbed another and threw that one too. Fucking dog tracks and film festivals. Transmission lines and air bases. It wasn't about building anything. It was about getting away with it and proving you were smarter than everyone else. I got up and kicked the slaughterhouse door. They'd be in France in watching the fallout. I kicked the door again and the latch broke. I might be a coward for thinking about leaving but at least I wouldn't take down the few weight-bearing walls on my way out, frail shims, matted grassroots swollen and floating in the water. I would at least have left behind something to cling to, even if it wouldn't have kept me afloat, I wouldn't take it from someone else. Not if I wasn't staying.

I threw up on the snow and wiped my mouth on a frozen rag left on the ground. It tasted like blood and I threw up again. There was no way that Britta or Astrid or the others knew. Tamara didn't like Astrid and she didn't trust Britta. I'll tell them, I thought. But what was I going to say? So there's this action that you may or may not know about and I really hope neither of you are cops or that you aren't friends with anyone who might be because I'm going to put a whole bunch of other people at risk by telling you this but…when I didn't really even know what was going on. I had to calm down and figure it out. I had to come up with a plan.

Or maybe I didn't.

I put snow on my face to cool it. While I was there a small yellow car started coming down the long driveway toward the farmhouse. I watched it without thinking. It was old with shot suspension, shaking on the dirt road and jerking in the potholes. I started walking back. I didn't give a fuck who was coming. Fucking puppeteers, bloggers and future law students. I passed a goat and hissed at it like a cat. Tawny eyes with thick black strikes. That's what Tamara should fucking have.

I was almost to the kitchen door when the yellow car stopped by the garage and a young man got out. I could see his brown shoulder length hair but didn't recognize him at first. I pulled on the kitchen door.

"Della," he called, "wait."

He loped toward me. I remembered him, some friend of Britta's from college named Bradley. He'd come through a few days earlier with some of the bike brigade organizers.

"Yeah?" I said.

"I left some textbooks and a pair of jeans drying by the fire. Have you seen them?"

"Whatever. I don't know. Go look around."

I let him go ahead of me and walked into the house, which was quiet.

"Is Black Francis here?" he asked. "I think I left the books in his room."

I vaguely remembered Tamara saying she'd sent Francis out to cut a new trail between his yurt and a different part of the creek.

"No. It's just me. Go look through his room."

He got his things and was on the way out when the idea hit me.

"Hold on," I said.

I gave him fifty dollars for gas and asked him to wait. I ran upstairs, grabbed my GPS, my rock hammer and my notes. I wrapped them in my red corduroy dress and jammed them into my messenger bag and whatever didn't fit I left. In the side pocket was the Pluto phone. I pulled it out, turned it on for thirty seconds and then back off. Next, I went to Jules's room and looked through every drawer until I found his passport. It was in an envelope with his birth certificate and I took them both. I went to Tamara's room and did the same.

My last sight of the farm was through the back window of Bradley's yellow 1981 Toyota as it crested Breaker's Rise.

I put the two passports and the birth certificate in a double sealed plastic bag with the last Hive phone, Pluto, and threw them in the river. I admit I blew a little air into the bag a little before I sealed it. Not enough to make it balloon, just enough to let fate take it one way or another. Then I called Star Bank Plaza One Visa and told them my card was stolen.

"How long ago?"

"Maybe a month," I said, "I don't use it much and didn't realize it until I called to check the balance. I got some cash out when I first got the card but I haven't used it since. The last time I remember seeing it for sure was when I stopped for gas in a town called Breaker's Rise."

"Did you use it there?"

"No ma'am, the machine was down. I paid cash."

They said they would cancel the card, send me another and have a company investigator contact me. I destroyed my notes and maps. Shredded them to spaghetti at the brand new Fed Ex/Kinkos/KFC. Then I pulled the SIM card out of my personal cell phone and donated the phone to a women's shelter.

Maybe Cady would have turned out just like Tamara and maybe not. There's no way of knowing. I like to think she wouldn't have. I like to think she would have been there that day in the car with me heading away from Breaker's Rise. I almost pretended she was but I knew I couldn't do that because she wasn't and that kind of fantasy leads nowhere.

When Credence saw me, he said I looked a little feral but otherwise okay. "Healthier, maybe even. Not bad."

But he didn't mean it.

"Like when you first came back from Davis."

Right after they blew up a building full of school kids and I lost my mind?

"There's a blush," he touched my cheek, "why do you think that is?"

"Must be that combination of science and emotional torment."

"Really?"

"No. Just a bunch of hippy drama."

The Czarina of Saturniidae flutters upward in a spiral of painted wings.

"Oh well, I guess that's unavoidable," he said and finished his coffee.

Hey, well, everybody, I got to go. They're having a sand-painting contest down the street and I think I got a chance. Wish me luck! And, oh, by the way, say hi to Grace and Miro if they ever come down from the mountain. I'd sure like to know what they think about all this. Maybe have them leave a note.

I stood. I didn't owe any of them anything. Not even an explanation. I went to my bank, fucking temple of predation that it was, and withdrew all my money. Since I had been living on the cash from the credit card, I had several paychecks in there and some savings. I caught a bus down to the travel agency in Redbird Square. They were having a sale on getting the hell out.

The window of the agency been redecorated with American eagles enjoying the wonders of Southeast Asia. White sand. Straw huts. Indonesian Sex Trade Barbie waits attentively on two birds of prey in festive shirts. PARADISE...IS ONLY AN OCEAN AWAY.

"You know, we're providing a list of realtors now with every ticket to Bali."

The travel agent with the coral skin was standing behind me with a red, white and blue slush puppie in hand and digging for her keys.

"We have a very popular package right now where local realtors actually meet you at the airport."

"I need a ticket to Laos."

In Laos there's a Plain of Jars where a race of giants kept their rice wine. The vats are carved of stone, some weigh over two tons and the land around them is pocked with bomb craters, trench systems, urns and shrapnel. I thought it might be comforting to be surrounded by the ruins of another civilization.

"I'll have to let the computer warm up," the agent said once we were inside.

I noticed one of the desks had several eagles in Hawaiian shirts lying on their backs with talons clawing the air. She set the slush puppie on the other desk.

"That's my next little project. It's for our Hawaiian packages. I already have the slogan."

A FOREIGN LAND...RIGHT HERE AT HOME.

I had a vision of little dark-skinned people getting sprayed by police gunfire, miniature sweatshops and border patrol, but that's not what they meant.

"What about Guam?" I said. "It's almost a state. Best of both worlds."

"We did Guam for Fourth of July. I wanted to do a military base, like a cute flyboy World War II theme, but we'd just done that for Japan."

The travel agent handed me a Lao tourist map of famous Buddhas, each one a gold triangle in a tangles of farm routes.

"These are good if you're interested in culture."

"Nope."

She handed another, Rivers: The Interstate of Laos, which was much better. She tried to hand me some city maps but I told her I'd make those myself.

"Aren't you the little adventurer," she said when I signed the paperwork.

I stopped in at work to get a free meal. Mirror was in the kitchen eating raw tofu out of a five-gallon tub with her hands. She asked me what I thought of the Farm, wrist-deep in milky water. I told her it was a lot like what I grew up around. I looked into the gulf for minute and thought about whether to tell her what I really thought. I wanted to explain to someone why I was leaving. Why I couldn't be a part of it anymore, or a part of anything. I considered just showing her a newspaper. We just sent in tanks and swept some foreign valley until it was soundless and still. A spokesman called it a clear victory for local democracies. I saw a picture. It looked like empty grassland when we were done. I closed my eyes. I saw thousands of baby rats run weaving through the rye and clover. Would I start there? Or at the box-mall-church, or the Farm or France?

Mirror said Mr. Tofu Scramble was gone. I sat at the counter across from his empty seat making my packing list. At lunch, Ed, Logic's Only Son came in and sat in Mr. Tofu Scramble's chair. He made a big show out of it, leaned back in the seat and ordered coffee. BLT on rye. Extra bacon. I thought about telling him the chair was a goddamned deathtrap and that the co-pays for the pain meds alone would kill him. But I just I let him lean against the creaking Hellmouth and after a while he slunk back into his old seat and wiped the counter clean where he had been.

Mitch set his the BLT down in front of him.

"So I guess he really left, eh?" he said, looking over at me.

"Yup. Bali. Or Thailand, I don't remember."

"Bali," He pulled a mint toothpick out of his pocket. "Didn't think he'd actually do it," he said and tore the paper from his toothpick.

He looked like he was about to cry.

"Oh, Della," Mitch said through the kitchen window, "I almost forgot. Tamara called looking for you. She said she'd call back."

"Cool," I said, "I want to talk to her too. I have a new cell, let me write it down."

I looked up the number for the regional offices of the FBI then passed it through the window to Mitch.

"Here, be sure to tell her to call me. I'll definitely be around."

On my way home I passed Devadatta. She was looking at an advertisement for a cruise line.

"Be a Part of It All" was written in pink script on an azure sky. A bald eagle circled the "a." The cruise ship was as white as a glacier and salmon jumped metallic and frisky around the prow.

"Those things are awful," she said.

"Floating zone of faunal annihilation," I pointed to the rippling currents behind the ship, "if you look closely you can see a skull on fire." I outlined a shape on the surface of the water. "I knew a clown who worked a cruise once. None of his clown friends would talk to him afterwards."

"I can't understand why anyone would go on one of those. I'm trying to practice opening my heart. It's probably pretty hard to be human if you haven't been before."

Devadatta shifted the strap of her shoulder bag. The spine of a biochemistry textbook showed inside.

"Would you go?" I asked. "Not on a cruise, I mean, but leave for real?"

"I've got another year of school. I'd want to be able to work. I hear they need nurses everywhere," she said. "So I'd wait."

I thought I heard her voice waver but it might have been my imagination.

My plane left the next day. I didn't see any reason to tell Credence and Annette beforehand. It was like with Mirror, there was no starting point for that conversation. I'd be gone before the argument took hold.

I walked into the house at dinnertime. They were in the kitchen. Credence had his cheek pressed against Annette's belly. She was sitting at the table with her chair turned sideways and he was on his knees. Violet and blue dusklight from the western window crossed them. Credence's face and hands, one on Annette's shoulder and another on her knee, looked like they were carved of sandalwood.

Dear Fellow Travelers and Attending Bellyfish,

While in earlier communiqués I hinted that the time had come to sever myself from your guidance, I must now make good and leave.

May we all meet one day on the banks of a river that flows through a country, which is neither Old nor New Honduras and celebrate our reemergence as citizens, lovers and family.

Until then, I will try to find a cheap cell phone plan with international coverage and no roaming charges.

Yours endlessly,
Friend of the Tiny Liver Hearts
Daughter of the Rat Queen

Nothing encouraging was said about the resiliency of life as it re-colonizes a wasteland—the sprig amidst the pumice; the independent coffee shop between outlet stores. I wanted something hopeful like that but I couldn't really think of anything I could stand behind. Goodbye. I love you. Get out while you can. I am. Della.

The next morning the sun shone down on the progressive micro-economy of New Honduras. It glinted off the environmentally sound building materials and played on the gutters and disconnected downspouts of Colony of the Elect. I walked down the wide wooden steps of Credence and Annette's house dragging a duffle bag behind me. I counted the leaves that blew across my path until there were too many to keep track of.

On the bus out to the airport I passed the new supermarket. All mud and sparkling windows. And Jimmy's apartment, which was probably already rented out for three times as much as she paid for it. They were stringing razor wire along the roofs of several buildings and it flashed in white ribbons as we drove by.

Two miles from the airport we hit a checkpoint. Crickets everywhere. Fluttering and jumpy, they made us all get off the bus. They wanted to know about our travel plans. I told them I was going to look at rocks. And then briefly described the fascinating process of marine sediment deposition, lithification and the general tendencies of limestone erosion. I was in the middle of explaining the intricacies of stochastic modeling for background extinction and why I wanted to see the metamorphic rocks of the Sop Phan Formation—which are considered Neoproterozoic–Early Cambrian in age—when they stopped me.

"Purpose of your trip?"

"Fun," I said.

They stamped my hand and moved me on.

Those final miles all I could think of was the Bellyfish and how I hadn't finished the bathroom tile mosaic and as we came into the terminal I felt like a fish myself, near the water at last.

The airport was packed. Some people were leaving the country but many, many more were fleeing inward, away from the urban centers, scrambling up onto the continental plate. I walked up to a wall of airline agents ticking away at their computers. Looming behind them were Pan-Asian girls with welcoming lips, Navaho sunsets and Maori whale hunters poised to strike. E-ticket kiosks were in rows to my left and I picked one near a poster of Tlingit Shaman and printed my boarding pass. Della Mylinek. Flight #222 to Bangkok. Continuing on to wherever.

After clearing security, I still had hours to kill. I mapped the public art (treating it as a permineralization of outdated thought and culturally relating it to the nearest food court) and I shopped online at the business center. I got Devadatta a molecular model set with glow in the dark carbon atoms and ordered a case of Rice Krispies for Annette. For Mirror, I got a rock-climbing manual with a lot of good tips on stable rigging.

I was starting to feel a little better. Like it was all a normal thing. Leaving the country after a long stint at school. Sending presents to friends. Missing a devastated homeland, which had been crushed to filaments under the wheels of unchecked hyper-mobile Imperial capital.

I ate caramel corn and watched TV because there was nowhere to sit where one wasn't on. The bomb threats were getting out of hand. They were getting called in everywhere. People who had a court date called them into the courthouse; people who didn't want to go to work called them in at their jobs. School kids called the schools. It was the best goodbye I could think of. One guy who had had an intervention done on him actually called in one to the rehab he had agreed to go to.

Sales were falling and they were running profiles on patriotic shoppers. Trotting out the last three independent business owners, each a black rhinoceros of the Serengeti, grazing numbly in the hinterlands, they put them in front of the cameras crying. Small businesses, they mewled, small businesses—but they kept getting cut off by ads for Wal-Mart's demi-anniversary sale so it was hard to hear them.

Somewhere about hour three they ran a promo for a show on the school bombing from the previous year, the one that happened when I was at Davis. Something in my mind flickered but I couldn't touch it. My heart started to beat faster. And it missed, which felt like swallowing but it wasn't swallowing. They said something about my flight over the PA but I couldn't hear it because I was at a different gate so I walked out into the terminal mall.

All persons traveling to Bangkok on flight 222, all persons traveling to Bangkok. Flight 222 is delayed. Please stay near your gate for further updates, all persons traveling on flight 222 to Bangkok.

I tried to focus on the color of the carpet and the sound of the jets taking off in the distance but something was pulling at me, something Tamara said about how symbols matter more than anything because it's the only real language we have left. How it's the only thing with any poetry in it and how history is really just a map of the destruction and creation of symbols. And I was thinking about it when they showed that promo for the special on the anniversary of the school bombing because that's the day I picked when the war started and I thought about how she was right, even though I told her she was wrong she was right. I picked that day because it was a symbol. Something awful, uncontrollable and random, and then I remember she said people would rather fund an empire than pay two cents more for plastic bags and she was right about that too because I saw it on the Wal-Mart campaign when we were standing out there with our leaflets and free coffee that tasted like water. I saw it then and that's why I left. Tamara said it. Nothing would ever change until they saw what the real price was, right when they ran their cards.

I walked between the terminals, getting on and off the conveyors and counting the replicas of clustered businesses at the end of each spur. But it wasn't until I was sitting back at the gate watching my sixth hour of television that I realized what was going to happen. Tamara and Jules were going to blow up the Wal-Mart near Superland™. They were going to do it on the day of the sale when all those kids were there. Just like that school and how it all happened last year. They were going to do it like I said, a trashcan fire in a tent, a bomb in the center because you'd never outrun the smoke with forty aisles of junk in every direction. It was a deathtrap. And more than that, it was a symbol. One you could even see from the golden valleys of France.

I ran to the payphones and called the Farm. Black Francis answered. He said everyone had gone back to town to prepare for the action. I called Tamara's cell phone but it had been disconnected. I called Mirror. She answered with her mouth full and I had to tell who it was twice.

"They're saying you're a cop, dude," she said and swallowed.

"Listen, I need to find Tamara or Britta or Jules or any of them. Are they staying with you?"

"Seriously, dude, are you a cop?"

"Are they staying with you? Do you know where they are? Would you please just tell me?"

"No—"

I hung up.

I looked around for crickets. They were everywhere, chirping and eating their young. I ran up to one and told him that I knew someone who was going to blow up the Wal-Mart.

"What? You need a day off too?" he laughed, licking decayed plant matter off his forewing. "You should just be glad you have a job."

The police operator said the same. I called the cable news desk too but I knew they wouldn't report it. For the past several days they had been following two immigrant families around while they shopped at threatened stores. The head of the Church of Enlightened Capital had been on every station preaching about the fearlessness of the American consumer. They weren't going to do anything.

I took one last look at the gate and ran. Down the center of the terminal mall, down the escalators and through the shiny phone bank rings by baggage claim I went, out the doors and onto the street. Where I caught a taxi back to town as planes arced above me flying pools of light over the Black Ocean.

It was night when I left the airport. The stars were clear and sharp through the taxi window and the terminal glowed behind, a swimming pool in the dark. We climbed out of the valley, angling through the traffic, and broke free for several miles before hitting the next checkpoint where we waited, with Bhangra rhythms pattering in the dashboard while the crickets asked us questions before careening again along the old rural highways and arterials past Pretty Little Hopes and toward the South Mall Hills.

I didn't try to stop my thoughts from racing. Instead, I directed them into the commercial intertidal zone where Wal-Mart was and tried to come up with a plan.

I had some cash, an old credit card, a field journal and an English-Lao dictionary. Everything else was in my luggage. The cab driver said he knew a cheap motel near Superland™ and I asked him to take me there. It was called the Welcome Home. It was about half a mile from Wal-Mart in the center of the Blackberry Massacre. Opposite the motel was a Holiday Inn Business Express and at the last minute the cabbie tried to get me to stay there but I assured him I much preferred the independently owned meth lab across the street and that's where he dropped me.

The woman who checked me in was flat-faced and part Samoan. She asked where my luggage was and I said the airline lost it. She smiled and pulled out a white plastic tub full of toiletries for sale and let me pick through for my favorite color of toothbrush. She didn't have any knives or duct tape though which was a shame cause it meant I'd have to buy them at Wal-Mart.

"What time's the curfew?" I asked.

"Eight PM unless you're shopping. Then you got to show a receipt."

It was 8:30.

Value Town Outlet Parkway was quiet. A strange wind seemed to come from passing cars and the regularity of the architecture, like it was a box canyon with its own weather. I pushed my hair out of my face several times but it kept blowing forward and I gave up, letting it whip my cheeks or float down over my shoulders in the suddenly still and silent air.

Ahead lay the Batholith, Wal-Mart. Cars dotted the parking lot and security cruised the lanes. I hadn't been there since the final days of the campaign when everything tanked and we were just hanging out for the ribbon cutting, watching it like a traffic accident. The last thing Credence had us do was to try to get future shoppers to sign onto a petition to "hold the company accountable to fair community standards." Credence loved that, "fair community standards," it was like some kind of organizer porn to him. As if everyone was going to sign that thing and suddenly discover their place in the constellation of class oppression. Little stars! Little stars! Blanched and atremble; unpattern yourselves—and each petition a prairie fire and all the signatures precious birds fallen and feeble rescued from the threadbare nest and carried gently home. Holding the hand of the dying. That's what we were doing.

I came to it. Crowning failure with more failure. Wal-Mart. In front of me, made of fake rock, unremarkable and low to the ground. I tried to focus only the physical appearance. Observe it as I would a trace fossil, a burrow. The white block letters, the teal background and a main entrance in front with a door on either side. It was constructed by a method in which the walls were poured then raised (by Egyptians) and structurally bound together by the roof. I heard that the fire department hates that kind of building but it's cheap and fast. Inside, there are five acres of retail space. The ceilings are about fifteen feet high and in the case of a moderate blast I imagined that smoke would race along the flame retardant panels until it hit the walls and moved down in a convective pattern to the floor and back up, making the exits the most deadly place to be in an explosion. Outside of the initial blast zone, that is.

I went through the main door and was confused by the brightness. I pulled out my notebook while my eyes adjusted and drew a box on the page with parallel scratches for the doors I had just come through. Then I meticulously walked up one aisle and down another making notes. In the middle of the household chemical / infant-toddler aisle a manager approached me. He was skinny with tan hair, acne scars and cornflower blue eyes.

"Can I help you?" he asked. "What is it you're looking for?"

A Candyland ride through the slaughterhouse?

"A knife and some duct tape."

He pointed me down a row and I went, counting the aisles and adjusting my sense of the floor plan. The center of the store was an intersection of accessories, electronics, small appliances and ladies' wear. A bomb in a backpack would do it. Especially if the ceilings were dropped and there was a strong supply of oxygen through the duct system.

I could easily see it on fire. The wicker dogs, the prom dresses, the camouflage strollers burning. It was beautiful and I couldn't remember why I wanted to stop it. I think that if I had a bag full of explosives, I might have let it slip, or forgotten it by the greeting cards and silver balloons with the superheroes on them and the ribbons trailing down to tie the fat baby hands to a generation of merchandising. I might have left it there. But I didn't have a backpack with a bomb in it and if anybody was going to blow up the Superland™ Wal-Mart, it was going to be me. Not some fucking crusty punk.

I grabbed the duct tape and a decent pocketknife and left. There wasn't much I could do that night anyway. Glance at the outside. Think. Everything else would have to wait until morning.

I slept with the sound of Vietnamese television coming through the walls and someone crying on the phone outside. Twice, I woke up thinking I was in Laos. When the sun did finally rise, I opened my eyes as if I had just shut them during a moment of uninterrupted thought. I washed with cold water, brushed and braided my hair and crossed the street for a continental breakfast at the Holiday Inn Business Express. There, I drank reconstituted orange juice with some low-level drug company reps and tried to clear my mind.

The New Land Trust Action was that day but I felt pretty certain that without the power outage at the airbase, not much would happen. And if it did, it wouldn't be on me. That whole thing may never have been real at all. I didn't know. There was also the possibility that Tamara and Jules might not even know yet that I'd stolen the passports, especially if they hadn't packed and were planning one final trip back through the Farm. They might still think they were leaving and going to land, exiles, fresh upon the Boulevard and that thought filled me with bliss but it had its dangers too because if they still thought they were getting out, they might act more viciously. Either way, I needed to prevent them from entering the Wal-Mart or get it evacuated if they did. My plan was to stay near the two main store entrances and look for anyone from the Farm going in or out. I was sure Tamara would be there. She couldn't help herself.

Steam rose from the Wal-Mart as the dew on the perforated metal siding evaporated in the morning sun. It was two hours before the store opened and the employees were already gathered outside. They shivered a little and some jumped up and down to keep warm while the manager, a tall man bald and shiny, read off the sales numbers from the previous day. Then he shouted out the national daily target and they got in a team huddle, did an Indian dance for greater poverty and went in.

I was standing near an embankment on the west side of the parking lot about a hundred feet from the doors. Ugly tight shrubs grew behind me, dense and tangled with beer cans. I sat down on the curb and waited. I killed twenty minutes wrapping my hands in duct tape like a boxer, for no reason at all.

The shoppers started coming. A huge SUV blocked my vision and I had to move a little farther back up the embankment to see. There were carloads of Mexicans with teenage children in sparkling t-shirts, pink and turquoise, laughing and swatting at each other and swinging mesh shopping bags. There were Ukrainian women wearing scarves pushing white-haired boys and black kids in close packs. There were metal chicks with tiny purses smoking cigarettes, guys just out of the army, and everywhere snarling siblings and strollers dragged by dazed white women, fat and depleted, to the front entrances of the store like it was a boat that could save them if they could only get on. They spilled out of the cars so fast my eye couldn't track them.

The doors were still locked. The manager I'd seen earlier was beaming on the other side and pointing to his watch. People pressed up against the glass as he began to unlock the first door. I walked along a lane of parked cars trying to keep an eye on both entrances. The manager unlocked the second door. The crowd split in two and moved forward. More people were coming every minute, like it was a hanging or something. More and more and more people and I couldn't keep my eye on all of them. Watching the whole crowd was now impossible so I decided to get closer to the doors.

Out of the corner of my eye I saw a pink-skinned girl with red hair. I moved toward her but she turned away. I crossed in front of a line of trucks and saw her ahead of me. She was working her way into the crowd. I pushed through into the center but couldn't catch up. Someone bumped me from behind and I tripped and people just flowed around me as if I were a rock in a river. When I got up, the crowd had shifted and she was by the door. I could see her face, her clear gray eyes.

It was Britta.

A few seconds later, I saw Astrid. She was in another part of the crowd heading toward the second door. An icy feeling came over my chest and ran down my arms. The skin on my head tingled like I was on speed. My eyelids were on fire. They were really going to do it.

Britta moved toward to the door on the right and Astrid to the one on the left. I was still about forty feet back, stuck in the crowd. I would never make it to the doors in time to stop them. I started yelling. It was all I could think of, to try to scare them off somehow.

"Britta!" I screamed. "Britta!"

Britta turned, her skin red and her jaw clenched. She looked right at me.

"Britta!" I yelled and the person next to me told me to shut up.

"Britta!"

She looked around quickly then began moving sideways through the crowd towards Astrid. I had never really let it in, what it would feel like to watch something like that, a real bomb exploding around real people. As Britta got nearer to Astrid and the crowd pushed them closer to the doors my hope dissolved.

I elbowed my way in and cut to the right.

"Astrid!" I screeched and someone shoved me.

They threatened to call security and I told them to do it.

"Astrid! Astrid! Britta! Astrid!"

Astrid stopped moving, her blonde hair lank, and scanned the parking lot. She saw me and she saw Britta coming towards her. I could see her lips whiten. She stood still and waited. They reached each other long before I got to where they were. And by then they were out of the crowd walking fast toward the far right corner of the lot. I could see the green Mercedes parked by a lamppost. I finally got through the crowd and ran after them but they were in the car and pulling out before I even got close. I yelled their names one last time as they drove away but they never looked back.

I was shaking and coughing, mostly from fear. I leaned over with my palms on my thighs and tried to catch my breath. The air felt like glass knives. I swallowed a couple of times to wet my throat then stood up. I had been crying and didn't know it. My nose was stuffed up and my face was hot and wet.

I turned back to the store. The front of it was swarmed and security was making people form lines but there too were so many of them so the knots at the doors just tightened. I started walking the perimeter in a semicircle to where I was before. I didn't think Britta or Astrid would come back but I had to stay for a while to make sure. After that it was somebody else's problem.

I pulled a muffin from the Holiday Inn out of my bag thinking I could eat it but I couldn't and put it back. Not until the adrenaline left my body, which would take a while. I could feel it beginning though. Someone passed me with a cart full of disposable electronics, steaks and diapers. That's when I remembered that it was the great maggot feast day and I didn't want to be there anymore. I was so pissed off I started to cry again.

People were acting like idiots. I pushed one of them from behind, a big old jock. I told him he stepped on my foot. It wasn't true but I felt better. It helped me turn the corner. Ten minutes later I was almost okay. I reminded myself I was beholden to nothing. I didn't live anywhere. I walked faster, skirting the heart of the crowd. I might even be on a plane that night.

There was a loud noise by the front entrance. Someone knocked over a barbeque grill and someone else was freaking out about it. I glanced up just in time to see Tamara slip in through the glass doors. She had a red backpack and her lavender hair was in pigtails. She was chatting with the security guard while she waited for the line to move.

I just stood there. I couldn't believe it. I couldn't breathe.

She looked right at me and smiled before disappeared into the store.

BITCH! FUCKING BITCH! FUCKING VANGUARD BULLSHIT POSER MOTHERFUCKING BITCH!

I ran as fast as I could for the doors but security stopped me. I told them there was a girl with a backpack, 5' 5", purple hair and that she had a bomb but they didn't believe me. Told me to wait in line. I pushed my way through to the other side and they grabbed me before I got there.

"Get a manager!" I said. "That tall guy I saw earlier. Or a cop, something!"

And they dragged out an assistant manager but he said they expected bomb threats on big sale days. I tried to tell them that this was different but they wouldn't listen. They just thought I was a meth-head or something and the silver tape on my hands didn't help.

I turned around and went back into the crowd and started telling the people in line. There's a bomb in there, I said, a big one, and I saw the girl take it in and she'll do it, I know her—but the right then the manager got on a bullhorn and announced that the store was filling up and they were going to have to start turning people away and, hearing that, people just blew past me with their eyes on the door and there was nothing I could say to stop them. Up front, the security guards were breaking out the liability waivers and people were signing them as fast as they could. Can one count for my whole family? Sure.

And I got in line too and forced my way closer to the front. A guy behind me started shouting, calling me names, but I kept moving until I was about ten feet from the doors. A guard handed me a white sheet of paper saying it wasn't their problem if the store blew up and I put an "X" on it and threw it back at them and was about to go through the glass doors when the tall manager came out. He said the store was full and that no one could go in until other shoppers left.

I told him he had to let me in, that my friend was inside and I didn't want to get separated. I said she had my asthma medication and I was having trouble breathing but he didn't believe me because I was shouting and people said they'd seen me running and that I was cutting in line. So I said please, please, I'm not lying, but a security guard came over and told him I was making bomb threats earlier and the tall manager put his hand on my shoulder. It smelled like baby powder and he told me to calm down or they were going to have to ask me to leave. Then I said the real reason was that the girl in the store was my sister and that she was a junkie and had just gotten out of jail for theft and that I didn't want to see her go back and that I saw her go in with a backpack and that I knew it was empty and that I was sure she was going to steal a whole bunch of stuff because she was good at it and they almost let me in but then they said no. And I said please, please, please let me in, and the tall manager put his hand on my shoulder again and someone behind me said I was probably trying to get to get at the kids' clothes before they ran out and I said I didn't have any kids and I told the manager I would leave them my bag and my ID if they'd just let me find her and that I would be quiet as a mouse because I was screaming then, and that I would buy diamonds and detergent and that it would only take a minute if they let me and they told me to step back. The guard's hand was on my chest and he said to calm down and I said I would and walked away apologizing, with my eyes darting through the crowd. I tried to make myself breathe evenly even though I was terrified and no one would do anything.

A white bus pulled up with New Life Community Church stenciled on the side. Kids poured out. They were just handing out those waivers left and right, passing them up and down the line. Little white papers, little doves, fluttering over the crowd of children, and everyone laughing and excited like it was their birthday or something. Another bus pulled up behind that one and I thought, I should leave. I should leave before it happens because no one's going to do anything and I don't have to watch.

I paced back and forth on the edge of the lot while I tried to think of something. I had to because it was my fault. If I hadn't let Tamara take the map, if I hadn't put the Wal-Mart right there in the center of it like it was the mountain at the heart of the world I wouldn't be there. I wiped my face on my shirt. Shopping carts piled high with the debris of nations rolled past and they let a few more people inside. Tamara wasn't out yet so there was still time. I knew she'd never blow herself up. Self-preservation was a religion with her. I started walking down towards the parking lot but as soon as I got too far away to see the doors I ran back up to where I was. I tried to take a long breath but couldn't hold it and coughed, gagging on the air.

More busses came with more children. They were bringing them in from all over the city. An hour must have passed while I was walking in small circles and Tamara still hadn't come out. I know because I was looking for her so hard my eyes ached. I knew she'd have to come back through those doors. And when she did I'd know it was about to happen and I could prepare myself. Because I wasn't prepared before. An undergrad told me, a pudgy girl with thick blonde hair walking back to her dorm. She said some people took over a grade school thousands of miles away. That there were hundreds of kids in it and that they were going to blow it up. It was like some sort of holiday or birthday. They were all waiting for something to start when it happened. And I didn't think they'd do it. I didn't think they'd actually blow up that school with all those babies in it. All on their birthdays, dressed for a party, I didn't think they would but they did.

I tried to map the cultural trends leading up to it but as I did they grew, interconnecting and weaving backwards and side-ways out to everything. Next to the megalithic institutionalized shredding of people's humanity, marked by tombstone malls and scabby hills, the Styrofoam gullets and flag-waving god-chatterers casting their votes for eternal paternity on the lap rapists—next to all of that, the intimacy between a terrorist and his target was almost a beautiful thing but I still couldn't solve that moment when they did it anyway so I grabbed more paper and widened my field of vision. I was mapping a basaltic flow of sub-cultural conflicts on individuality and Marxism when a large bomb went off in the courtyard outside my window. It shook the building and left my windows rattling. I ran out. Someone screamed and I flew down the stairs with the blood in my ears pounding and everything sounding like it does on when you're on nitric oxide and I burst through the heavy front doors onto a quiet autumn quad. The sun was everywhere and the leaves were just turning gold and red and falling like open palms to the waving grass.

I stood in front of the Wal-Mart with the banners waving and the white papers flapping and the lines swelling all the time and I knew what I was going to see. People were honking by the front of the store and security was trying to get some of the cars out and I was crying and hitting my hips with my fists.

Then I saw Tamara. She was coming out of the store with her arms full of bags. The red backpack was gone. I knew it was just a matter of time.

I could have screamed but it wouldn't have done anything and I could have tried to get them to evacuate the building but if they hadn't let me in before they wouldn't now and she was just walking away and there was nothing to do but watch and I didn't want to because I had already seen it, last year when they said it was far away over the Black Sea and past pools of green light but it wasn't. It was my neighborhood. I think the school kids were black and that's why it didn't get covered here and that's why they were all speaking a different language. It was slang. And now they are celebrating it with a sale to commemorate the ribbon cutting with fifty percent off for school kids but it's only today because it's their birthday and they're singing songs to little African birds and I have to do something. I stopped pacing and moved toward the crowd again. I wanted to say goodbye because someone should and you can't expect the parents to be there and I want to see their faces and sing happy birthday for them, all those sweet little liver hearts, as they march into the store the second it's unlocked by the regional manager smiling bald and shiny because he opened late because the district manager told him Jesus was gonna be there and he believed him but he wasn't so he waited while the kids pressed their sweet black faces against the glass and passed notes (I wish I knew what they said but I can't read Cyrillic and they wouldn't show them to me anyway) I'm going to wait by where the carts are and I'm going to sing happy birthday to each and every one of them with their name and not just a verse for all of them together but one for each even though I can't pronounce some of their names like Prichnikovaya and don't know how to spell the made-up ones like Levonda. Lavonda? And I want to say it right because it's the last time they're going to hear it and I want them to know I did my best.

And I ran at the crowd but they grabbed me again and said to leave or they were calling the cops but I didn't want to leave the little liver hearts because you shouldn't be afraid like that, not when someone needs you, you should be able to look them in the eye, even if they're dying and you're scared and you can't do anything, you shouldn't run even if they're howling and bleeding, you should stay and sit with them while they go

238

because someone should and you just shouldn't be afraid like that, enough to leave them alone like that when they only have a few minutes left, you should be there.

So I ran back up to where I was and sat down with the fear like acid inside me, on fire with tears streaming down my face and duct tape wrapped so tight around my hands they were numb. I sat there because there was nowhere left to go. I was at the spine of the world. Turning away was as bad as leaving, or hiding in a college, or a restaurant, or clutching the torn shred of a failed movement or pretending to build one out of spectacle. It was all the same. I turned to the store, fixed my eyes on a patch of cement that ran along the front and waited. I knew what was coming. I saw it every night. People filled their carts and packed their trunks and every time a bus pulled up and kids ran out I made myself stay because even though I knew there was a timer on the bomb, I didn't know when it was set to go off and I didn't want to look away.

The sky changed color and the variegated tones of the cars in the parking lot shifted every few hours. I sat there all day, burning. I saw Tamara across the lot. She was watching too but I didn't care anymore and she went away. She was just there to see if I still was. I know her. She's like that.

It got dark and the crowds thinned. The streetlights turned off and the emergency lamps came on and the Wal-Mart was still lit, bright and white, as the employees walked out to their cars and drove away. The tall manager came out last and locked the doors and left and I sat there listening to the quiet. I thought I heard the trickle of water in a culvert but I don't know.

I'm not sure how long I was there before I realized nothing was going to happen. Nor do I know how many times that thought came to me before it stayed. It would hit me, suddenly; Tamara's not going to do it. She never was. She wouldn't. And then that thought would get replaced by slivers of her speech glued into a new constructed meaning and I could see that we had only seconds, that she would do it, and then I would know beyond any doubt that the Wal-Mart was about to explode with all those kids inside. I'd wait with every muscle tense, my heart splayed helpless, a jellyfish on the sand. And then nothing would happen and I had no idea why.

Tamara might have planned to bomb the Wal-Mart and run into a technical snag. Or she might have changed her mind. Maybe she was just buying rope and forgot her bag inside. Maybe it was all going to happen tomorrow—I sat through every possibility, each a wild universe, a bomb threat? A Buzz Lightyear? O my monks, all is burning... The fear dissipated and the shame rose then it went the other way. Countless times, when I was on the verge of leaving, my thoughts would take a new form, new sight or sound or feeling or just a desire for it all to be true and the whole thing to blow up so that I wouldn't have to wait like that anymore. And all of it would come back, the terrible conviction, and I'd run after it until it vanished again and I fell clutching, and what was the all that was burning? I saw a thousand specters and grabbed at 999 of them.

Hours after the store closed, a station wagon drove out onto the empty lot. It slowed to a stop in the middle and a man got out of it. He was in his forties, stout with thin hair. He came around the other side of the car and waited. A young girl climbed out and he handed her the keys. She got in the driver's seat and he looked around, probably because it was past curfew. Then he got in beside her. She tried to start the car but it stalled. She tried it again and it went a few feet and stalled. Finally she got it going and lurched forward. She drove in a shaky line, then slammed on the breaks and stalled it again. I watched her like there was nothing between us, like we were inside each other.

At the end of an hour she could keep the car going. She drew lazy circles on the grid of the lot before pulling into a parking space and getting out.

After they left I was alone. I heard bullets and felt deep tremors in the earth but I didn't move. Cady sat beside me and I was afraid that if I stirred for even a second, she would be gone. I stayed that way all night and let her leave on her own. Some things are so sad that they have no name. I have tried to name them and I can't. I sat there and watched those things dissolve into that wasted land.

People will do anything. Smash a kid's head against a rock. Maim silverbacks and drag them across a square. Run through landmines to protect someone they've never met. Waste their bodies on grace. A high wire, a hurdle, a diving plane. It's chemistry and people are shifting compounds, not elements like I thought. Sitting up all night, watching the Wal-Mart fail to blow up, I saw an endless spectrum. I don't mean some soft sell about life on the banks or shades of gray. What I saw was a spectacle. A death chamber. A chandelier. A thousand rooms. By the edge of an industrial park with my face burnt and my swollen duct-taped hands, I finally joined the human race. I became a tenant in that house.

I was not afraid of horror, I was afraid of beauty, of what it could do to me if I let it. I felt like a sun, expanding and brighter than anything. My fingertips burned and my red eyes looked over the emptiness. I cut the tape off my hands and watched the skin turn from white-blue to pale pink as blood flowed back into them.

The parking lot glistened, a black frozen lake. There was light atop the subdivisions. I stood up and fell over, scratching my face and neck on the clipped branches of the tangled shrubs. When I got back up my legs were on fire. I stamped my foot and millions of nails went through my sole fast enough to shatter my clay femur and I fell again.

There was a trickle of water. I hadn't imagined it. It was quiet enough for me to hear it and I followed the sound. I climbed over a mound of bark chip landscaping. On the other side was a drainage pipe through which clear water ran. It was a culvert under some kind of utility road. But the road had moved, curving now to the left and wider. The old cement was torn away and the ribs of the pipe left exposed, oxidizing in the open air.

I limped over to it and knelt down to get some water on my forehead. I was in a land between, not over the Black Ocean, not on the shores of New Honduras, not in the forests of Grace Mountain. A ghost on the site of the Blackberry Massacre.

I unbraided my hair and combed it with my fingers then washed my face for real. My sweatshirt was filthy so I took it off and held it in the icy water until it was soaked then used it as a rag to clean my calves and arms and to wipe my boots. Then I left it there at the mouth of the drainage pipe and walked, bare-armed, out onto a side road that fed into Value Town Outlet Parkway.

There were a few cars on the road and some busses. People were going to work. I stood around at a bus stop for a while listening to people talk. Some kind of Southeast Asian language, Cambodian maybe. They were dressed like Mexicans and had hard plastic names tags. Señor Chankrisna. Señor Nath. Señoritas Boupha and Thirith with their lemon and cherry striped ponchos, their black pants and passing around a pack of Cambodian cigarettes with a white hawk on it. I watched the bus doors open and fold shut behind them. I didn't get on. I waited as groups came and went.

I saw men in satin union jackets, hungover and red. I saw bleached blonde Latinas with fake violet nails embedded with rhinestones tapping their fingers, clicking them against hard vinyl purses. I saw black, white and Filipino nursing assistants in Hawaiian scrubs, tall and wide with bent backs and thin gold crosses laying like silk over their clavicles. I can't say what I saw. I saw mean children and scared men and disoriented women in wigs from costume stores and pressed and shaven Arabic men with wedding rings and polished shoes and groups of teenagers swinging themselves into place, throwing back their heads with their mouths open, their arms along the seat backs as they passed, stuttering out of sight.

I got on the bus at noon and rode it into the older part of the city. I walked down the street with all the pawnshops, looking in the windows. I saw a whole wall of burning TVs. Fire on every screen. And I saw my own face flash by, a person of interest. But that was just another storyline too so I kept walking.

I ate lunch at a burrito cart on the south side of town near the water. That's where I saw the paper with my face on it. In the picture I was blonde and my hair was tied back. It was my ID photo from Davis. It didn't say much, just that they wanted to talk to me in connection with the bombings. I thought that made a lot of sense. I would want to talk to me too if I were them. But I wasn't and sat on a bench near the water and thought about other things.

I walked further south along the new promenade under the sweet gum and crape myrtle trees until it dead-ended by a convenience store. A boy with a skateboard was hanging around by the dumpster talking to people when they came out. He had on a plastic trench coat and a t-shirt with a big white skull on it. I went over to him and asked him what he was doing.

"You want to buy me some beer?"

"Sure," I said and he started to hand me money but I said I'd pay for it.

He shrugged and inclined his head toward the store. He was maybe fourteen. His face was bony and his hair was dyed black and growing out strawberry blond at the roots.

I got the beer and we went down by the river.

"Do you like The Misfits?" I said, pointing to his shirt.

"I just like the shirt," he said and opened his beer, "don't really know the band."

His skateboard was tipped up, pivoting gently beneath his two forefingers.

I pulled out a beer and opened it.

"What are you going to do tonight? I don't mean it in a weird way. I'm just curious."

"Get drunk. Skate around."

"Will you go home?"

"Probably."

"Why? Do you like being there?"

"My dad sucks."

"Does your dad suck worse than all this?"

I waved my arm across the water and the city and everything I saw.

"Maybe," he said, "I don't know."

I took one more beer and let him have the rest. The sun was setting and I wanted to say something helpful but I knew he wouldn't understand so I said something stupid that made no sense because I had been thinking things all day and there was no way I could explain them and I shouldn't even have tried.

"Everything's on fire," I said. "The guy who won't sell you the beer, your dad, the Ravage all around us, your feelings about the music you like, it's all on fire."

"Well, I wish it was on fire for real," he said and kicked his board down, "because this all sucks."

"Yeah, well, me too. I wish it had all burned away so I wouldn't have to watch."

He put the beer under his arm and headed off in one direction toward an apartment complex that I'd passed on my way down. I headed off in another.

It took me an hour to find a pack of crickets imaginative enough to believe that I should be taken in to custody. It wasn't penitence. It was just a lack of options.

By the time I turned myself in I was pretty run down. No electrolytes at all. My hands and face were chapped and I had a lot of scratches but I was as lucid as I have ever been, clear and attentive. I watched each person who came and talked to me and could almost see the flames licking up around them.

I was held as a possible terrorism suspect. Grace and Miro were so proud they could barely stand it. Like it was lefty Christmas just for them. Viva North Pole Libre.

There was a lot of debate about the timeline of events and my whereabouts. Some of which could have been solved earlier if anybody in my family talked to cops. But they don't. Years of training. They said Grace wouldn't even tell them my middle name.

"It's Rachael," the FBI guy kept saying, "we know it's Rachael. It's a matter of public record. You're not keeping anything from us. Della Rachael Mylinek. I'm holding her ID right here. Public record."

Credence said she made him cry but he probably just said that to cheer me up. He said every time they'd ask Miro a question, he'd get that look like he was watching snowflakes fall. Credence gets that look too sometimes.

I saw Grace for a few minutes. My mother is beautiful. Her hair was the color of late fall when all the red and brown leaves are turning black but haven't yet, should have and haven't. I bet she did make those crickets cry.

The papers said I was a scientist, which was media code for Nuclear Secrets so everyone had to watch computerized models of mushroom clouds on TV for days. There was even a site where you could type in your zip code and see a model of your local fallout patterns under the current weather conditions. Which were changing.

"I'm wanted in connection with a series of terrorist attacks," I told the guy who brought me my Gatorade. "You should be scared of me. I'm a geologist."

Grace always said I was good at entertaining myself.

They put me in alone so that I didn't convert the masses.

I didn't ask why they thought I was a terrorist. And I didn't answer when they asked why I didn't ask. In one particularly intense interrogation I decided to give them a brief history of the planet. Starting at about 4.6 billion years ago and sweeping gracefully up to the present. My favorite part is the 2 billion years between the prokaryotic and eukaryotic cell. It's riveting, really. I get excited. I did it once when I was drunk at Davis and nobody talked to me for a week. But the FBI loved it. I could tell.

What became clear after several meetings with the agents was that they didn't really have anything. It was mostly the panic I caused in the airport when I failed to board at the gate. Apparently, they pulled my bag off the plane to Laos and blew it up on the Tarmac to just make sure there wasn't a bomb in it. Then the terminal went into a security shutdown and the cameras went live and my face was everywhere.

Over the next two weeks a lot of people came to my defense. Coworker Franklin said I always showed up to work on time. My professor from Davis flew up with copies of the *Journal of Paleobiology* for everyone and talked about the rigors of academia and the immense pressure on doctoral students. Mirror denied that I was antisocial and went into elaborate detail about my behavior at the party. She even dragged the Russian guy to sign an affidavit saying I was with him that night. They asked if anyone else had seen us together, which I thought was pretty funny.

In the end they didn't release me because of any of that. Some apartment manager caught Jules and Tamara rifling through people's mail and they got busted for identity theft. They were awaiting arraignment at the county when the bag I threw in the river washed ashore south of the city. Finding the last of the Hive phones sent the crickets into a chirping frenzy. The wireless company's records showed that the phone had been used near Breaker's Rise, which matched with my stolen credit card report. Tamara's face was on security camera footage from the dog track and that, along with the lack of alibis for the time of the bombings, pretty much sealed it.

I suppose I could have jumped up and down and claimed to be the art director of the consumer apocalypse. Gone down with ship and all. But I wasn't the one who bombed those places. I just thought they looked pretty on fire. Sort of. Now that everything is it means less.

When I got out I spent a few days with Grace and Miro up on the mountain. They never asked me what my role was in the bombings or about Jules or Tamara. That way they could pass a lie detector test. They're still secretly hoping I am a terrorist with a more far-reaching plan. Something vast, tied to a huge underground of new Internationalists. Mostly though, we talked about Credence and Annette and the soon-to-be-here Bellyfish. And about Southeast Asia because of my ticket to Laos. There was a substantive discussion about the transition of former colonial provinces to fledgling communist governments without a stable economy or adequate cultural reference points to sustain them.

"You can't expect a thousand years of oppression not to result in rage when the power dynamic shifts," said Grace.

"I don't," I said. "If it shifted now I'd probably want to blow up a small star."

She kissed me on the forehead like I was ten.

Coworker Franklin said I could have my job back. He'd cut some deal with the new owners to keep on any employee who could get it together enough to get a food handler's card and I already had one. So, despite being recently held as a terrorist, I was a model employee.

My first day back in town and out of jail, I went down to Rise Up Singing to see what it was like. The sign over the door said RISE in fatigued metal and there was a new mural, a big social realism piece with a remodeled house in the center and a thick red line over the top that turns into dashes then disappears into an endless sunlight. But it was all one big ember so I started working there again. I didn't care which little piece of orange carbon popped out and cracked at my feet. Hello! Imbue me with meaning! I'm a little piece of gender identification. Crack! I'm a down-in-the-gutter art intellectual. Thwizzz… (the tiniest of voices) I'm a nineteenth century neo-classical vagabond. Phit. I'm a spaceship. It just didn't matter.

Mirror quit outright.

"Fuck Franklin. That fucking fish killer. And fuck the new owners. If I wanted to have a food handler's card, pull micro beer and listen to Enya, I'd go to fucking college."

Mirror didn't seem too broken up about Tamara going to jail either.

"Whatever," she said, "she's always been a little faggot. I'm just glad she's not as much of a hippy as I thought, you know, with that farm and the goats and all."

I don't know for sure why Tamara and Jules didn't take me down too except that "whoever did it" was getting a lot of credit in the subculture, mostly for the urban targets and names of the terrorist groups, my tattered little flag. I don't think they wanted to share the attention. When Tamara and Jules actually got charged, it was Bastille Day in the squats. Better than a police riot. I personally know of at least three vegetarian restaurants and a record store where they were gods. I even heard a coffee shop in the Midwest. The Breaker's Rise Two. Free vegan corn-meal blueberry muffins for life. Credence says there are even t-shirts with them looking all punk rock on the front with the bombing sites listed like tour dates on the back. I haven't seen them. It's the kind of thing I would normally wear. Not in this case, but in general.

I told Credence that and got a lecture on the difference between strategies for political change and merchandising.

"I'd still wear it, if I didn't know them. I'd wear it."

"It's moronic."

"It's the purest form of communication."

The t-shirt, the bumper sticker, the bomb. The undifferentiated ocean of brutality I had been drowning in had undergone a change. It was as violent as it had ever been but it wasn't personal. The waves were not random. They were simply the rocking back-and-forth of actions and reactions. The slogan, the talking point and the bullet were all elements, atoms, leaving behind banded marks. It ebbs and crashes, pulling grass, sand and small animals into the sea. I know shouldn't care, that it's just erosion and happens to everything. But I do, I still care, I still cling to the shore.

Credence and Annette painted my room pale gold for the Bellyfish and hung mobiles, stars and birds that circle across the skylight. I lie in bed and I watch them for hours. I still stay awake and listen to the world at night.

Mirror suggested I try cranial sacral therapy.

"You should totally do it. I also know this dude who did it after a really bad head injury. He said it made him dream in magenta."

Instead of retributional geology?

Mirror said when she first met me she thought I was a little out of my mind. I told her it was true. I hadn't watched a school full of children get blown up a thousand times. I was less settled than I am now.

As a local celebrity, I was asked by a teacher at an alternative high school to come speak to his class about the history of the earth. About how we think the moon was made. About comets and asteroids and extinctions and how the sea was filled with ammonites and how there wasn't any grassland and that planets die like everything else—babies, continents, solar systems. I don't have the part after that. Just like with the skateboard-goth boy down by the river, I don't have a god or a country hiding in my hands. I don't even have a saying or some kind of joke. Consider the lilies…(voiceover to be drowned in howling winds of the holocaust). So I decided to bring in a bunch of concretions and some rock hammers and let the kids bash the hell out of them. It seemed like as good a finale as anything else.

The principal stopped us in the hall. Behind her were construction paper flowers and soccer trophies in a glass case under a banner that said "Welcome Home, Birds of Prey." I was momentarily sorry the school had not been on my target list.

The teacher introduced me as Professor Mylinek, eminent geologist and former terrorism suspect, which she didn't think was funny. They wanted to see my notes and have me sign a waiver so they could videotape the class in case they needed to turn it over the FBI. They also confiscated the rock hammers so we had to have the kids take the concretions outside and smash them on the sidewalk. They looked like a bunch of angry seagulls. Which was pretty great too. Any fossils inside those rocks were destroyed but it felt good and the principal got it all on camera through the window of the science lab. The teacher said that's what the kids liked best, feeling dangerous. But I still saw the gulf between us, a short lifetime of thoughts. Future soldiers and tiny liver hearts, universes. Atoms.

The day before the war started, Annette accidentally knocked over a metal bookshelf in the basement. She was trying to kick some heavy boxes across the room because she couldn't lift them and one of them got stuck. She got mad and shoved with her foot and the whole shelf came down. I heard the noise from upstairs and ran.

"Annette!" I yelled. "Annette!"

When I opened the basement door, she was crying. The bookshelf was on its side and medical reference books were everywhere. She was back up against the wall in the corner with her arms crossed trying to hold still. She was okay, but as I moved closer she shivered.

That morning I'd gone with her to the doctor to look at the Bellyfish. They put us in a dark room and the radiologist coated her belly with clear jelly.

"It helps get better pictures," she said.

I sat down and looked at the monitor. It looked gray and pixilated like an old TV.

"Well that's one of their heads," the radiologist said. "They're big babies."

Annette's face looked blue in the monitor light as she watched the Bellyfish.

"See that, Della?" her voice was soft and crackly. "That's her little arm."

A little starfish arm moving like every direction was forward.

Annette took the bus home and I walked. I looked back at her standing at the bus stop. She's like one of those women on the posters in the Ethiopian restaurants, the ones the North African tourist bureau puts out. Noble and frightening. I could see her throat and fingers wrapped with gold raising her arms. Teff blowing like sand from her clenched fists.

The light changed and I crossed the street, cutting through Redbird Square down to the river. It was Friday and the beginning of a three-day weekend. Normally it would have been busy but it wasn't and busses passed half full. Taxis waited in line.

All week they had been showing maps on TV. Newscaster Ken was finally learning how to pronounce the names of smaller nation states that had long been on the periphery. The stores sold out of water and the city was emptying. I walked to work and counted the vacant houses, all with kitchen lights on, all with the original trim restored.

Mr. Tofu Scramble said when they took the bars off the windows in Old Honduras there was a big party. They roasted a soy pig and the first hundred through the door got a house. He did, anyway. Told me he could live for ten years in Bali off the sale. I told him I hoped he wouldn't have to. He was right about the time to get out, though. It had passed. You could feel it.

When I heard the bookshelf crash, I thought it had finally started. So did Annette. She couldn't stop crying. The impact of the encyclopedias and reference books and that heavy metal shelf, all hitting the cement floor at the same time, made the house shake. I thought it was a car bomb going off somewhere nearby. Annette didn't say what she thought it was.

When the shelf went over it hit a hanging lamp that I'd rigged up to make it seem less like an interrogation chamber down there, mostly because that's where I would be living. The lamp was still swinging back and forth when I opened the basement door, which was another reason I thought something else had happened. Annette stared at it, transfixed. I couldn't get her to look at me.

I remember telling Jimmy about how it was when I first met Annette. How she'd scared me because I didn't really know any black people. I only knew how I was supposed to feel about them—Now, Della, when you meet a Person of Color, make sure you look them in the eye and open your palm so they can see that it's only a sugar cube.

"It's like that everywhere in one way or another," she'd said. "It was the same for me. You can live in one valley and think the people in the next are a totally different species."

Annette constructed of tiny mirrors.

Miro told me when he was a boy he had a pet rabbit. They moved into a neighborhood where it was all Slovenians and the first week he was there some boys ripped open its chicken wire cage in the yard and killed it.

"My parents told me it was a dog."

"What did you do when you found out?"

"Nothing," he said. "It's not really any different, people, dogs, when the thinking is that way. It's the same isn't it?"

"Yeah, but how can you even sit there knowing people are like that?"

"They were kids too. I'm sure they're different now."

"Yes, but how can you fucking stand to live in this world?"

"Della…"

I was at work the next day when the war officially started. There were planes and sirens and traffic jams. It was just after the lunch rush, which was mostly tempeh reubens and carrot-ginger soup. The new owners were falling all over themselves trying to make friends with the staff, who were working like they'd been pressed. The restaurant was busy because carrot-ginger is the only soup of the day we have that isn't gross and everyone gets real excited about it. One guy calls every day at 11 AM when the soup goes up to see what it is. When I told him it was carrot ginger, he acted like I had found him a kidney match.

The construction on the patio was almost complete. Broken bricks and recycled concrete glued into green resin so that in the rain it would look like river rocks. Chains of colored lanterns dipped across the courtyard and crisscrossed high and off-center over where the shed had been.

The siren went off about 3 PM and no one knew what to do. There wasn't a basement. Someone said to get under the tables and stay away from the windows but no one did, not even the person who said it. When the first blast hit, everyone ran. Mitch was standing in the street looking up at something and pointing. I could see her green eyes staring straight into the sun when the second blast hit. Then I saw her running too.

I ran out the side door and made it into the doorway of a brick building across the street. A bus trying to veer away from a collapsed wall of an apartment complex hit a telephone pole and it went down. Sparks shot into the sky as cables snapped and whipped around etching electric meanders in the sky. Some hit water and blue light shot up the poles and across the sidewalks that were wet from an earlier rain.

I crouched in the doorway, pressing myself back into the corner, but I could still see the street. There was a large crack as a bolt of white current shot laterally through the air and contacted the metal streetlight on the other end of the block, blowing it to pieces and engulfing a car underneath in lavender flame. Particles oscillated faster and faster as the heat rose and I thought for a second I could see the real shape of things, the radiating blackbodies incandescent and brilliant, the seamless stream. The Rat Queen shook her fur free of beads and pennies and the Saint with the Black Tears lifted her robe. Thousands of new planets spun out from underneath, filling the sky like clouds of fireflies.

Annette says I'm too hard on the world, that I only see one side.

Grace says I'm afraid of my own longing.

I looked around at the smoke and people. I couldn't find any hate in me anywhere. The world is a violent child none of us will get to see grow up.

I decided to love it anyway.

Acknowledgements

I imagine that every writer hopes to someday be able to pub-
licly thank those who made their work possible. I am fortunate
enough to get to do that here. The list is long, I ask you to bear
with it. Each one of these people deserves to have their name
shouted from the rooftops but this is the only the soapbox I got
so here goes...

While working on the first draft of *Zazen* I received enough
food, printer ink, and cash from friends to support me for five
months. These months were essential to the creation of this
novel. No first-time novelist knows for sure if they can finish a
novel until they do and without that time I might have stopped
halfway. There are periods when it's easier to wait tables with
part of a novel in the drawer than to try to break through your
own mediocrity. But, because of the remarkable gifts of my
friends, I had no excuse for not trying. Thank you. Now I can
say I am a novelist. Angus Durocher, Geov Parrish, Sascha
Krader, Laurel Hoyt and the Salathaus folks, Doug McMullen,
my parents, Christian Fennesz, Tess Lotta, Bill Ferrell, Dennis
Shaw, and Lamalani Siverts—you have made my life better.

I would also like to thank Beulahland and Staccato Gelato
for letting me sit for hours and hours while I wrote. If you're in
Portland, Oregon, give them lots of business. They deserve it
for putting up with people like me.

And... (deep breath) another thank you to these writers,
readers, and editors for their kind encouragement—Mike Mc-
Gonigal, Mike Daily, Jon Raymond, Pete Rock, Michael Kroetch,

Jeff Gordinier, Jay Babcock (who published *Zazen* online before anybody at *Arthur Magazine*), Laurent Blain, Jason Waugaman and all the Godless Moravians. In particular, I would like to thank Alex Ney who took the photo for the cover and read each version of *Zazen*. Because of his dedication, I was never truly alone with the manuscript. It was a phenomenal gift. I want to thank Karin Bolender, who talked both Jay Babcock and Laurent Blain into reading *Zazen* in the first place. And, of course, my profound thanks to my editor Richard Nash, a man whose faith in both the future and the future of the novel is boundless.

And last, my family: Blake Wright, Stefan Jecusco, and Violet Veselka. Blake, who, first as my husband and then as my friend, never stopped backing me up and moved his schedule to take Violet with little or no notice so that I could keep writing. And Stefan, who sacrificed his own artistic time for mine. While always a believer in art first, during the four and half years on *Zazen* it was my art that came first. I owe the world a debt for what he did not get to make in that time. My world has been entirely changed by his presence.

Finally, love to my daughter Violet who lost many evenings of my attention. Sitting next to me on the bed while I wrote, she watched more Miyazaki films and Justice League episodes than any child should. Once, when Violet was five, she asked me about Della and what she was like. I said Della was afraid that the world was full of sadness and that everything beautiful just got hurt. Violet looked at me for a second then said, "Yeah, but Della's wrong."

Della is wrong. Violet's right.

I am in awe. Thank you all.

Vanessa Veselka has been, at various times, a teenage runaway, a sex-worker, a union organizer, a student of paleontology, an expatriate, an independent record label owner, a train-hopper, a waitress, and a mother. Her work has appeared in *Arthur, Bust, Bitch, Maximum Rock 'N' Roll, Tin House,* and elsewhere. *Zazen* is her first novel.

Dear Reader,

This is a Red Lemonade book, also available in all reasonably possible formats—limited artisan-produced editions, in trade paperback editions, and in all current digital editions, as well as online at the Red Lemonade publishing community: http://redlemona.de

A word about this community. Over my years in publishing, I learned that a publisher is the sum of all its constituent parts: yes and above all the writers, and yes, the staff, but also all the people who read our books, talk about our books, support our authors, and those who want to be one of our authors themselves.

So I started a company called Cursor, designed to make these constituent parts fit better together, into a proper community where, finally, we could be greater than the sum of the parts. The Red Lemonade publishing community is the first of these and there will be more to come—for the current roster of communities, see the Cursor website at http://thinkcursor.com.

For more on how to participate in the Red Lemonade publishing community, including the opportunity to share your thoughts about this book, read what others have to say about it, to learn more about Lynne Tillman and her novels all of which we now have back in print, as well as to share your own manuscripts with fellow writers, readers, and the Red Lemonade editors, go to the Red Lemonade website: http://redlemona.de.

Also, we want you to know that these sites aren't just for you to find out more about what we do, they're places where you can tell us what you do, what you want, and to tell us how we can help you. Only then can we really have a publishing community be greater than the sum of its parts.

Let me also note the following editorial credits. I edited this book, Nora Nussbaum copy-edited it, and Daniel Schwartz proofread it.

Regards,
Richard Nash
Publisher